Frat Around and Find Out

DEVON McCORMACK

PEACH STATE FRATBROS, BOOK 1

FRAT AROUND AND FIND OUT (PEACH STATE FRATBROS #1)

ALSO BY DEVON McCORMACK

LUST

TWISTED RIVALRY

THE GUY NEXT DOOR

BFF: BEST FRIEND'S FATHER

BETWEEN THESE SHEETS

TIGHT END

TROUBLE

1

Lance

"LANCE, YOU GOTTA get dressed! Hurry!"

"Dude, weren't you supposed to be back here already?"

"We're heading out soon. Come on. Chop, chop."

As I rush through the Alpha Theta Mu house, I keep having to tell the guys, "I'm moving as fast as I can," while my fellow frats give me hell about how behind I am.

The past few years, I've never had an issue holding down a job, attending classes, standing as the fraternity's president, and making it to the all-important TaskFrat challenges to remind all the rival frats who's the baddest frat at Peach State. Unfortunately, for whatever reason, Peachtree Springs decided to start construction on the highway today, which had me backed up for thirty minutes on my way here from having lunch with my parents, and I've been freaking out, since I don't want to let my team down on the first challenge of the season.

I scramble into my room, hurrying to get into my TaskFrat Challenge outfit, as per the email we received earlier in the week, which lists the guidelines and dress code for the event.

As I slip on the G-string, noticing just how revealing it is, I'm relieved we're still enjoying the warmth of what's been a lovely Georgia September. I'm also feeling surprisingly confident about my body as I check myself out in my closet floor-length mirror. Although, this outfit seems unusually skimpy for a challenge. Not that we haven't had to wear ridiculously revealing outfits in the past, but the most we've ever gotten down to is Speedos. Still, it shouldn't surprise me, since Beta Pi is in charge of today's task, and they're known for their sexy-themed parties.

And hey, guess everyone's gonna get a good view of how fortunate this bulge is.

A knock at the door draws my attention away from my crotch, and maybe because I'm so used to the humiliating outfits TaskFrat puts me into, I don't even think twice when I call out, "Come in!"

Ash Fuller, my best bud and fratbro, enters, wearing his G-string and his Alpha Theta Mu sleeveless crop top that matches the one I'm heading to my drawer to fetch.

"Someone was cutting it close," Ash says, plopping down on the edge of my bed. "I was about to see if one of the sophomores would be willing to step up in your place."

As I find my crop top, I say, "I'm shocked I'm willing to do this humiliating crap."

"You know you love the attention. Who signs up for TaskFrat Challenge if they don't?"

Fair point. The TaskFrat challenges are essentially a series of task-based games that Peach State frats made up to create a safe version of hazing for entertainment purposes, while posting pics and vids of the events on socials is like free advertisement for future pledges.

"And some of the noobs want their turn in the spotlight," he adds.

"They'll get their chance for the bigger games." I toss off my shirt and swap out. "And what's it gonna look like to the rushes if the president isn't out there representing us?"

"Been president for three years, and you're some kind of PR wiz all of a sudden."

"You know it," I joke, checking out my skimpy outfit in the mirror. My muscles are really bulging today. I flex my abs. "I make this look good." I wait for Ash to confirm, but he's quiet, stirring some insecurity. "I look good, right? You're my bi bro. You're supposed to boost my self-esteem."

"Does my straight best friend need some confidence today?" Ash asks. "I have praised your body more than enough the past week. You're looking like you put in some serious workouts now that we have our own fitness room."

"You liking the gun show?" I flex my biceps, which I've given plenty of attention to as well.

Ash hops up from the bed and approaches. "Oh my! Such a big, strong, straight man. I'm so turned on right now. Is that what you needed?" He doesn't even pretend to be enthusiastic—that's Ash for ya.

"You be glad your boyfriend isn't here to kick my ass for you drinking me in like that," I tease.

"Oh yeah, he'd be real intimidated."

Colin, his boyfriend—former Alpha Theta Mu alum, now at Emory Law—is swole with muscle, used to be a tight end for Peach State, so I definitely couldn't compete with that. And really, our relationship isn't like that at all. Still, gotta give my fratbro hell.

"Whatever," I say. "If I were queer, you know you would have hit this."

"Keep telling yourself that, man."

"What is this talk about?" I hear from behind us as two of our Alpha Theta Mu friends, Marty and Payton, head in, Payton in his outfit, Marty wearing athletic shorts.

"Are you out of your mind?" Marty asks. "I come by and you're talking about messing around behind your boyfriend's back?"

"What?" Ash says. "I would never…"

Marty cringes. "What? Yeah, of course, I know you wouldn't. I'm saying you shouldn't be goofing around like that when we're about to be late."

The challenge doesn't start for another hour, but for some events—like today—some guys from each frat need to show up early to help set up the venue.

"So come on," Marty says. "You can talk when we get back about how Ash would never have fucked Lance even if he was the only available man on the planet."

"Aw, douche," I snap.

"Yes, I am clean and useful, thank you very much. Now, Payton, just grab one of them, and I'll get the other. Let's get them to the car. The guys put me in charge of getting you all to the venue on time."

Of course the guys would choose Marty. He's the goodie-goodie of Alpha Theta Mu.

But we're not leaving yet.

"You're not in your G-string." I motion to his shorts.

"They're obviously under these."

It's a well-established tradition that the skimpier the outfits, the more of a boss move it is to show up at the venue sporting them like it's no big deal. This is something my buddy Marty is aware of. We're not gonna be the guys changing out of shorts and jackets in the parking lot like a bunch of cowards. We're fucking Alpha Theta Mu.

Marty drops trou and tosses his shorts at me. "Happy?"

"Much better," I say, and then the four of us drive to

the location.

The TaskFrat challenges are typically at one of the Peach State frat houses, but once in a while we'll have a special occasion when it's held at another venue. For the debut game this year, we're meeting at the local park a few blocks away. When we arrive at the parking lot, the place is packed. It's a full-blown pre-TaskFrat tailgate.

"Kind of early for this," Payton says, since people don't usually start arriving during setup.

"You sure we got the time right?" Marty asks from the driver's seat. Payton scrolls through his phone.

"We definitely got the time right," Ash says.

I notice the guys from the other frats are wearing regular tees and board shorts.

They would never…

"You think we misread the dress code?" Marty asks.

"No," I say curtly, since I know for a goddamn fact that I wouldn't have misread that.

"What is going on?" Marty asks. "Why aren't the other guys wearing this? You think they have them on under their shorts?"

"Nope," I say.

"The fuck?" Payton says.

I already know exactly what's going on.

And I suspect I know who's to blame as I recall a comment my Sigma Alpha archnemesis offered at the last TaskFrat Challenge Committee meeting: *"Wear something pretty for me at the next challenge, okay?"*

"Ty Lancaster," I say through my teeth.

"What?" Ash asks. "How would he have done this?"

"He's buddies with Morgan Frax, Omega Psi's guy who's in charge of sending out the tasks. Ty must've talked him into doing it."

"I'm not getting out of the car," Marty says as he parks.

"Oh, come on," Payton says.

Marty points out the window. "They've got their phones out and looking this way. They've been told this is what's gonna happen."

Marty's right. It seems everyone's noticed our arrival, and they're already chuckling, clearly anticipating the big reveal.

Heat stirs in my chest and flares in my cheeks. "I can't believe that asshole duped us like this. And I fell right for it."

Even worse, I'm jealous that it's a damn good prank. When he's good, he's good.

"Hey," Ash says. "This isn't your fault. Someone had to prank us. And we got them last year."

And we got them good too, thanks to the help of one of our guys' beloved family pet hog, Jasper. Jasper is like a people-person—a people-hog, I guess—but that's hard to tell when all two hundred and fifty pounds of him are tearing toward you. We let him loose in the Sigma Alpha house during Greek Week. We'd already sprayed the guys' costumes with lavender, which apparently Jasper adores. So all the frats and sororities had to do was set up lawn chairs and enjoy the show as Sigma Alphas with ripped togas or in the buff hauled ass from their house like they were running from Michael Myers.

"And what we're wearing is not that weird for a TaskFrat event," Ash adds.

He's right, but at least when we've worn Speedos, all the other frats were wearing the same.

"Do we have time to go back to the house?" Marty asks. "Or maybe I can get someone to bring us a change of clothes."

"We're barely on time as it is," Payton says.

"They clearly don't need us for setup," Marty adds.

It's true, but in the back of my mind, I hear a familiar voice, one that's with me every day, here for me, encouraging me along.

"Sometimes you just gotta own it."

"We have to own it," I say, the way he would have.

"Huh?" Marty asks.

A powerful determination rises within me. "Everyone in this car, when we get out, we are strutting like we've never strutted before."

"Fuck," Marty groans, since of the four of us, he's the most self-conscious.

"Ash, text the guys at the house so they can change

before they get here. But we're already here, and we're not running. We all look hot as fuck in this, and if we act cool, then Ty Lancaster and his Sigma Alpha goons can laugh it up all they want, but they'll know they didn't get the best of us. Then we stomp their asses in the competition."

My confidence in my plan surprises even me. I never considered myself much of a leader. Hell, even running for president of Alpha Theta Mu was a joke until it wasn't. But the longer I've been in the role, the more natural this leadership has felt.

"Everyone on the same page here?" I ask.

Ash shrugs. "Colin told me I look hot as fuck in this earlier, so I feel good."

"Not a huge surprise for an exhibitionist," Payton teases, but that's true. So it'll be great having Ash at my side.

"I…hate…this," Marty says, gripping the steering wheel like he's considering bailing. "Can I at least keep on my jacket?"

"No," I insist. "No fear. Give them nothing."

He sighs, but he must know I'm right.

"On my count of three," I say, "we get out. Fucking own it. We all in? Marty?"

He takes deep breaths, his hands locked on the steering wheel as he seems to be trying to control his anxiety. "Don't expect a miracle," he says.

"Fair." I take the lead, getting out on my side. Ash and Payton follow, and then Marty gets out, stripping out of his jacket, but still wearing his discomfort on his face. Despite his hesitation, I've always been able to count on him to have my back. And today is obviously no exception.

As laughter erupts, plenty of phones are out to capture our humiliation.

Ash is smiling and waving to guys we know—not trying to act cool, just genuinely giving zero fucks—so I follow his lead. I say hi to some frats and sorority sisters, scanning the crowd until I notice a pair of eyes on me near a thick oak.

Ty Lancaster, you fuck.

Standing with his crew, his dark-brown bangs curled over his forehead, he folds his arms, grinning that charming-ass smile that always seems to win the girls over.

Since Algebra II freshman year, we've been competitors, each of us trying to outdo the other's grades to the point where acing a test without nailing the extra credit question wasn't an option. I became frat president sophomore year, and then he became president of Sigma Alpha his junior year. The moment we were both competing on frat row, that took everything to a whole other level.

I take measured breaths, reminding myself to keep

my cool. No need to show weakness in front of the other guys. I hold my head high and head across the grass, my guys right behind me, clearly for support. As I get close, I notice he's sporting a nice bronze tan, his cheeks slightly sun-kissed. The guy can even make sun damage look hot.

When I settle in front of him, he says, "Hot G-strings, boys," and winks.

Getting under my skin is like his superpower. That heat in my chest radiates—I can feel it emanating off my flesh.

"Guess it helped knowing Alpha Theta Mu wouldn't hesitate to step up to the challenge," he says with pride.

He knows because Sigma Alpha would have done the same.

He sizes me up. "You been working out, Lance?"

"He has, actually," Marty replies on my behalf.

"Yeah," I add, "so if your goal was to get all the Alpha Theta Mu guys laid, I should say congratulations."

His smile shifts into a subtle sneer.

"We know that's not exactly your talent, don't we?" he claps back, which earns a few snickers from his guys.

And damn, what an ego bruise. Ty is a sex god. Can get any girl he wants. Hell, he could get guys too if he was into that. And I'm just…well, getting laid is not my strength. I'm more the fumbling guy who can't keep a girl's interest for long. But also, I'm not into one-night stands, something Ty enjoys on the reg.

We stare each other down before he says, "Come on. Admit it, it's kind of funny. I got you good."

"Obviously. We're here, aren't we? But seems like that's what you had to do to try and intimidate us so that you can win this challenge."

"If it works, maybe you guys weren't gonna win anyway."

"We'll see, won't we?"

"We don't have to see. Sigma Alpha slayed last year."

"By a hair," I remind him, though I hate that while we were neck and neck throughout the school year, they clinched it in the final challenge and were declared victors. "Plus, you had a lot of your best guys graduate. Bet it's making you a little nervous."

I study his fellow Sigma Alphas, noticing them showing the nerves he's not willing to right now. I move closer, getting in his face. He doesn't flinch, both of us standing our ground.

"I'm not afraid of being a little nervous," he says. "That's what makes it worth it. Gives me an edge so I can really appreciate how it feels to kick your ass."

Something about Ty showing his competitive side brings out mine too. I'm so worked up right now, my adrenaline off the charts—so much so, I can barely tell the difference between my competitive spirit and being pissed at him for duping us.

We're still staring each other down, refusing to break

eye contact. Like so many things with us, even just looking at one another has become a staring contest neither of us is willing to lose.

Ty's lips curl into a smirk before he leans closer and slightly to the side, whispering into my ear, "Getting awfully close. Careful. You remember what happened last time we were too close."

My cheeks flush, and I glance around to make sure no one heard him. No one seems to have caught on, or maybe they don't realize what he means because I doubt he would have shared what happened last spring, just like I haven't told my buddies.

We share another look, a glint in his sparkling blue eyes, and I imagine he's reflecting on our pervy secret.

I wish I could say more, but I can't do that without revealing too much to the guys around us. I'm about to speak when the crowd erupts in hollers and shouts.

I turn to see some Alpha Theta Mus getting out of their cars, wearing their own G-strings and crop tops.

"Ash, didn't you text them?" I ask.

"I did."

Jason, one of our Alpha Theta Mu bros, rushes the crowd, arms high over his head as he hollers, leading the charge, reminding me that I really do have the best frat.

I turn back to Ty, unable to keep myself from looking at his lips, thinking how close they were that morning. How hot his body was, pressed up against mine. He's still got that sparkle in his eyes, like he's thinking about it too.

And as our fellow frats get the crowd going wild, I whisper, "Try not to get too excited."

His smirk expands into a smile, and as frustrated as I was with him when I first arrived, now there's a rush. Partly because I feel clever. Partly because I have one over on him.

And partly because there's something fun about sharing this secret.

2

Ty

A FEW YARDS away, Ryan, my friend and fellow Sigma Alpha, blindfolded and holding in his hand a spoon with an egg on it, walks on his knees toward a table set up for flip cup. I stand in a circle with guys from other frats, waiting for him to tag me so I can continue to the next part of the course.

Not every TaskFrat Challenge is an obstacle course, but they're the easiest to start the year with. Each frat develops its own challenges, which are voted on by the committee before we organize them to ensure they gradually increase in difficulty throughout.

Lance's friend Ash isn't far behind Ryan.

"We're right on your asses," Lance says from beside me.

I glare at him, then glance lower, getting a look at his tight cheeks in that G-string. Since he arrived at the park, I've been impressed he hadn't backed down. He and his guys could have easily driven off as soon as they realized we set them up to look like fools. Or he could have gotten out of that car, acting humbled and embarrassed, but instead he held his head high and absorbed all the laughter and mockery. Lance Fehn has always had a way of impressing me—not that I'll ever tell him that.

"Like what you see?" Lance teases as he catches me still looking at his ass.

"Thinking I should have found something less flattering on you, is all. I've already noticed girls checking that ass out since you got here. Have a feeling you'll be cleaning up at the afters."

"The only one I notice checking out my ass is you."

"I've kind of already had you, so…"

Our gazes meet again, both of us surely thinking about our little secret. The thing that must be on his mind as much as it's on my mind whenever we see each other.

It happened last May, after Lance and I got trashed at an Omega Psi party, which was really our big mistake. Omega Psi is known for being wild—we've had to discipline them for a few of their pranks and for hazing the year before last. They were also fined after their prank against Lance and me, when we woke up the morning after the party, naked and bound together in stretch wrap, facing one another. Embarrassing as fuck for me since, on top of having a hell of a hangover, Lance thought there was a rock wedged between us.

Only it wasn't a rock. It was my morning wood. An interesting predicament for our straight asses.

"You didn't have me, just to be clear," Lance says.

"I definitely marked you, didn't I?"

When we were trying to escape our predicament, despite my hard-on, we did our best to navigate the situation. We weren't careful enough, though, and before either of us knew it, I shot all over the guy.

Lance chuckles, again glancing around, though I'm careful whenever I bring it up not to say anything that would clue anyone in.

"I told you not to," he insists.

"I told you to stop squirming."

"I was trying to get out."

"You got something out, didn't you?" I say, and his face turns bright red. I'm so proud of myself for making it that shade. "I notice it still makes you blush when I bring it up," I tease, loving every second of it. Wild because at the time, I thought it would be the thing I'd never live down. But now it's our fun dirty secret.

A few hollers catch our attention.

A fellow frat takes Ryan's spoon and egg, and Ryan feels for one of the several Solo cups on the table. Once he finds one, he downs the drink, then takes extra care setting his cup on the edge of the table, only to miss it entirely during his first attempt at the flip. Ash is next to hand off his spoon and egg with one of his teammates. As he feels around for the cups, he inadvertently knocks a few over before settling on one. Unfortunately, he manages to drink and get his flip in fast, earning cheers from the crowd. He removes his blindfold and races toward us.

Fuck.

"Hope you enjoy watching this ass running toward victory," Lance says as Ash tags him.

I grunt, unable to keep from looking at his bouncing ass cheeks as he's off to the next part of the challenge. My dick shifts in my shorts—I assume because Lance has ignited my competitive streak by heading on before me.

The crowd around flip cup calls out again—Ryan's successfully landed his flip, removed his blindfold, and is now starting toward me.

"Come on!" I call out to him. "You're a linebacker for fucking Peach State! Act like it!"

Ryan really throws his weight into it, and I position myself to sprint off because I fully intend to own Lance's perky ass tonight.

"Come *on*, Ryan!" And the moment he tags me, I dash off like my life depends on it.

Lance is already at the next obstacle, a wide kiddie pool full of blue Jell-O. He searches through what looks like stuffed condoms.

I grab the letter with my team color from the table:

Find the flag in your team's color and take it to the next station to hand off to your teammate. If you take a decoy from the pool, your team is disqualified.

Not loving that our color is fucking teal.

I hurry into the pool, watching as Lance pulls a ball from a condom and discards it.

"Right on that ass," I tell him, which earns a quick look before he continues making a mess of himself in the Jell-O, which hasn't fully congealed.

The noise from the crowd grows as people catch up from farther down the course. Some of them are shouting for me, some for Lance, as we scramble to find our flags. I drop to my knees, hurrying through a few decoys that are annoyingly close in color to teal.

Finally, I find the flag and spring to my feet. Lance must've found his at the same time because as I leap up, he appears right next to me, and I inadvertently hit him from the side, knocking him off his feet. He goes tumbling back into the Jell-O.

"Oh fuck," I say as I catch my balance, then turn to make sure I didn't hurt him.

On his ass, he props himself up with his hands, emerging from the Jell-O, drenched in blue goo. "Ty Lancaster, you shit!"

I didn't mean for that to happen, but I have the upper hand, and I'd be a fool not to take advantage. "Sorry, bro," I tell him before rushing off to hand off my flag to my next teammate, feeling like a bit of a dick, but real good about our lead.

"YOU REALLY KILLED the challenges tonight," Jodie, a Phi Lambda, says as she bats her eyes at me, her attention giving me an even bigger ego boost.

As if I need it.

Sigma Alpha is enjoying all the praise. Not just with the game, but our prank, which has set the bar for the rest of the frats for the year. I must admit, part of what makes the challenges so fun is getting to be competitive with Lance.

And now that I'm standing in front of this hot-ass girl I should be making some moves on, I surprise myself because instead, I'm scoping the after-party at Alpha Theta Mu so I can rub our victory in his face some more.

And, of course, apologize to him for what he must think was an intentional trip.

"Who are we looking for?" Jodie asks.

I thought I was being discreet, but clearly, not so much.

"She hot?" Jodie asks, and I see the question in her eyes, the probing, trying to see if she's got competition, or more importantly, if there's no competition because I'm that into another girl.

"I'm looking for a he."

"Oh really? I haven't heard. But based on what you just said and how you've been flirting with me for the past ten minutes, I'm guessing you're bi?"

"What?" I ask, shocked by her conclusion. Though I shouldn't be, given how I phrased that. "I meant, I'm looking for Lance Fehn."

I don't bother explaining who he is, since he's active around campus. And it's clear by her expression she knows whom I'm referring to.

"He's a friend," I clarify.

"Oh," she says with a laugh, sounding relieved, since it means she can continue her pursuit.

And I'm relieved too because I could have blown my chances, and she's too hot to miss out on. Fortunately, I keep my cool long enough to link up with her on Instagram before I make my way through the party, toward the DJ booth, where I figured I'd find Lance since he loves DJing for the frats. He's chatting with Ash, both still in their G-strings and crop tops.

Doesn't surprise me about Ash because the guy loves attention. Lance, though, is usually more reserved, but tonight he's baring those cheeks and abs, his crop top and hair a little wet but not covered in blue goo anymore, so he must've taken a shower.

Funny because most of the guys from their team have cleaned up and are fully dressed.

Just like when I saw Lance strutting around in that G-string at the event, I have to hand it to him. The guy has a way of turning around any bad thing.

As his gaze meets mine, his eyes narrowing as he smirks, I find myself getting…excited. I chalk it up to my body associating him with that morning when he accidentally rubbed one out for me, thanks to those asshats at Omega Psi.

"Didn't bother to change?" I ask in my typical asshole fashion as I approach the DJ table.

"Didn't see the point. Told you I looked damn good in it."

He really fucking does.

"Yeah, well, doesn't look like hitting the gym did you any favors tonight."

I shouldn't enjoy teasing Lance Fehn as much as I do, but I can't help myself, especially when he makes it so goddamn fun. Even as he stood there, giving me shit for the prank I put him and the Alpha Theta Mu crew through, I knew he was impressed. As he should have been. Although, he's right. I'm gonna have to be ready for whatever he and his frat have in store for Sigma Alpha now, but that's part of the fun of pranks, right?

"I would say what didn't do me any favors was when you tripped me into the Jell-O," he says, quirking a brow. "Low blow, dude."

"That was an accident." At his glare, I raise my

hands. "Honest on that one. I wouldn't do you dirty like that."

He studies my expression as though trying to decide whether he can trust me.

"Hey, I'm just trying to keep you from siccing a hog on my guys again," I joke. "Besides, I'd never lie to someone I fucked around with."

"We have *not* fucked around."

"You know they say when someone doesn't use contractions, they're probably lying."

"I have a sneaking suspicion they don't teach that in cybersecurity classes," he says.

"Just something I've seen in shows. And you remembered my major? You really are obsessed with me, aren't you?"

"Like you don't know mine?"

Medical engineering.

"Um…like chemical engineering or some shit?" Now I'm the liar, and the way he's looking at me, I figure he knows. "I feel like you're trying to get off the subject of when I got my cum all over your abs."

"One of these days someone is gonna hear you and think we messed around."

"And then what? I'll have more interested guys approaching me than before?"

I can tell he's having to keep from rolling his eyes.

"Tell me, am I the last person you messed around

with?" Before I asked, I told myself I was just giving him hell, but as soon as the words come out, I'm genuinely curious.

"I've been out with girls since then," he insists.

I find that hard to believe. "Come on, Lance. You're not the kind of guy who's gonna charm the pants off a girl, take her back to your place, show her a good time, and then try to politely get her to leave as quickly as possible."

"I'm not *you*—is that what you're saying?"

"Hey, I am very polite about when I ask her to leave."

He laughs. "I bet you are, Ty Lancaster. But I don't know. I'm thinking tonight might be my lucky night. Got this new gym body pumped, and already had a few girls come up to me because apparently, this G-string is catching more interest than I guess you imagined."

I grit my teeth. I wasn't just saying that when we were at the challenge, but I also wasn't actually trying to improve his sex life. Although, what the hell? If he does get laid because of it, good for him. What does that have to do with me?

"Well, I'm sure you've attracted some interest, but we'll see if you can seal the deal."

He winces, his brown eyes piercing. "Just because I don't vibe with a lot of girls doesn't mean I couldn't go home with one if I wanted to."

"Oh really?" Now he's out of his depth. I've known the guy for years, and that's just not him.

"I'm a fun, sexy guy." He runs his hand through his dirty-blond hair—a little blonder now, like it usually is after the summer. I must admit, he makes even doing only that much look sexy. Whatever *it* is, Lance has got it.

"I didn't say you weren't." Once again, I'm surprised as the words escape my lips, and his wide-eyed look suggests he is too. I quickly go on, "I just don't think that's you, is what I was saying."

"I can work it when I need to."

"Really? You're just gonna hook up with a hot girl tonight?"

"It's senior year. I'm a stud these days. You don't know me as well as you think you do."

"A stud?" I snicker. "Okay, sure. Prove me wrong. I'd love to see that."

He shrugs, and I can fucking see the bluff in his goddamn eyes. I want to just call him out on it, but before I have a chance, he grabs a Jell-O shot off a tray, downs it, then heads over to one of his Alpha Theta Mu buddies. They talk briefly, and then the guy takes over the DJ table while Lance chats up a group of girls.

I notice my hands clenching up. This is so not him, and I don't think he'd even enjoy it, so I don't see what he's trying to prove other than pissing me off because of some dumb comment I made. Which…is so us. And normally, this would excite me, but as the girls laugh at his jokes and move closer to him, I'm starting to be pretty fucking annoyed with the guy.

I could be doing the same thing, shooting my shot, finding the next girl to spend a fun night with but who will wind up texting me on and on about wanting to get together for coffee or maybe dinner. I've played that game plenty of nights, and sure, it's a rush.

Lance might end up having a great time, and it's none of my damn business either way, but even as I'm trying to play beer pong to distract myself, I keep glancing at him. When I see a Phi Lambda girl with her arm draped over him, whispering in his ear, it makes a burning sensation flare in my chest.

He's hitting that competitive nerve again, trying to prove me wrong. Could have kept my damn mouth shut, but now he wants to make me mad. Why? If anything, our rivalry is playful, in good fun, but damn, *this* doesn't feel fun.

He seems to make a point of heading right past me with his arm around this girl. As he nears, he winks. "Night, Ty. Hope you have some fun tonight too. Might want to check under your bed for a hog, though."

Motherfucker.

A strong emotion pulses through me. Part of me wants to grab him and tell him this is so fucking stupid, that he's gonna regret this in the morning, but I could be wrong. She could be the best night of his life for all I know, and maybe when she starts messaging him for coffee and dinner, he'll be eager for it and suddenly have a girlfriend.

Why is my chest so tight? What does it even matter if he has a girlfriend?

Good. For. Him.

But if I'm really so fucking chill about this, why am I crushing my Solo cup in my hand as they make their way upstairs to his bedroom.

He's fucking mine. I marked him.

The hell did that come from…?

3

Lance

"Morning, sweetheart," I hear, my eyes flitting open and discovering Angie at my side.

I groan as I feel the first signs of a hangover, and her lips slip into a sneaky expression.

Before last night, I'd seen her around campus and at events, but it wasn't until after my conversation with Ty, when he was so sure I'd never mess around with a girl the way he would, that I started chatting her up.

"When did I pass out?" I ask, rubbing my eyes.

"Less than halfway through *Wicked*. But you said you've seen it before, so I didn't feel the need to wake you up."

"I vaguely recall making it to 'Popular.'"

She laughs. "Yeah, I'm surprised my singing along didn't wake you. So what do you want to do now? Morning BJ? Or would you rather go down on me? I don't think I'm ready to be fucked again."

"Wait, what?" I ask, my headache making me particularly confused.

I glance over myself, fearing I'll find myself naked like in some kind of college movie where the guy didn't realize he'd hooked up the night before. I'm slightly relieved to find myself in the pajama bottoms and tank I changed into after we came to my room.

But only slightly.

Angie laughs again. "I'm kidding. The look on your face!"

"Oh…"

In the short time I've known her, I've discovered she has an interesting sense of humor. Like when I confessed to her I'd gotten myself into a jam with Ty by saying I would try to hook up with a girl, she immediately said, *"We should go back to your room. He won't know the difference."*

I'm hoping Ty bought it. That, despite how he thought I would never do something like that, he was sitting there wondering if he really knew me at all. Maybe even jealous because Angie is hot as hell—the kind of girl my brain can't compute having in my bed right now. Although, it makes more sense knowing we didn't do anything together.

"You mind if I have breakfast here?" she asks. "I'm hungry, and I've been awake for the past thirty minutes."

"Of course. After the favor you did for me, I owe you."

"I think you should owe me more than breakfast, but it's a start," she teases with a wink. "Speaking of which, this is probably the first walk of shame I've done without having messed around with someone. It was fun, though."

She has this bright, beautiful smile, and, it bears repeating, she's hot as hell, yet there's zero chemistry between us. But she seems like she'd be cool to be friends with.

"Now, come on." She crawls over me and jumps down from the bed, starting for the door. "I'm legit starving."

I tail behind her as we head downstairs. Angie immediately attracts the attention of some guys who are watching *Judge Judy* in the main living area.

"Hey, boys," she says like a girl who's never met a stranger before heading into the kitchen, where Marty and Ash are eating breakfast.

Ash smirks, and Marty is wide-eyed like he thinks I shouldn't have been able to attract a girl as hot as Angie. Even Frat Cat, cuddled up in Marty's lap, looks to see what's up.

"Hey, Ash," Angie says.

"You know each other?" I ask.

"We were in a study group for Electrodynamics," Ash replies.

"That's right," she says. "Do you all mind if I just

make myself at home? Just let me know what I can and can't eat."

"You're a guest," Marty says. "Help yourself."

She does a double take. "Such a gentleman. Thank you." She heads to the pantry and starts to search through while Frat Cat climbs on the table to keep an eye on our guest.

"Hey, Prez," I hear behind me and turn to see Ash's stepbro-boyfriend approaching. Emory is about an hour from here without traffic, so he makes sure to drive up here for the weekends so he can spend time with his man.

With a towel around his waist, his hair still wet, and shiny wet patches across his chest, Colin must've just taken a shower.

"When the hell did you get here?" I ask as we hug.

"Around two in the morning," he says, pulling back.

"So we've been up all night," Ash adds, and I notice the huge grin that suggests it hasn't been so terrible for him to be up that long.

"I'm surprised to see you guys down here, then."

"Boy's gotta eat," Ash says.

"I think you were eating just fine earlier," Colin says, heading over to his boyfriend.

"Oh, gross," Marty says, stopping his spoonful of Raisin Bran inches from his mouth. "Please, I'm trying to eat."

"Can't help that I can't keep my hands off my man," Colin says as he manhandles his boyfriend from behind before burying his face against Ash's neck and taking a gentle nibble, making Ash blush.

"You two seem fun," Angie says, closing the pantry, holding a protein bar.

"Oh, sorry," Colin says. "I didn't see you behind the door. I'm—"

"As if I wouldn't know a former tight end for Peach State when I see one, Colin Phillips." She shakes his hand. "The pleasure's all mine."

Marty's expression is twisted up as he glances between Angie and me. "Wait. So you spent the night with Lance?"

"Yeah, Lance just showed me the night of my life."

Ash's eyes bulge. Marty's jaw drops.

"Angie," I say, "you don't have to do that with these guys. We're all cool."

"Then in that case, he was trying to be a dick to Ty Lancaster, and I agreed to help if he'd watch *Wicked* with me."

"We never really agreed on that part."

"That was really my plan from the start. I've already made my other friends watch it with me too many times."

"Wait, what happened with Ty Lancaster?" Marty asks.

"Eh, he was making this big deal that I could never do what he does and have a one-night stand, and I wanted to show him up."

"You don't do what he does," Ash points out.

"That's none of his business, is it?"

The guys get a kick out of that.

"Guess you had to get him back after that prank last night," Colin notes.

"Even the guy who wasn't here knows about it?" I ask.

"Yeah, everyone was posting about it in my feed. Pics are hot, though. You should be proud."

Marty cringes. "I feel like maybe we're all operating off different definitions of pride."

"Couldn't you guys have just left the park?" Colin asks.

I reflect on the moment when I made the call, when I could hear Kacey in my head, saying, *"Sometimes you just gotta own it."* He's been gone for so many years, yet I still follow the words of wisdom my big bro left me with before I lost him.

"Just some advice I heard once," I say, not wanting to bring the mood down—or upset myself—by getting into it.

"Well, it definitely made the night extra sexy," Colin says before refocusing on Ash. "And you looked especially sexy." He continues fondling his man, offering a few kisses along his neck. Ash closes his eyes, rolling his head back as he gets into it.

Everyone in the kitchen gets so quiet, I can hear Marty gulp and Angie tear open her protein bar.

"Sorry, that's rude," Ash says as he snaps out of his blissed state.

"None of us were complaining," Angie observes, fanning her face with the bar. "But if the show's over, I should be heading out. I told some friends I'd meet them for pickleball."

She rounds the kitchen island and stops beside me. "We should hang out sometime. I'll hit you up on Insta, *big guy.*"

She winks playfully, and as she leaves, Marty looks shocked, though he waits till she's gone before he says, "Wow. Like *wow* wow."

"Looks like Ty Lancaster can't give you any hell about your approach," Ash adds.

"The *big guy* was a joke," I insist. "There's no vibe there, but she seems like a fun person to hang out with."

"What?" Marty seems bewildered. "Angie's hot."

"Come on," Colin says. "Being into someone isn't just about their looks. It's a connection. A spark. And you know it when it's happening...or it sneaks up on you." He gives Ash a pointed look, which makes my fratbro glow.

I can't help myself. "Colin, you graduate and suddenly you're…what? The wise elder of Alpha Theta Mu?"

"Depends on whether or not Ash thinks a wise elder is hot."

Ash sneaks a look to Colin. "It's definitely hot."

Marty glares. "Pretty confident Colin could have said just about *anything* and Ash would have said that."

"Yeah," I say. "But we can't fault him. Colin can be pretty fucking charming."

Ash confirms with a nod.

"Okay," I say, "can you guys let me finish my breakfast and get out of here before making me vomit it back up?"

Ash groans. "It's been a week."

"From what you said when I first came down here, it's maybe been an hour."

"Hey!" Marty snaps. "Let them have their fun. It's not their fault you got friend-zoned in record time."

Asshat. He's got this cocky smirk on his face, so pleased with himself for the dig.

"As president of Alpha Theta Mu, I banish you from this house."

We all enjoy a laugh, and with Colin here, it reminds me of some of the best times I've had at the frat with my buddies.

4

Ty

"Get that set in, come on, really kill it," Ryan urges as I pump barbell reps. I start to strain, and he encourages me along. "One more, bud."

I force the final rep before my friend steps in, hoisting the bar up and resting it on the rack.

"Fuck." I sit up, catching my breath. "I'm just trying to stay fit, not sign up for the team."

He snickers. "You're fit, man, but you ain't this fit." He flexes his biceps, his cut-open tank giving me a view of the impressive musculature he's crafted over his years of training. When it comes to his body, Ryan doesn't play around, which is why we work out at a gym a few blocks from campus. It's never as busy as the one at Peach State, and it has updated equipment—musts so my linebacker buddy can keep on top of his game. "You sure you can't come tonight?" he asks. "We have a hot party planned, and I think the president deserves to enjoy it."

"Nah. I've got work, and then I have a paper I need to work on, and it's better I do it this weekend so I don't have to think about it next weekend during TaskFrat and afters."

"Fair. We gotta crush Alpha Theta Mu again. Get a good enough lead on them, and they won't be able to get as close as they did last year."

"Two years in a row would be nice."

"Under your leadership, if it even needs to be said."

"It definitely does. Especially knowing how much it'll crawl up Lance Fehn's ass."

I remember how satisfying it was seeing the Alpha Theta Mu prez getting all worked up as we reached the final challenges last year—how passionate he was, how hard he tried…and then getting to feel sweet victory when Sigma Alpha still slayed.

Ryan grins. "You two are ridiculous about that stuff."

"We both enjoy a little competition."

"A *little?*" He angles his head, pumps his brows.

"Okay, maybe more than that," I admit.

Really, it's not only about the competition. I enjoy our verbal sparring, the way Lance takes what I give him and serves it right back. Even as annoyed as I was when he found a girl at the party last weekend, I had to hand it to him for how he showed me up and stirred enough jealousy to keep me from being able to focus and land my own fun for the night.

Though…I guess that wasn't just about the girl he found, but about those weird thoughts I had about him being mine because I marked him. Still not sure what that's all about. Maybe some primal impulse to dominate my rival. Yeah, that must be it.

"And it's not like you can judge," I add. "You do the same when you're on the football field."

"Don't start comparing the silly TaskFrat challenges to football because I will throw down. Now I know you're just stalling, so lie back down and let's hammer out this last round. I want to see those pecs peccing."

"That's not a thing."

"Down!" he insists, the way I imagine his coaches do when he's slacking.

"I love it when you take charge like that," I joke, but I lie back on the bench and pump out the next set.

Once we finish up, we hit the showers, then meet back at the lockers. I've got my towel around my waist, but Ryan is still drying himself off with his, not giving a fuck about having his dick out, wagging about. He doesn't really think much about baring it all—here or around the frat—I'm sure because he's spent plenty of time throughout his life naked in locker rooms.

"Keegan and Jaxon are planning to hit up the gym tomorrow too if you want to meet up," Ryan says.

Keegan's our Sigma Alpha bro, a sophomore we took under our wing last year. One of our other frats, Jaxon, has enlisted him to help him put on some more muscle, so they've been hitting the gym pretty regularly.

"If you think I'm gonna jump into another day of you drilling me like you did today, you are out of your mind."

"You can thank me when you're strutting those gains and landing more girls."

"No problem in the girl department already, thank you very much."

"I mean, you've seen Lance's bod now and the way he rushed off with that girl. Careful, or he's gonna be the one nabbing all the hotties."

Ryan's expression is playful, but his words burn at something in me—this threat that has me guarded.

"That is not happening," I say through my teeth, acknowledging that I'm more worked up by that than I should be.

After we finish up at the gym, I go straight to work to knock out my afternoon shift at Junkie's Pizza Place. It's not far from frat row, and being Friday, it's hectic, but a good day for tips.

I'm in the zone, really hustling for my tables. I grab two pizzas from the back counter, and as I'm making my way down the hall, the restroom door is flung open and a guy comes storming out, pushing me. The side of my arm slams against the molding that runs along the opposite wall, and the pizzas I'm carrying tumble to the floor.

Fuuuucckkk…

The guy—older, maybe in his forties, in a button-down and tie—glares at me like it's my fault he ran out of there like a stampeding rhinoceros.

"Watch where you're going," he snaps with the sort of attitude that makes me want to step to him, but I remind myself this is fucking work. I'm a goddamn professional.

"Sorry, sir. It was an accident."

He checks himself over. "You got sauce all over my shirt."

There's like a speck on his button-down.

"What's going on here?" I hear behind me and turn to see my manager, Cheryl, approaching. "Are you both okay?"

"Why don't you ask this shitshow over here who just dumped pizza all over me?" the asshole says.

Cheryl takes a breath, then tells him, "I think it's time for you to go. I can smell the alcohol on your breath, and I know this employee very well, so I have a feeling I already know who was responsible for this."

He glares between us, before groaning. "Fine. This place is crap anyway."

He leaves in a huff, and as Cheryl looks me over, she takes my arm. "Are you all right?"

I notice a pink spot where my arm hit the wall. "I'll be fine."

"You should probably get some ice on that."

"It's nothing."

"Are you sure? You can take the rest of the day off, and I can cover for you."

I mull it over. "That would give me some more time to work on my essay. Would you mind?"

"Of course not. We'll get this cleaned up. Then get some ice on that and clock out. I can handle all this."

I help clean up but don't put ice on my tender tricep. Just want to get away from the place so I can decompress.

I hop into my car, and without thinking, I pull up a familiar name in my contacts.

Grant.

It's been three years since my uncle passed.

But he wasn't just my uncle.

After my dad left my mom, and didn't want to have fuck all to do with me, Uncle Grant stepped in to help Mom raise me. Then, seven years ago, he was diagnosed with frontotemporal dementia. The majority of people don't struggle with it until their mid-forties, but apparently, people can get it in their thirties too, which we learned the hard way. It progressed rapidly.

He was everything in the world to me.

My fucking hero.

The guy I could call whenever things were going good or bad in my life.

The first person I would want to tell about the crap that guy just pulled in there.

There's a part of me that wants to hit the Call button, remembering those times shortly after he died when I could at least get his voice mail.

But we're long past those days.

I could call Ryan, but I don't want to spoil his night before a party, and it's kind of late to call Mom, so I stuff it down with all those shitty emotions I've gotten so good at packing away. Instead, I tuck my phone back in my pocket and drive to the library.

It's barely past seven, which gives me a good stretch of quality time, and it'll be easier to concentrate here than at the frat with a party going down.

As I reach the third floor, I see a familiar face. Lance Fehn keys away on his laptop at a table by himself, the same table I'm used to seeing him at with his best friend, Ash Fuller.

I return to that weird-ass thought I keep having about him. That I marked him, so he's mine. A strange sensation swirls in my chest, and I do my best to ignore it as I approach him. Could use a little of our banter to cheer me up right about now.

When I reach the table, I sling my backpack around, resting it in the chair beside him. The moment I catch his gaze, his eyes light up, the way Ryan's or Keeg's might when they see me somewhere. Like a good friend, not a rival.

"You planning to slight a Sigma Alpha party tonight?" I ask.

"Maybe I lost the invite," Lance jabs before smiling. "I have a project I need to work on. And I've had so much going on lately, I needed a sober night to come and get it in. What's your excuse? Shouldn't the president be over there, setting up for his own party?"

"Not like my guys don't know how to throw a party. And I'm in a similar boat. Taking on a lot this semester. Rush was killer, so need to get some work in before bidding this week."

His gaze lowers. "Dude," he says, reaching out and placing his hand on my arm.

His touch catches me off guard, and I notice the dark bruise from banging my arm earlier. I should've iced it.

"Oh." I tell him about the asshole, relieved to have someone to talk to about it.

"That sucks. People are pretty cool with me at the rec center because it's people from school, but I used to work at the mall, and it's amazing how shitty people think they can be to customer-service workers. Like we aren't even human."

"Right?" I say, the sting of that moment still affecting me, but my eyes are drawn to where Lance still has his hand on my arm.

He must realize it's weird too because he pulls away.

"So…" I draw out as I sit in the chair adjacent to his. "How was that girl you were with at that party last weekend?"

"Angie?"

"Oh, are there others? Have you just been lining them up since the last time I saw you?"

Tension builds in my chest, which…what the fuck is that about? It's really not any of my business, but if that's true, why am I so curious?

He chuckles. "There haven't been any others," he says, not answering my first question about Angie.

"You seen her since then?" I press.

"We were supposed to meet up again, but she got sick, so I don't know when that'll be."

"Told you," I spit out.

"What?"

"All that fuss to prove me wrong, and you only proved me right. You didn't just hook up with a girl and leave it at that. You got your little Lance feelings all over it, and now you're gonna date her, aren't you? You know it's cool if that's your thing. You didn't have to try and prove anything to me."

Why do I sound so worked up over this? And why is my heart racing? Feels like I'm pissed at him, but I don't really have a right to be. It's like there's something twisted in my brain that thinks because I came on the guy once, that somehow he's mine and shouldn't be messing around with anyone. Which is wild because I've never had that feeling about anyone I've messed around with except him—

No, wait. What we did wasn't messing around.

Fuck.

This must just be leftover jitters from that asshole at work upsetting me earlier.

Lance eyes me strangely, as though he can read these wild thoughts, which I know isn't what's happening. "Well, maybe you were right about that," he finally says. "I was trying to get you back for the prank and winning the TaskFrat. And I guess it worked because it got on your nerves, didn't it?"

He has no idea, and I don't really either, considering this is a weird thing to be thinking about my Alpha Theta Mu rival.

"Sorry you had a shitty day at work," he says, again catching me by surprise.

I appreciate that even though the number one person I would have wanted to talk to isn't around anymore, at least I had someone who could hear me out.

"Thanks, man," I say, probably the most sincere thing I've ever said to Lance Fehn, which makes me feel strange, so I groan. "Anyway, I'm done harassing you for now. Gonna find a spot and actually knock some of this shit out. Good luck with your work. And hope you have a fun date with Agatha."

I'm already walking away when he calls out, "Angie."

"Yeah, whatever," I say, trying to act like I care less than I do.

5

Lance

"IT'S WILD GOING to an Omega Psi TaskFrat Challenge fully clothed," Marty says on our way over, my crew leading the way. The streetlights illuminate the block, which is crowded with Peach State students in spirit wear, heading to the host house for the challenge.

"Let's not assume we'll be in these clothes by the end of the night," I remark, since I know this frat well enough to be suspicious.

"Remember last year, they had us in BDSM outfits," Payton mentions.

"I didn't forget," Marty says.

Payton smiles. "I thought you looked good in your harness."

"And no compliment on my ass at the last event?" I ask. "That hurts my feelings."

"Wow, Payt," Ash says. "I don't think you complimented any of us on our asses. You ain't safe."

Payton rolls his eyes. "I was busy trying to keep that damn string from riding up my ass, thank you very much. And we already know who had the sexiest ass, at least according to the comments on that Phi Lambda girl's vid on socials."

My cheeks warm because damn right it was me, but mainly because of the particular angle she shot me from, which proudly displayed my assets.

"Not doing those squats for nothing," I say as we reach the Omega Psi house.

As I survey the crowd gathered on the front lawn, I catch myself looking for the Sigma Alphas. I've seen Ty around since our run-in at the library, but just in passing.

In all the time we've known each other, he's never stopped to chat with me like that. Although, we only stop and talk for the digs and to remind each other we're gonna kick the other's ass in TaskFrat. Normal amount of interaction for frat rivals, I'd say.

"Angie planning to be here tonight?" Ash asks.

"Yeah, she's feeling better and caught up on work, so she told me she'd swing by."

It makes me reflect on how Ty kept bringing her up—how jealous he must've been that I got with a hot girl like her. I could have told him there was nothing going on between us, but he was being such a dick, and when he pretty much assumed we were getting together, I didn't bother to correct or clarify. Besides, it's really none of his business.

"Hey, guys," I hear, and turn to see one of Sigma Alpha's own approaching—Dax.

He's the Sigma Alpha who hangs around our frat most. Honestly, though, I'd be surprised if there's a frat Dax doesn't hang out with because not only is he cool as hell, he's also made lots of friends with benefits since he transferred to Peach State last year.

He hugs it out with Ash, then makes his way around the crew for fist bumps.

"What's up, man?" Ash asks.

"Getting into trouble. The usual," he says with a wink. "How's Colin?"

In the time I've known Dax, he's made interesting comments to Ash and Colin, which makes me wonder if something happened between them. Well, at least if he got to witness some fun they shared since that's the kind of thing they're into.

Ash catches Dax up a bit about his man, and then Dax asks, "You all figured out how you're gonna prank us back yet?"

"We haven't had time," I confess. "And for it to be any good, we need to sit on it a bit, wait until you Sigma Alphas have let your guard down. And when we do have a plan, you really think we're gonna share it with you?"

"I could probably get it out of someone," he says with a confident smirk.

"Well, guess you're gonna have to find out the hard way," I tell him.

"Hard way happens to be my favorite way."

As the guys get a kick out of that, Ash asks, "Speaking of your frat, where the Sigma Assholes at?"

"Ooh, I don't know that I can tolerate that from an Asshole Theta Mu."

Before Ash can reply, I spot Ryan, who's hard to miss, with Keegan and—of course—Ty Lancaster. They're standing in the crowd with their team, just a few yards away.

"Let's go pay them a friendly visit," I say, unable to help myself.

"Can we not do this tonight?" Marty asks, but I'm already leading the charge.

"Well, if it isn't last year's second place," Ty says when he notices us.

"If it isn't the number one assholes of Peach State."

Ryan places his hand on his chest. "Our wounded hearts. Ready for us to stomp your ass again like we did last time?"

"Ready to make you eat those words," Marty says.

There's my competitive Marty.

Ryan's eyes widen in a way that takes me by surprise, like he's feigning shock. "Wait a minute." He sizes the group up. "You guys are disqualified, I think."

"Wait, what?" I ask.

"Yeah, for sure. Fuck, you didn't get the memo? You were supposed to wear the same outfits as last time. Oh, hold up. I got you." He reaches into his back pocket and retrieves a pink G-string. "At least one of you can play. Mart, it gonna be you?" Ryan and the other Sigma Alphas are all smiles, feeling real proud of themselves for that one.

"Have you been carrying that around all night just so you could make that joke?" Marty asks.

"Damn right. Kind of missing seeing the pretty boys running around in their sexy little outfits."

Not sure if it's the way he said that, which was a little too convincing, but Ty and Keegan wince at the same time before Ryan approaches Marty, waving the G-string close. "Come on, Mart. Put it on and look sexy for me again."

"Hey, Payt," Marty says. "You have that clip of when Ryan got that wedgie from the Bulldogs. Maybe we can make it go viral again."

Ryan scowls. "I just want you to know, after we annihilate you tonight, I'm gonna go home and stroke myself off thinking about all your sad, loser faces."

Keegan and Ty glance to one another, once again not exactly thrilled at where Ryan has taken the…insults, I guess?

But this is kind of Ryan's thing.

There are a few more barbs exchanged, the usual

kicking-ass sorts, before we get back to our conversations within our groups.

Ty approaches me, saying, "You manage to get together with *Amy*? Or is she still pretending to be sick to get out of having to date you?"

"Angie," I remind him.

He glances around, seemingly annoyed. "Yeah, sure, whatever her name is. So you been on this date?"

Again with his weird interest in Angie. Not like I probe about all the girls he's hooked up with.

"Not yet."

"Sorry, sounds like she's giving you the runaround. You poor, pathetic thing."

"You just can't stand that she's interested in me and not you."

"What?" he asks, his expression twisting up.

"Hey, Lance!" I hear from nearby and turn to see Angie heading over.

Oh, this is about to get interesting.

She sidles up beside me, hooking her arm around my waist and drawing me close. "Hey, stud," she whispers in my ear in a way that gets the hairs on the back of my neck standing on end. "You know, I'm eager to get together…do what we did last time."

I press my lips together because she's talking about watching *Wicked*.

Despite being a little thrown, I know what she's

doing. She knows I was trying to show Ty up, and now she's ramping things up in front of him.

"What do you say?" She's flipped on a sultry voice that, I must admit, even though I haven't felt like there's been anything more than friends here, is making me blush.

I notice Ty, his jaw tense, his fists balled up, assuring me I was right about him being jealous.

"I think that would be hot," I reply.

"Oh, hey, Ty," she says as she rests her hand on my torso, sliding down in a seductive move, like she's really trying to put on a show for him.

Ty is practically shaking, like he's liable to haul off and punch me. Wow. He must really wish he could get with her. Makes me feel kind of great right now.

"Good luck tonight," she whispers close again before biting my neck. She smiles at Ty before heading off, leaving me feeling like I just put Ty in his place.

He starts like he's about to say something but then closes his mouth. "Good for you, man," he says through his teeth before turning away.

"Oh, hey!" I call out, and he turns back to me. "Your arm better?"

He shows me the spot that was bruised last time. It's mostly faded.

But that doesn't set him at ease. He still seems un-nerved over Angie's stunt.

How the hell is Ty fucking Lancaster so worked up from thinking I have one attractive girl who wants me, when he can have pretty much any girl he wants?

Before I have much of a chance to think on that, ominous music starts playing, the house lights dimming before a green glow emerges from under the front porch.

"This is definitely Omega Psi's style," Ash notes.

By that, he means weird and creepy.

The front door opens, and several cloaked frats step out onto the front porch. One pulls back the hood, revealing Reagan Spears of the TaskFrat Committee.

He approaches the front steps. "Tonight's task will be about collaboration and teamwork. You will each be paired with those you are competing against, sharing a victory with another team. Please designate your team captains for tonight, and they will start off the challenges in the house. Once they have completed theirs, they will head out and pass the next part along to their team, who will stand by in the back of the house, where the next part is set up and will be revealed."

"You can't tell me someone from the drama department didn't come up with this shit," Ty whispers near me, and I can't help but chuckle.

Unsurprisingly, the Alpha Theta Mus quickly agree that I'll serve as team captain for the night, and Ty's chosen for his team. The designated captains meet by the front porch, and the TaskFrat crew place hoods over our heads so none of us can see as we're led into the house.

While under the darkness of my hood, Reagan goes on to explain the task before we're separated into pairs, with guides escorting us to rooms in the house.

"Okay, okay," one of our guides says as though this is the last thing in the world he wants to be doing tonight.

"Who am I partnered with?" I ask.

"It's me," Ty says.

Of course it is.

"What I'd give for a gag," the same guide says.

His voice has a deep, resonating timbre. Very distinctive.

We keep going until we're stopped, and then the guides cuff my wrists in front of me, my ankles together, then lock us together around the waists, my ass against Ty's pelvis.

I can't help but reflect on the other Omega Psi incident Ty and I shared. I can only imagine what he's thinking as the guys finish securing us into whatever weird-ass thing this is before one of the guys removes my hood. I glance back as the other frat with us removes Ty's.

"You guys can't start the task until we leave the room, got it?" says the guide who spoke as we were coming to the room. Given that this is his gig, he's young, either a pledge or a sophomore.

"Got it," Ty and I assure him before he and the other

guide head out, closing the door behind them.

Glancing over my shoulder, I notice an envelope dangling from Ty's neck on a lanyard, which according to Reagan's rules, we aren't allowed to open, since they're instructions for our teammates once we get out of this.

"This is strangely familiar," I tease, giving Ty hell simply because I can.

"I can't imagine what you could possibly be referring to," he teases back with a smirk, which is nice to see given how hostile he seemed earlier when Angie was around.

Funny that, despite all our shit-giving, and as fucked up as that thing was that happened during Omega Psi's prank, it somehow makes me feel closer to him than I really am. Maybe because in my messed-up brain I associate getting off with intimacy—and whatever the reason, as much as the guy can wind me up, I also feel pretty chill with him too.

"This is definitely an Omega Psi challenge," I say. "They do love tying shit up."

"And I can't help thinking it's not an accident that we wound up on the same team. Someone here probably got a kick out of that too."

"You're probably right." I struggle in my restraints. "Do you see a key or anything?"

"No."

I wiggle around some more.

"Can you stop doing that?" he asks.

"Well, maybe if I wasn't doing it all by myself."

"No, can you stop—"

I feel something against my ass and freeze in place. I recognize the sensation. Too well.

"Holy hell. Ty, what the fuck?"

"I'm not doing this."

"Okay, I obviously get how erections work, dude."

"You just call me *dude*? Are we fighting already? We're supposed to be working together."

I can't get my head around this. "Why am I making you hard?"

"I didn't say *you* were making me hard. You're just rubbing up against it like wild."

"Oh, it's my fault again, is it? This is sounding so familiar."

Ty sighs. "Just, will you focus?"

"You don't want me to move, so I'm having a hard time understanding what I am supposed to do."

"Just stay perfectly still, no sudden movements. And you should listen this time, since you know what happened last time."

Fair point.

I still my body, trying to focus. We're wasting time chitchatting. "Come on. The other guys are probably halfway out of theirs by now."

"Okay, it's cuffs, and they got one locked from my

wrist to this waist restraint, but I have a free arm, so it's likely they put a key on one of us. Probably you because that's the kind of shit Omega Psi puts into these things."

"Now you're making up excuses to feel me up?" Even though I know we should be focusing on the task, I couldn't help myself.

"Shut it." He rifles through my pockets. "Aha! Found it!"

"Our hero," I joke as he unfastens the cuffs around his other wrist, then starts on mine.

"See what happens when you listen to me?"

I roll my eyes. "Yeah, don't expect that to happen often."

"Okay, I can't get your ankles in this position. So you're gonna have to." He hands me the key.

"No problem." I start to bend down, and he stiffens even more.

"Whoa, whoa," he says.

"It'll take me two seconds."

"It could take me one and a half."

"Then just do it. It's not like I'll be telling anyone about this, any more than that shit that happened last year, right? Besides, we have to get our ankles free at some point, and I'm not falling behind in the score because of you."

I bend down, disregarding the potential danger of, apparently, Ty's impending ejaculation. A rush of adrenaline courses through me—I guess I'm just really excited that we're about to break free.

"You good?" I ask.

"Nearly."

We have another set of chains fastening us at the waists, and as I turn to get to the lock, my eyes are drawn to his bulge. "Oh my God, Ty, seriously with that thing."

"Look who's talking," he says.

"Huh?"

I follow his gaze to my crotch.

In the frenzy of trying to get us out of the locks, I hadn't really noticed, but I'm sporting a stiff one too.

It makes me freeze for a good moment as I try to make sense of why I've got a goddamn rock in my pants, but Ty says, "The challenge, Lance."

I get back to unfastening the lock on the waistband tying us together.

The other thing…that's something I'll work through once we kick ass at this task.

6

Ty

DESPITE LANCE'S AND my efforts, we weren't the first team captains to free ourselves, which led to our houses coming in second place, behind Beta Pi and Zeta Tau.

But losing tonight's challenge isn't the reason I'm so on edge right now. At least, not only because Lance and I could have given our guys extra time if we hadn't been so obsessed with our dicks. More because I'm trying to figure out what the hell that was all about.

I couldn't look at him through the rest of the challenge, too worried that just glancing at him might cause me to spring up around everyone. But now I'm hunting for him at Beta Pi's afters.

"Shots, shots, shots," Ryan chants as he collects Jell-O shots from a Beta Pi pledge, handing them off to me and the rest of our teammates.

I down mine before continuing to look for my rival. I better not find him in some corner, making out with

Angie. Not when we have to discuss whatever the hell happened tonight.

It was one thing when I had morning wood and got off on him during that Omega Psi prank. I thought it was just because of the friction, but what happened tonight clearly wasn't because of morning wood. For whatever reason, having Lance Fehn's ass against my pelvis had me harder than I've been in a while. And more importantly, it wasn't just happening to me.

I find Lance with his friends, and as soon as he spots me, he slips away, into the kitchen.

You really think you're getting away from me that easily?

I tail him like a stalker, and when I round the corner, I see him downing a shot from a tray on the counter. As I approach, he swallows it down.

"Um…" he says.

"We should talk." By how pissed I sound, you'd think he'd decked me, not given me an erection.

He nods, glancing around uneasily.

I spin on my heel and start through the house, and though neither of us is wearing a big sign proclaiming what happened earlier, it sure does feel like it. I guide him to the second floor and into one of the rooms the frat makes available when people want to mess around— well, at least if you're in the know. And I'm always in the know.

As soon as Lance closes the door behind him, he searches the room like he's trying to avoid eye contact. "Funny," he says. "This is where people usually come to…"

Fuck, even knowing what typically happens in here, I didn't connect that with this thing that's happening between us. It makes this even weirder, doesn't it?

We're both silent for way too long, in that way that makes an already awkward situation that much more awkward.

"You wanted something?" he presses, which annoys me since he must know why I brought him here.

I glare at him. "You think I wanted to give you a guided tour of Beta Pi? Come on, Lance."

He raises his hands. "Hey, I'm not assuming anything."

"There are at least two things we can safely assume." I glance pointedly at his crotch.

"That really isn't an assumption, though, is it? We *know* that happened."

"Yeah, well…" Fuck him for being right. I get to the point. "So…you got hard?"

I don't know why I posed it as a question. Maybe because I want to hear him confirm it really happened.

"Don't put this on me," he says defensively. "You were hard first!"

"That's true, but that doesn't change that we were both…"

"I was there," he snaps. "I don't need a recap."

I'm glad he's freaking out too, since it's how I'm feeling right now. I run my hand through my hair. "You seem pretty chill about this, but I've never had anything like it happen before."

"That's not really true. You're the one who kept calling it 'messing around.'"

"As a funny bit. I wasn't actually thinking that's what it was. I'm not a perv."

"I mean, it seems pretty pervy now." His expression twists up, but he's smirking.

Smirking at a time like this?

If he didn't look so adorable, I'd be so pissed right now.

Adorable? What is he doing to me?

"Okay," I say, trying to focus on the issue at hand. "I got hard for you twice…apparently. At least, that's how it seems. Or…maybe it was simply because of the way we were rubbing against each other, and I'm overthinking it."

Lance considers this. "True. Maybe it was something about that positioning. Our bodies were really close, and the cuffs thing was kind of sexy in and of itself, right? We could have been getting chubbies for that, not each other. Not that there's anything wrong if we were. My best friend is bi, so it's not like it's a big deal."

"No, it's not a big deal at all. Just feels like something

I would have discovered before now, you know?"

"Yeah, I do. Like, I've kissed a guy before, so—"

"Wait, what?"

That's new info.

"Dude, we're in frats. Stuff like that happens. We go to parties and play spin the bottle. We compete in TaskFrats where we rub against each other. Sometimes pranks happen, like waking up and having you come all over me and—" He doesn't finish his thought. "Why did you make that face when I said that?"

"Huh?" I hadn't even realized I was doing anything, but I must admit, there was something about him saying I came all over him that was…intriguing. In a way that surprises me as much as the rest. Well, maybe getting less surprising the more this stuff keeps redirecting to Lance.

"Your eyes got wider," he explains. "You seemed…excited about it, not that I know what you'd look like when you got excited…outside of how you get when you're winning something…or…" He shakes his head. "Whatever. This is so stupid. I told you, I've kissed a guy before, and it wasn't all that. So I know I'm not attracted to guys. I'm not saying you can't be, and if you are attracted to me, I totally respect that."

So he's experimented and felt nothing?

Maybe I'm wrong?

"Maybe you just weren't attracted to that one guy, though," I say.

"Possibly. But we could also be overthinking this. You sound as surprised as I was by it, so maybe…"

"What?"

"You've had sex with so many girls…you could just be super horny. When was the last time you had sex?"

I consider this. "Start of the semester, I guess. The first party."

"Not the weekend before last?"

I grit my teeth. "No, I didn't get as lucky as you that night."

"Well, maybe that's what it is for both of us."

"Both of us? You had sex that weekend."

"Oh…well…" He wears an adorably sheepish expression.

"Wait, what?"

"So…that Angie thing…"

My gut twists up just hearing him say her name.

For a guy who's considered himself straight, this sure doesn't feel straight.

"Nothing ever happened between us," he mumbles, tucking his head toward his chest. "I told her how you said I couldn't hook up like you, and then she was helping me prove a point."

Despite how I've been freaking out up until we came in here—thrown off, to say the least—now I suddenly feel relieved, and also cocky as hell. I fold my arms, giving him a look that makes him roll his eyes. "Oh really?"

"Hey, don't use that against me. I was being nice telling you that—that because I didn't mess with her and I've been too busy to jerk off, maybe that's why I'm getting hard."

"Because you haven't gotten off in a while?" I ask, pondering the new information. Maybe between school and work and my frat responsibilities, I wasn't attending to my sexual needs either, and that's what's messing with my head. "I hadn't thought about that. Maybe it's just that we haven't gotten any action in a few weeks. Which is wild, given all the action I got over the summer on my Miami vacation."

He scowls. "Okay, I didn't come in here and share that so you can brag about all the sex you got on your summer manwhore trip."

"I think I might go into details just to hang it over your head the way you were trying to hang getting with Angie over mine. Fair is fair."

"Ty, since you love winning so much, you got this one. I didn't hook up with her, and you were right when you said that's not the kind of guy I am. Are you happy?"

Given how stressed I was when I practically dragged him in here to sort this out, I do feel better. I shouldn't enjoy being right about him as much as I do. But it's a pleasure that gives me a little twitch—another symptom of not having gotten off with a girl in a few weeks. And not tending to my needs myself for a few days, I guess.

"So if we're cool now," Lance says, "I'll head back to the party, and we'll pretend that hard-on incident didn't happen…and neither did that first incident."

As soon as the words come out, it's clear he's second-guessing his initial reasoning.

"Yeah…" I say, echoing his skepticism.

"Hey, we don't have to make sense of it all tonight. Why don't we take a minute, think about what happened? If there's something for either of us to figure out, it'll happen another time, right?"

True. This isn't something that we'll resolve in a single conversation. And by how quickly and calmly he came up with that, I know why the guy's the president of Alpha Theta Mu. Guy can think through a complicated situation. It's a good call, something I respect him for.

"Go get lucky and see what happens," he says.

"There's nothing lucky about what I do, Lance." Reclaiming my cocky attitude helps me leave behind the anxiety I came to the party with.

He chuckles. "Okay, not surprised with that rock in your pants," he says, referring to what he believed my dick was at first when we were bound together by Omega Psi last spring. "Think I'm gonna start calling you Rocky."

"I kind of like that nickname, Stud."

He laughs, shaking his head. "Whatever. We should probably get back to the party. We cool?"

"As cool as rival frat presidents can be."

He approaches and starts to put his hand on my back, as if to lead me out of the room, but stops himself. "Maybe I shouldn't push our luck. Let's just get our horny asses downstairs and play some beer pong."

"Sure, Stud," I tease.

We share a laugh, and it's nice being able to laugh with him again, especially after how in my head I've been since the challenge.

When we return to the party, I find I'm calmer, though I'm still trying to process it all.

I may give Lance hell about some stuff, but he's not an idiot, and he could be right that this is all just from being so fucking horny. I could find a girl, and we could rush back to one of our places and get this out of the way.

But tonight, I really just want to hang with him because once again, I'm reminded that despite how much hell we give each other, we get each other on some level. And it's comforting that, whatever the fuck is going on, Lance is open to talking about it.

After the party comes to an end, I head back to my room, still thinking about our conversation. Maybe I do just need to get one out of my system, and then all that stuff will clear away and I'll never get a boner for Lance again. And then we can both move on, and tonight will be one of the most awkward conversations I've had in my life.

I strip down, grab some lube from my nightstand, and lie in bed. I get situated and start thinking about Deidre. She's the last girl I hooked up with, and it was like fucking fire. Sparks flew as we tossed around my bed. She was near weightless and just wanted to be pounded. I ran out of steam toward the end but had to push myself to keep going, passionate about making sure she came. And fuck, when she came…

But just as I'm really getting going, the image of Lance springs to mind. The way his ass was pushed back against my pelvis, wiggling about.

I try to ignore the thought, but suddenly, when I'm trying to think about messing with Deidre, all I can see is Lance under me, his sexy body, that great view of him in his G-string.

I envision him taking my cock, his expression all twisted up. Heat rushes to my face, and I find myself not resisting the fantasy. If this is something I'm into, then I want to know. And it's not like I'll ever have to tell Lance about this little innocent fantasy. Besides, it'll probably make me soft the longer I think about it.

So I really get in there, imagine him calling out my name, letting me toss him around on the bed—no, begging for it. It's the kind of fucking we would share— wild, competitive, sweat-filled fucking. In my mind, he's not holding anything back as I take him. Make him mine.

"Yes, you're mine," I mutter as I realize my cock is stiffer than I can remember it ever being while I've jerked off.

In my dirty fantasy, his mouth is hanging open as he calls out my damn name and—

I grunt as my hips thrust forward repeatedly, cum shooting out, shocking me as I feel the warmth against my goddamn chest.

I never fucking shoot that far.

What the hell?

It takes me a minute to recover as the cum keeps spilling out in a second burst that lands on my navel, and then I collapse, my mind spiraling back through the intense fuck I imagined sharing with Lance.

Oh, fucking hell.

7

Lance

"HOW HAVE YOU been?" Mom asks.

After my Biomedical Microscopy class, I had some free time, so I decided to give her a call. I make it a point to give my parents a call whenever I can. Since we lost Kacey, we all know we must take advantage of every precious moment since we never know how many we'll have left.

"Work and school," I reply. "Been hectic the past few weeks but managing."

"And how was TaskFrat? You haven't mentioned it. Do I need to expect Shirley to send me a video of you in a…I don't know…what's worse than a G-string?"

Shirley is Mom's friend, who apparently is active enough on social media to catch when one of the latest TaskFrat TikTok videos is trending.

"No G-string," I reply, which gets her laughing.

I tell her about the event last Friday—conveniently leaving out the bit about having a raging boner for Ty and our subsequent conversation at Beta Pi. She doesn't need to know I haven't been able to stop thinking about Ty Lancaster.

And not in my usual, fun-rivalry way.

I've tested our theory that it might be from lack of jerking off…several times. But it hasn't done anything to keep me from blushing whenever I think about what happened. My dick plumps up every time I think about the way he was rubbing against my ass during the challenge.

"It sounds like it was fun," Mom says.

Fun isn't the word I'd use for any of this. Just *weird*.

"So I imagine Ty wasn't too thrilled that you were tied with him," Mom adds.

This is what I get for having a healthy relationship with my mom and telling her about all the stuff in my life. I love her, but fuck, should've known I couldn't talk to her about Ty too much without potentially piquing her curiosity.

"Yeah, he wasn't thrilled. But hey, I'm planning to meet Ash over at the library soon, so I'll call you later and we can chat about your day some."

"I feel like you're avoiding something, but your mother knows you well enough to let you sort it out, and I'll talk to you about whatever it is when you feel like."

"Okay, Mom," I groan.

We exchange I-love-yous and goodbyes. I feel bad for

cutting our call short, but I wasn't entirely dishonest. I am meeting Ash at the library, like I usually do on Tuesdays. At the same time, it's not some urgent thing I needed to get off the phone with her for. But hey, it'll give me extra study time, so I head over and get to it.

Ash isn't here yet. Figure he's swinging by the student center cafeteria to grab a jumbo chocolate-chip cookie, his favorite, and I do my best to concentrate on my Signals & Systems work.

But concentration hasn't been easy the past few days, and all I can think is that I should just ask Ash about these things I'm feeling. Who'll understand better than my bi guy? Still, Ash is smart, and if I say something that indicates I'm having these feelings about Ty, then I'm revealing something about Ty, without his consent, which I would never do.

Fuck. But how can I bear dealing with these thoughts all by myself?

I focus on my work, starting to feel like I'm able to get Ty Lancaster out of my head again, when I hear, "Hey, Stud."

There's that familiar warmth in my cheeks again. I turn to see Ty standing at my side, his gaze right on mine, and I glance away quickly, like I'm afraid if he looks into my eyes, he'll see how I'm starting to think I was wrong about it being from not getting off.

"Hey, Rocky…" I drag out as he makes himself comfortable in the chair beside mine.

He's quiet for an uncomfortably lengthy amount of time, so I add, "What's up?"

"Good."

"*Good* isn't a response to what's up."

He searches around the library, which is fairly empty, but it's not like we can just chat about anything we want in here.

"How you been?" he asks.

"Fine… You?"

Silence again. And I'm left thinking, what the hell is going on here?

"I think we need to talk." He leans closer, whispering, "I—"

As his breath hits my ear, my skin pricks with sensation, and I recoil from him, catching him by surprise.

"Man, personal space," I say.

"Sorry." His forehead creases because that's not something I've requested from him before.

I notice the way he's looking at me, and it's weird, like this is the first time he's ever seen my face. I want to crawl out of my goddamn skin and slip away, but also, don't want to move. Don't want him to stop.

"Sorry I'm late," Ash's voice comes from nearby, and Ty and I break eye contact. "The cafeteria had a line because they only had one guy working the register." He sets his stuff down on the chair opposite mine.

"Hey, Ty…" Ash glances between us, seemingly trying to make it make sense since it's not like I'm best friends with the guy.

Smart as Ash is, I doubt he could guess what's going on right now even if he tried.

"I, uh…" Ty responds.

He's not thinking fast enough, and I worry he's gonna make things as awkward around Ash as he has around me, but fortunately Ash doesn't press, and instead says, "Oh, I know what you guys are talking about."

"What?" Ty asks.

I can tell by his panicked expression that he thinks I went off and told my best friend about our conversation the other night, so as Ash settles in his chair, I try to psychically convey to Ty that Ash doesn't know what the hell happened, and that he won't unless Ty says something.

I'm expecting him to get angry about thinking I blabbed, but his expression relaxes. "I guess he is your best friend…"

"Ty, why don't we talk about this later?" I ask, trying to get the guy to shut the hell up because Ash isn't a dummy, and he's clearly catching on that something's up.

"I would have preferred you told me before you told him," Ty goes on, "because this isn't just about you."

"Ty," I say sternly as Ash glances between us. He

might not have suspected anything before, but now he definitely is. "Just official TaskFrat stuff," I tell Ash. "So it's something we should talk about another time, Ty."

Ty's cheeks pinken—it's nice not being the one blushing for a change—but Ash just shrugs, seeming to buy the cover. I hate lying to my best friend.

"Yeah, I guess it's something we can talk about later," Ty says. "Maybe you can meet me over at Sigma Alpha."

I should agree, but if I let him leave now, after everything that just happened and everything I've been thinking about since this past weekend, it'll drive me wild. I won't be able to think about anything else, let alone study.

"You know, maybe we should go ahead and get this sorted out now." I push to my feet. "Ash, do you mind?"

Ash's expression twists up. "It's not a big deal. Get your stuff done."

I put my book and notebook away, and then we head toward the main stairwell doors. Ty looks anxious as fuck.

"Where do you want to go?" I ask him.

"One of the meeting rooms on the fifth floor," he says, I'm assuming because that floor's never that busy.

I'm relieved we're gonna discuss this right away, since I'm in too much suspense about what he wants to talk about. When we reach the fifth floor, we find an empty room without anyone else on either side, then head in and close the door.

Ty glances around.

"You looking for recording devices?" I ask. "So you can give me a secret mission?" I'm trying to make light of a tense situation, but he glares at me. Doesn't seem in the mood. "Any other day you would have thought that funny," I remark.

"Yeah, well, today's not any other day."

Then there's awkward silence again.

I head to the other side of the main table that takes up most of the room, and I set my backpack in one of the swivel chairs. A thousand clever remarks run through my head, but since Ty's not in the mood, I wait for him to get to the point.

And wait...

And wait...

He runs his hand through his hair, messing up his bangs, then starts for the door. I think he might be about to head out, which would make this whole situation even stranger than it already is, but then he spins toward me. "Lance, you were wrong."

"I wasn't expecting an accusation to start. What was I wrong about?"

"I don't think I'm just horny as fuck."

Shit.

"Friday after the party, after we talked about it, I was actually jerking off..."

I cringe. "Is this something we need to get into?"

"It's relevant," he insists, so I let him go on. "I was thinking about this girl I hooked up with over the summer. Hot-as-hell blonde in Miami…"

A pulse of rage rushes through me, the sort I might have had for him any other time when I knew he was having this incredible sex life, but now I'm wondering if some of this jealousy isn't because *he* was with that girl, but that *she* was with him. Is this how he felt about Angie?

"It was incredible," he says. "Like fucking-for-hours kind of fucking—"

"I don't need the details of your sex life. And why did you bring me in here to talk about how you were jerking off thinking about this girl? Sounds like I was right, and yet you said I was wrong. I'm so fucking confused."

"Because I started thinking about *you*," he spits out, and I'm so thrown, he might as well have told me the building was on fire.

"Me?" I ask, barely able to make sense of the thoughts in my head.

"Like…here I was, thinking about one of the hottest sexual experiences of my life, and then suddenly I'm thinking about you."

"Bet that killed the mood real fast," I blurt out.

I don't even know why I said that. After what he

shared so far, I know that can't be the case, yet a part of me just can't accept the weird-ass thing that's been going on between us the past few days.

But as we make eye contact, his expression even more serious than when he's trying to stomp Alpha Theta Mu's ass during a challenge, I'm aware of how much my being there didn't kill the mood even before he says, "I came harder than I've ever come in my life."

There go my cheeks again.

"You were thinking about…what? Us messing around?"

His face twists up. "Do you really want to know?"

"The hell? I didn't want to know any of this, but if you're gonna share this much, I don't see why you need to stop."

He hesitates, as though some reasonable part of his brain knows better than to share, before he says, "Fucking you, Lance. I was fucking you. Like giving you the time of your life, watching you enjoy every inch of me. Jesus, are you happy?"

Happy isn't the word I'd use, but my face is burning, and my dick is getting pretty stiff, the two events assuring me that what happened between us and what I've been thinking about between last Friday and today isn't a fluke.

"And," he continues, "I've been trying to give myself some time to think about *why* I was thinking about you, but now it's like burned into my fucking brain, and it's just, like, haunting me at this point."

"You wanted to fuck me?" It's hard to tell if I need him to confirm what he just said or if I *want* to hear him say it again.

"No, I was trying not to think about that," he says, then, "But…yes. A lot. Like right until I blew."

He quiets again, and as uncomfortable as the silences were before, this time it feels unbearable. He won't even look at me.

"Lance, I've never had to deal with something like this before, but I think…no, I *know*, I want to act on some of these things. And I'm wondering if maybe I misunderstood that first time…"

"When you came all over me? Yeah, maybe that should have been some kind of indication for both of us."

He glares at me again, and I realize why. "Whoa, I wasn't making a joke," I assure him.

"Just saying I should have probably put two and two together. I know your erection was probably because you are this fucking prude who hasn't had sex in like a million years, but mine—"

"It hasn't been *that* long."

He snickers. "Dude, now *I'm* trying to lighten the mood."

And really, I'm glad someone is trying because this

shit is way too serious right now.

He takes a breath. "I know you probably don't have those kinds of feelings for me, and I guess since you're the first person who experienced what was happening to me—"

"Twice."

He smiles again, and fuck, what it does to me knowing I can make him smile like that.

Why did I just think that…?

Wait, why is that thought surprising me when I keep having these kinds of thoughts?

"I've never felt this way about other guys, Lance. And I've pulled up images online, but it seems it's just you who gets me going."

I swear, it's like the guy is trying to poke at my inner…whatever the hell is making me interested.

"And I don't know what to do about it," he concludes. "Sorry if I'm making this too weird."

"You're definitely doing that."

He huffs, nodding, avoiding eye contact.

And…I can't deny something's happening for me too. "I guess this would be a good time to tell you that whatever's going on with you, I…get what you mean."

His gaze cuts right to me.

"And I don't know what's going on either, but even while you've been talking about this…" I indicate my crotch, and it catches his gaze.

"Oh…"

"Yeah…"

"What are we gonna do, Lance?"

That's the million-dollar question.

"Right now, it's all in our heads. We haven't actually done anything with each other, so what if we tried and we didn't even like it?"

"That's true," he says. "Like with this girl I met in San Antonio. I thought we'd have a great time, but then we kissed, and there just wasn't any chemistry there."

"Sure," I say, once again fighting back that knee-jerk irritation at hearing about one of these girls he's done stuff with.

"What if we try to mess around, see what happens, and then we'll know for sure."

I nod. This isn't an erotic thing. It's practical. We both have questions, and this is the surest way to get answers.

He licks his lips, and fuck, now I can't take my eyes off his lips.

"Yeah," he goes on. "Chances are we get a little grossed out and move on. But maybe it doesn't mean anything about the two of us as much as that there could be something for guys, right?"

"Yeah," I say, though I hate the thought that we might mess around and it won't be as satisfying as I have a feeling it'd be. But am I really suggesting me and my

Sigma Alpha rival mess around to sort this out?

I mean, it feels like the only right way to do it but also like I'm in way over my head.

"You free later?" he asks.

Oh, we're on, aren't we?

8

Ty

THIS IS A mistake.

I shouldn't have told Lance about my fantasy, but once we were alone together, I couldn't keep this all in my head anymore. I had to tell someone. Anyone.

I definitely shouldn't have encouraged us to meet at Sigma Alpha to mess around, and Lance shouldn't have gone along with it. But before he left the meeting room, he said, *"I have another class, and then I'll meet you at Sigma Alpha."*

This has huge mistake written all over it. It could wind up being an epic fail that leaves both of us, or one of us, embarrassed as hell. Although, if there's anyone I trust to experiment with, it's the guy who kept secret what happened last spring.

I return to my frat house, telling myself I'll get some work done on a group project I have in Ethics, Law, and Policy, but it turns into mindless scrolling on socials.

Nothing takes the edge off, though, so I start pacing

my room like I would before a big exam. Biting my bottom lip, I check my phone for what must be the hundredth time. Lance's class must've ended thirty minutes ago, but he hasn't texted me to let me know he's on his way.

Maybe now that he's had time to think about what a stupid idea this is, he's changed his mind. Can't say I'd blame him, but my heart sinks at the thought of not exploring this, of being left wondering what the hell is going on. Just as bad would be having a guy I've considered a worthy adversary suddenly looking at me differently whenever we see each other at TaskFrat challenges or around school.

No, he wouldn't do that to me.

I start texting him, then stop.

Fuck, if he's looking at his phone, sees the ellipsis come up, he'll know I stopped, so I go ahead and send the question that's burning on my mind.

Still coming over?

I stare at the text feed, waiting for a response, when the ellipsis appears, indicating Lance is replying, giving me some relief that at least he's still talking to me.

Then it stops.

Then starts back up.

Then stops again.

When it doesn't pick back up again, it's soul-crushing. This has been my fear all along—that he wouldn't come. And he won't. I can feel it in my bones.

Once he had time away from me, he must've gotten his head on straight—as if anything is straight about any of this—and decided he couldn't follow through with messing around with a guy.

I wish he would just say that, not leave me wondering what he's thinking.

I know it's a shit idea—if he needs space, I should give it to him—but I'm not letting him get away without telling me to my face, so I grab my keys and wallet and start for the door.

When I open it, I freeze in place. Lance is standing outside, wide-eyed, his phone in his hand.

As seems to be a familiar pattern for us the past few days, I'm thrown. "I thought you weren't coming over," I blurt.

His lips twist into a frown. "I considered it. Got to the door when you texted and figured this was my last chance to bail." He smirks awkwardly, and all the frustration I'd worked up dissolves. Having him here brings me visceral relief.

I step aside so he can come in, then close the door.

"You want something to drink? I have some beer, White Claw…"

"I could have a White Claw."

"I only have peach-flavored. That work?"

"This is Peach State. Why would we have any others?" He smiles, disarming me in that way he has.

I fetch two White Claws from my mini fridge. We pop them open and take sips. When Lance finally pulls the can away from his mouth, his tongue slides across his bottom lip, making my mouth water.

Yup. No question. This guy definitely does something to me.

"You got anything stronger?" he asks.

"You kidding me? What you want? Tequila? Gin?"

"Vodka?"

I crouch down and grab a small bottle of Absolut from the mini fridge.

Lance takes a much bigger gulp from his White Claw, and when I hand over the vodka, he screws off the top, pours a shot's worth in the can, swirls it all together, and takes another drink. Guy's got the right idea, so I do the same with my drink before setting the bottle of vodka on top of the mini fridge. When I finish mixing the vodka, I take another healthy, much-needed drink, enjoying the way the vodka stings lightly against my tongue.

"This would have been better to have in the library." He takes another sip.

"Tell me about it."

"So…I know we said we'd meet here and figure this out, but we weren't exactly clear about the specifics."

"That's because I don't know what we should be doing." It was one thing to agree to meet up and do something to make sense of what's happening between us. Another entirely to actually do it, so now we're just standing around, uncomfortable as hell. "I don't imagine we could be much more flaccid right now," I joke.

"So maybe we figured it out." His gaze meets mine, his cheeks that familiar shade of pink I've seen more the past few days. It stirs something in me that makes me aware we definitely haven't figured it out.

"Maybe we get into my bed." I try to sound chill—emphasis on *try*. "See what happens."

His brows tug closer together. "This how slick you are with girls?"

"I'm actually disappointed because if I turn out to be bi, I'd hate to think this is how bad I'll be at seducing guys."

He laughs, breaking that tension once again before his expression turns serious and he glances at me, like he's wondering whether he should have taken that as a joke. I can't really help him there because I'm not all that sure myself.

He sets his can down on my nightstand, then sits on the edge of my bed. "Okay, let's get this over with. Sit down next to me."

I place my drink beside his and join him, keeping about half a foot between us. Some part of me is clearly still afraid of running this test, which makes me think that's the very reason I need to do it.

Meanwhile, Lance is doing that thing where he's not making eye contact. He's not comfortable.

"Relax," I say, "I'm not gonna lunge at you and start making out."

"Yeah, that doesn't sound like the way to do it." He cringes, as though he's disgusted by the idea, which is more than a little insulting.

"If you're not into that, then maybe this is a bad idea."

"We agreed this is the only way to know if this is something we're into, right? Are you butthurt because I don't want to jump right into making out with you?"

"No, but it doesn't help that you made that face when I suggested it."

"I don't know what face I made, but you saw my dick earlier when we were talking in the conference room, so I wouldn't take it as an insult."

He's right. I'm overly defensive, which somehow has nothing to do with him and everything to do with him at the same time.

"Maybe we just, like, touch each other a little. Like before," I suggest, but I can read the apprehension all over his face at the mention of touching him, and it's a real buzzkill. "This was a shit idea. If you're uncomfortable, just go, and I can find someone else. I'm sure plenty of guys would be willing to help me understand what the hell is—"

I barely noticed him move, but now he's got his hand on my thigh. My body's stiff as he glances at me uneasily.

"You said we start with touching? Is this okay?" He pats around my thigh, keeping his touch as unerotic as possible. "There. I'm doing it. I'm doing the thing," he says, like he's trying to make a joke out of it.

His face is bright red, and he won't look me in the eyes, but even being silly about touching me is clearly working as my dick lengthens in my athletic shorts.

Lance doesn't look, though. "That doing anything?" he asks.

"Um…"

His gaze finally shifts to look, and his jaw drops. "Oh…"

"Yeah…"

His hand settles on my thigh, which only makes me stiffen more, and he doesn't take his eyes off it for a few moments. When he does, his gaze meets mine and he gulps.

Though there was little doubt before we began our little experiment, there's no question in my mind as his touch lingers. His thumb caresses against the fabric of my shorts, so I have to shift slightly to let my cock finish swelling.

"Are you okay?" I ask him, since it's hard to gauge based on his expression—frozen in place, hasn't changed since we locked eyes.

He breaks eye contact and leans back, so I can see the bulge in his pants. He slides his hand closer to my crotch, then over my cock, before stroking back and forth. His gaze has returned to my cock, and he licks his lips. "This okay?" he asks.

"Does it look okay?"

He chuckles nervously before his expression turns stone-cold again. "Lie back. If you want, that is… I want to try something, but not if you'd rather not."

I trust Lance. This is just as strange to him as it is to me, and if my lying back helps us untangle this, I'm willing to give it a whirl. I relax back, and he slides his hand from my cock up to my waist.

"This still okay?" he asks.

"That you took your hand off my dick? Not really."

He huffs out a breath. "I meant, can I feel it under your shorts?"

"Oh. Uh, yes, if that's something you want to—"

"I. Do." He slides his hand under the waistband of my shorts, moving toward my cock until I can feel his warm fingers against my flesh.

My body vibrates—partly from his touch, partly from anticipation—as I'm wondering what he'll do next. He gets a handle on me, and unlike when he put his hand on my thigh at first, I can tell there's nothing playful or silly about this touch. He wears a determined expression as he strokes me some more.

Fuck, it's sexy.

I roll my head against my bed, enjoying the way he's pumping me.

"That's good?" he asks.

"What does it feel like?"

He snickers, his grip firming as he strokes more confidently. "Can I pull your shorts down?"

"Don't you dare move that hand." I intended for that to come out playfully, but there's so much truth to it that it sounds more like a threat. I tuck my thumbs in either side of my shorts and push them down, revealing my hard-on, and he keeps his hand in place as he sees my cock in the flesh.

"No underwear," he notes.

"In case something happened."

His lips curl into that sexy, familiar smirk. "Looks bigger than I remember."

"Last time you saw me naked, I'd already come, so…"

And there's that beautiful pink shade again, something I can only appreciate for a moment before he pumps me again.

I can't stifle my moan. The way the sensation pulses through me makes my body quiver, and I relax back as he keeps on working me up faster. My hips jerk with his movements as a series of sensations burst in waves through me, rushing up my body, radiating out of my chest.

"Fuck, you're good at that, Lance," I say, and my encouragement makes him speed up.

"You get harder when I jerk closer to the head," he says, and that he even notices that thrills me. I love how he's paying attention to my body and movements, and it's no surprise how close he's getting me.

"It's kinda dry," he says.

"I have some lube…"

"You mind if I just give it a little spit? Sometimes that's what I do when I'm jerking off."

"That sounds hot as fuck."

He leans down and spits onto the head of my cock, running his hand through it, the moisture slicking across my flesh, coating me so he's able to pick up his movements even more.

It's definitely over for me.

"Lance, I'm about to—"

"Do it," he says as we lock eyes once again. With his free hand, he hikes up my shirt, keeping his movements steady. I don't see any of the doubt or uncertainty he came into this room with, only this primal part of himself committed to taking me to the end. It's as though he's intuited exactly what I need before I—

"Fuck, fuck…" My body erupts in a series of fits as I bash my fists against the sides of the bed, rolling my head back as the climax is so intense before I feel the warmth rush across my abs and chest. I figure that has to be the last of it, but the sensation lingers as a second burst lines my waist.

As my climax relaxes, Lance is still going, but my cock feels too sensitive, so I seize his wrist. "Ooh, ooh, no no, that's good," I tell him as the sensation eases up.

I catch my breath, recovering from the intensity of what he just did, accepting that there's no fucking way any of this is simply about a fantasy. This is clearly something my body wants, and now that I've experienced it, maybe *needs*.

As I come back down from the high, I notice I still haven't released Lance's wrist. And he glances at my cum-soaked torso, licking his lips again before saying, "I guess we sorted that out. Maybe I should go now."

He pulls away, pushes to his feet, and starts for the door.

What the hell?

9

Lance

I RUSH TO the door, overwhelmed by everything that's happened—from what I felt for Ty when I first saw his erection, to getting the idea to stroke him off, to finishing the job.

What started off as curiosity turned into a damned obsession. A mission to get to take him all the way. Reading his body and studying his cock made me feel a delicious rush.

In the moment when I was making him stiffer in my grasp, I wasn't myself but a sex god, with total control over Ty's pleasure. I was feral with desire, not using my head. Just acting off these innate impulses that drove me until he came all over himself.

And when I saw him soaked with his cum, all I wanted to do was lean down and take a quick lick. I nearly did until, in a moment, I was no longer hypnotized by his cock and able to regain my senses.

Even though Ty said he wanted me to jerk him off,

went right along with my suggestions, I worry I pushed us too far. He wanted to experiment, maybe have me rub on him, not have me jerking him to finishing on his chest.

And oh, how he finished, the white streaks across his perfect flesh.

I'm at the door, grabbing the knob, when Ty says, "Lance, wait a minute."

I whirl around to face him, and he isn't wearing his shirt anymore. Guess he threw it off so he wouldn't get it soaked in the cum that's still over him.

My mouth waters as I study the little spots glistening on him.

Ty blinks erratically, like he's struggling to recover from what was obviously a mind-blowing orgasm. "Did I do something wrong?"

"*You?*" I'm offended by the question. What could have been wrong about the way he lay there, writhing about and moaning while he let me pump one out of him? "Not at all. I just didn't mean to make it weird and get so into it…"

"I told you I wanted you to do that, and you think *you* made it weird?"

He's right, but this whole experience was like another person stepped into my body and took over. Even now as he's acting so nice about it all, I'm waiting for him to say something like, *What the hell got into you?*

Instead, he says, "Seriously, are *you* okay?"

I'm used to Ty being cocky or a bit of an asshole, but now I'm seeing a rare expression for him—concern, for me. And I must admit, it's nice.

"I…don't know," I confess.

He moves closer, and my gaze drifts across his torso, taking in the streaks of white. I lick my lips again, wondering where this impulse to run my tongue through it all is even coming from.

He rests his hand on my arm. He's touched me before, but it's never felt like fire grazing across my flesh.

"Lance, come on. After what we just did, pretty sure there's not much you can't talk to me about."

"So you're fine with how far it went?" I study his expression, searching for any sign of regret or discomfort.

His eyebrows shift with his smirk. "*Fine* isn't really the word I'd use." He strokes across my arm with his thumb, and my dick perks right back up. "And obviously, if you don't want to do anything else, I get it, but I'd hate to be rude. Feel like it's my job to make sure you get off before heading out."

The way he's drinking me in, I can only imagine how the women he's been with have felt when he's set that look on them. I check the bulge in my pants, which is fucking straining, because I don't know if I've ever been so swollen in these jeans before. Part of me thinks I should bolt while I have the chance. But with everything that's happened, and how hard I am right now, I'm too curious to deny myself this.

"But," he adds, "if you've changed your mind, that's totally fine too. I'll be disappointed, but I'll understand—"

"No, it's fine."

"*Only* fine?" His smirk shifts into a grin.

Given everything that's happened, it shouldn't shock me that he'd want to do this too, but my mind can't accept that he's anything other than my straight rival Ty, even with all the facts I have that tell me that can't be right.

He runs his hand down my arm, caressing until his touch breaks away from my skin and gravitates to my crotch. He applies gentle pressure, and my cock pulses with the sensation as he moves even closer.

The twist of his lips as he rubs along my shaft sends a burst of excitement pulsing through me. "Mmmm…you like that?"

"Clearly."

"Then I bet you'll really like this…" His touch abandons my cock while he unfastens my belt, then unzips my fly, sliding his hand beneath my trunks, gripping my cock.

A rush shoots up my spine, goose bumps pricking across my arms as he gets hold of me, his eyes meeting mine as he offers that first stroke. My mouth falls open as waves of sensation pulse through me before he strokes back up and there's another wave. He moves slowly at first, like I did when I was trying to get a feel for what I was doing.

"You did a really good job with my cock, so I feel like I have my work cut out for me."

He offers another sweeping movement, running the full length of my shaft, and I tremble from the excitement it stirs.

He chuckles. "That's what you like, isn't it? I like it more toward the head, but you like feeling it all the way to the base, don't you?"

He's not wrong. It's something I had to work out while I was jerking him off, studying his expressions and the way his breath hitched. Now he's doing the same to me.

He leans closer, whispering in my ear, "Uh-huh. Think I'm right."

The way his breath hits my flesh is too much for me, and I roll my head back, embracing the sensation.

"Fuck." I moan.

"Oh, you like that too?" he asks, guiding me until my back's against the door. He firms his grip on me as he whispers, "Dirty Lance learning a lot of new things about himself too today, isn't he?" His lips graze my earlobe while he continues working my cock, the pressure in me intensifying quickly. "Showing me things about me, and now it's my turn." He stops stroking for a moment, and my body goes into panic mode as I search around to figure out what he's doing before he runs his hand through the cum on his torso.

"You want a taste?"

I feel so transparent. Like he's reading my goddamn mind, and I don't even have a problem with it because he can't know how bad I want to taste him right now.

He raises his fingers to my lips. "Go ahead. Take it, Stud."

I lean forward, running my tongue on the bottom of his fingers, but as the taste hits, I move forward and take his fingers into my mouth, sucking gently. My chest swells with excitement as swirls of sensation spiral through my body.

How could such a simple act get me so worked up?

While I finish sucking up his cum, he spits in his free hand before wrapping it around my cock. Keeping his fingers in my mouth, I moan.

"Yeah, you really had a good trick up your sleeve there. Had to steal it."

His slippery palm moves faster, up and down, driving me wild as I keep sucking on his fingers even though I've lapped up every bit of cum.

"I think you're getting close," he says as my ass clenches from all the pressure, moving toward the urgency until he moves close to my ear again. "Come on,

Lance, give it to me. Let's see what your load looks like."

And with those words, it's over for me as my body erupts in a fit. I press my hands tight against the door behind me as the pressure finally releases.

Ty snickers. "Fuck, that's it," he says, and once I manage to open my eyes, I see him watching my cock, surely as fascinated by seeing me come as I was with him.

I pant, trying to catch my breath as Ty's gaze meets mine.

Despite all the discomfort and uneasiness I had after getting him off, the satisfaction on his face takes all that away. Now I'm just blissed out, accepting that I'll have to figure out later all the confusing bits.

"Well," I say. "I guess we learned a thing or two from this session after all."

"Maybe more than just two, but yeah."

I laugh, noticing how much the tension I had coming into Sigma Alpha has eased up.

"So…what does this mean?" I ask.

"Means…I think you need to swing by again so that I can determine…" He leans closer. "Exactly how sensitive these ears of yours are."

Once again, I feel my nerves vibrating with excitement with how he's stimulating them.

"Seriously, though, we're going to do that again, right?" I ask.

I must sound so goddamn pathetic because I'm desperate.

"Lance, I still have my hand around your dick. What do you think?"

"I mean, I don't know. Don't you usually hit it and quit it with girls?"

That's my real fear. I know how he is, and if this is the last time he's ever gonna touch me, fuck, what the hell am I gonna do?

"Maybe that's the issue," he says, studying my expression. "I haven't hit it yet."

And there go my cheeks again as I recognize a familiar, determined expression.

"So much for thinking we're straight, huh?" I ask, which makes him laugh.

Because yeah, that was as not straight as it gets.

10

Ty

"YOU NOT GONNA answer me?" Ryan asks, pulling me out of my thoughts.

He stands beside me in the gym locker room, assessing himself in the mirror.

"Huh?" I'm more than a little distracted. It's been hard to think about much else since Lance came over and we fucked around the other day.

Whatever doubt I may have had about what's happening between us has evaporated. What we did in my bedroom was explosive. And not just because of the way he worked my cock, but even getting him off, feeling the subtleties in his movements, the way his expression locked up as he came…it's something I haven't been able to get off my mind.

And now I'm supposed to get back to my life and act like everything's normal? Fuck that.

"My chest looks bigger, right?" Ryan puffs it out, his towel at his side, since—as usual—he's not bothering to cover up.

It's interesting that, even though I'm discovering this side of myself, I'm not even remotely attracted to my friend.

Not a thought I would've ever had before, but since my experiment with Lance, how can I not? Sure, I've known guys like Ryan are attractive. I've been around plenty of hot guys, but none of them got me worked up like my Alpha Theta Mu nemesis. Although, maybe it's just because I never woke up tied to any of them, marking them with my cum. Or because none of them have ever looked at me with those intense brown eyes.

"Your chest and your arms are a lot more swole right now," I assure Ryan, who winces.

"That was like pulling teeth."

"I'm sorry, man. I've had a lot on my mind the past few days."

"Anything you want to talk about? Or you gonna stew in it and deal with it yourself, then tell me all about it?"

Ryan gets me. I'm not the sort to show my hand, especially when I'm dealing with shit. I tend to keep it all in, stuff it down until I resolve the issue. Then I share it with friends. Probably not the healthiest way to do it, but that's the way I've always been.

"It's—" I nearly say, *It's nothing,* but I would never say that about what I did with Lance. Not when it was *everything.* "I'll tell you about it at some point, I'm sure," is the most I can give.

"Okay, man. You know I'm here if you need any-thing. In the meantime, I'm gonna be an amazing friend and tell you that your pecs are looking hot as hell today. Whatever girl you wind up with at Omega Psi's party tomorrow night, tell them to thank me for how hard you got these." He grips my pec, and I'm impressed at how firm the muscle is. He's right to credit himself for how he's pushed me.

"What muscles can *I* grab onto?" comes from nearby, and a smiling Dax rounds the corner of the row of lockers. Wet and with a towel around his waist, it's clear he's coming from the showers.

"Hey, man," Ryan says, approaching Dax and hug-ging it out, not seeming to give any fucks about the way his dick's waving around as he pulls back, something Dax clearly notices.

"You just get here?" I ask as we fist-bump.

"Nah, I've been here for a bit."

Ryan and I glance at each other because it's not so big a gym that we would've missed him.

"I got a good workout in," he assures us, sporting a mischievous smirk. The guy fucking oozes charisma and charm. I thought I was good at getting laid until I saw Dax's skills. Prolific is an understatement. He's also just an all-around cool guy.

Two guys pass behind him, one in a tank, the other in a polo and holding a backpack. They head for the exit, and the one with the backpack says, "See you around, Dax."

"Yeah, text us later," the other follows, turning enough that I can see the glint in his eyes, which keeps me from having to speculate about what Dax was up to.

"What did you hit today?" Ryan asks Dax. "Arms? Shoulders?"

God, I love him, but he can definitely come across as the oblivious jock sometimes.

"I hit glutes," Dax jokes. "Hard."

"Yeah? Let's see." Ryan steps around to check out Dax's ass, still not seeming to pick up on what Dax was insinuating.

"I was fucking those guys who just passed us," Dax explains, putting our precious friend out of his misery.

"Oh…" Ryan says, his eyes widening. "That makes more sense."

"But you guys clearly got in a good workout today," Dax notes.

"Yeah, this isn't like peak fitness. Planning to put on thirty, but look at these guns." Ryan glances back at the mirror, flexing for himself.

"Damn," Dax says, admiring his physique. "Looking thick as hell."

"Come over and give it a little feel."

Dax doesn't pass up the opportunity to feel up a guy, so he takes Ryan's bicep and gives it a squeeze. "Like a rock."

Is it weird that even the word *rock* reminds me of Lance because of what he thought during that first…encounter?

Ryan grabs Dax's hand and moves it to his abs. "You'd fuck this, right?"

"Oh my God, Ryan," I say.

"I'd probably want you to fuck me," Dax says, "but since that's not happening, I suggest you take a pic of this and add it to your Insta stories."

Wild to see Ryan joking about fucking around with a guy, having no idea what I was up to earlier this week.

What I can't seem to get out of my head.

Ryan stands a little taller, clearly pleased with the compliment as he fetches his phone from his locker and snaps a few pics. "See, Dax appreciates that I just need my ego stroked every once in a while. My best friend could learn a thing or two."

"It's probably better coming from someone who would actually fuck you," I say, "but I'll take the best-friend note under consideration. Maybe we can add it to the minutes at the next frat meeting. Meanwhile, Dax, I noticed I haven't gotten a compliment after this guy just put me through it in there."

"Okay, okay," Dax says. "I'd let you both fuck me,

but it'd have to be at the same time. That better?"

I'm tempted to say, *No way I'm fucking anyone other than Lance.* But of course, I can't say that, and it's a weird-ass thing to even think, especially when I don't even know if he'd want me fucking him.

"I don't need your pity fuck," I insist.

"Why you turning down Dax's pity fuck?" Ryan asks. "You accept them from girls. That seems homophobic." He's got that playful expression on his face. The guy loves giving me hell.

"Fuck off, you big frathole," I tease, and Dax and Ryan are in stitches.

We chat a bit more, get dressed, and head out. When I get into my car, I check my phone to see if Lance has messaged.

We've exchanged a few DMs on Insta. Just checking in. Yesterday, apparently there was a big to-do when one of Ash's gerbils escaped, and they thought Frat Cat might have been a killer.

But neither of us brought up what we did. I'm hoping I'll get to see him at Omega Psi's party tomorrow night.

Maybe we could even sneak into another room and mess around some more...

Of course, if he's decided he doesn't want to mess around, I'll understand. But fuck, I hope he'll want to.

When I don't see a message from him, there's a

pinch in my gut. I tell myself it could just be the tension Ryan worked up with that planks finisher.

But there's panic mixed in too—that maybe Lance brought up that part of his day and not the messing around because he doesn't want to do anything again.

Wants to forget about it.

After all, after he got me off, he was quick to head for the door.

Maybe I should have let him leave instead of getting him off.

I consider DMing him, but I don't want to hound the guy, and we messaged yesterday, so I should be able to manage twenty-four hours without texting him again.

I pull it together and head to work.

It's a rather uneventful Thursday afternoon, and I'm only into my second hour when I discover Ash, Lance, Payton, and Marty being seated in my coworker Jerri's section.

Lance knows this is where I work. Is it strange that I'm hoping he was the one who suggested they come here tonight?

Maybe because he wanted to see me again.

Why does that set off fireworks in my chest?

I could get Jerri to swap out with me so I can take their table, but…why do I feel nervous about approaching? The hell is that? I'm Ty Lancaster. I don't get nervous about flirting. Though flirting with a guy after hooking up with him…I've never done either. Not that it matters. And I'm always cooler than this.

"Well, well, look who it is," I say, approaching the Alpha Theta Mu crew.

"Oh no," Payton says. "We about to get food poisoning for a week, bro? Maybe some cyanide on top?"

"Tell me, is that just for the pizzas?" Ash asks. "Or are we safe with calzones?"

"As an employee here, I would never tell you that. But since you asked, I'd also never tell you what I'm gonna do to the calzones."

The guys share a laugh—well, all but Marty, who looks anxious.

"Mart, don't worry. I'd never kill you. Someone needs to run back and let those pledges know who did it."

Despite the banter, I notice that the guy who's usually the first to give me hell has been quiet, and my gaze meets his for the first time.

I've had those brown eyes set on me plenty of times before, but it's different now that we've messed around. It sends a pulsing sensation through me, like a message my nerves are carrying to tell everything in me that we're close to that delicious experience again.

Still, I'm tense, since I can't really read his expression. I thought we were fine, just taking some time to process everything, but with him sitting there silent, not being his usual playful self, I'm wondering if maybe I'm wrong.

"Sorry, Lance, we weren't expecting a president, so we didn't have the red carpet rolled out," I tease, since I have to rag on him a bit or the guys are gonna be sus. I'm also hoping however he reacts gives me some insight into what he's thinking.

Lance smirks. "We'll start with some waters. We prefer to be hydrated if we're gonna be writhing in agony from cyanide poisoning."

His jokey retort sets me at ease. "Three waters coming right up," I say before spinning around.

"There are four of us," Marty calls out.

"I noticed."

Of course I'm gonna get them all waters. Marty should know by now that my teasing is just that.

I let Jerri know I'll be taking their table, then serve them for the night along with my other tables. Lance and I keep exchanging looks, and I see him keying into his phone at one point, so when I get a moment, I sneak a peek and find a DM on Insta:

LANCE: The cyanide was lovely...you could hardly taste it with the crushed pepper.

I chuckle. Fuck, this guy is fun.

ME: I know what you're doing with all this talk about me poisoning you guys. Coming for my job.

LANCE: I'd prefer just to be coming.

ME: Mean it, Stud?

LANCE: Are you fucking kidding? It's all I've been thinking about the past few days.

It's like he knows just what I need to hear.

ME: Is that why you're stalking me at my job?

LANCE: *laughing emoji* I tried to talk them into another place, but I can't help that Junkie's has the best calzones. Also didn't know if you'd be working.

ME: So you were trying to avoid me?

I'm giving him hell. But also probing to see if there is any discomfort on his end. Because if there is, I'd never want to push.

LANCE: What? No. I didn't want to bother you.

LANCE: I know how you are with girls.

ME: Well, neither of us knows how I am with boys.

ME: I just wanted to give you time to think about what we've done.

ME: Make sure you're comfortable.

And now I'm texting too much.

Lance doesn't reply right away, which makes me nervous. Like if he doesn't want to get together again, some part of me will suffer.

As soon as the bubble pops up, adrenaline pulses through me.

LANCE: If we both keep waiting for the other to text, we're gonna be waiting for a long-ass time.

I could start bouncing around the break room, I'm so excited.

ME: In that case, I guess we do need to meet up again.

LANCE: I agree.

I notice Cheryl coming from the kitchen, so I slide

my phone into my pocket and get back to work.

When I take the check to the Alpha Theta Mu crew, I give them the appropriate amount of hell. And while I chat with them, Lance and I keep glancing at one another, enjoying this little secret we share that none of his buddies know about—I doubt could even guess given the interactions they've seen between us.

As they're heading out, the place is getting busy. It's not even a few minutes since they left when I feel another vibration in my pocket, and I take a look.

LANCE: You want to meet up at the Omega Psi party tomorrow?

There it is!

ME: Do I ever...

I THROW ON a shirt, checking myself in the mirror in the en suite bathroom of my room. Most of the rooms in our house don't have one, but being a senior and the president, I have priority for the perk.

I study my arms. I'm filling this polo out nicely.

I tell myself I'm being my usual vain self, but I know I secretly hope Lance will think I'm looking good. That this will make Lance eager to sneak off with me for more trouble.

I grab my phone off the counter and notice it's pulled a Memory from photos, which immediately makes me tense up.

I'm tempted to leave it. No reason to dredge any-thing up tonight. But it's been three years. I can handle whatever's in here.

I click on it.

I'm used to seeing the old pics of Grant and me. Going on fishing trips. To Six Flags. Universal Studios. Go-carts. Sometimes it's pleasant to reflect on the good times. But this picture isn't from those days. It's Grant sitting on the couch, looking pale as hell, his gaze not meeting the camera as I hook my arm around him and smile.

My chest tightens, and I press my palm against it. I quickly close out of the Memory, but the floodgates have opened and the memories are back, a montage of everything from the disorientation and confusion to the fall…to steadily losing more and more of him each day. I fight back the tears as I instinctively start to pull up Mom's number, but I stop myself.

No. I can't do this to her. I refuse to do this to her. I must deal with this shit on my own.

It'll pass. It always passes.

I tuck my phone in my pocket, telling myself I just need to get out there and live my life. That's what Grant would have wanted.

But fuck, it hurts like hell.

11

Lance

"OKAY, ASH," I say as I knock on his door. "Come on. Get off the phone with your boyfriend and let's get to the party."

Ash opens his door in his underwear, a cute pair of red trunks. "About that…"

Behind him, Colin plops down on the bed, shirtless, waving.

"What? I thought you weren't gonna get here until later tonight," I say.

"I finished with my work early, so…here I am."

"Sorry," Ash says. "He surprised me. And then we got a little dickstracted."

"Sounds like you won't be rushing off to the party, so I'll head on, and if you two can manage to pry away from each other at some point, how about you come meet us at Omega Psi."

"Thank you for understanding," Colin says. "It's not easy not getting to spend every night with my man."

"I understand that. I mean, not about spending them with a man, but with someone you're with romantically."

Their expressions twist up similarly, in that way couples do sometimes because they've been together so long, although these guys were like that even before, which I guess came with the stepbrother territory.

I blush. "I should have stopped after saying I understood."

"You really should have," Ash teases.

"Okay. I'm gonna go party. You guys enjoy…whatever you were in the middle of."

"Thank you, Prez," Colin says.

"I'll see you in a bit," Ash adds before closing the door, I'm sure to get back as fast as he can to fucking around with his man.

Normally, I wouldn't be in such a hurry to get over to Omega Psi, would tell the guys to finish up and walk over with me, but tonight I obviously have more on my mind than just having a good time with my buddies.

I want to see Ty.

After messing around on Tuesday, I was so in my head the rest of the week, wondering if maybe Ty was gonna hit it and quit it when I really didn't want him to quit it. What we did has awakened something in me, this curiosity I never considered might be lingering inside me. I keep imagining how tragic it would have been if he'd let me walk out the door that day. Not getting to feel his hot breath against my flesh, his grip around my shaft. I was relieved when we saw each other at Junkie's once he assured me he wanted to see me again too.

When I get to the party, I find Ty playing beer pong with some of the guys on the back porch, and as soon as his team claims victory, his gaze travels around, as though he's looking for someone. When his gaze settles on me, a smirk plays across his lips.

And now I'm smiling too.

He grabs a guy near him and pulls him into the game before slipping away. Taking a Solo cup off the table, he approaches. "Well, well, well…Alpha Theta Mu's president, in the flesh. Well, maybe not as much flesh as I'd like to see, but still…"

I laugh, but even as he smiles, there's something else in his expression too. Something feels off. Or maybe it's just in my head.

He glances around before giving a subtle head tilt to follow him, and I do. He leads me into the house, like when we were at Beta Pi, and then into a room, closing the door behind us.

He looks unsettled, agitated. Has something changed? Is he more nervous about this than he let on when I saw him at his job?

As he nears, he studies me in a way that assures me that whatever the hell I thought he might have been questioning isn't the case.

"So…" I drag out.

"You trying to make it awkward?"

"Isn't it already?"

He slides his hand over my crotch, rubbing his palm against my cock, which is already hardening. His forehead creases. "Stud, you're not getting turned on by me doing this now, are you?" he asks, his tone dripping with sarcasm. "All worked up now that you know what I can do to that cock?"

His words ignite something deep within me, and I'm shocked to find he's gotten me even harder.

His gaze locks with mine briefly before wandering, and again, I'm caught off guard. Something's up for sure.

But he pushes me back toward the wall and starts unfastening my belt and fly.

"Ty, I—"

"I swear, you keep on like this, I'm gonna make you shut up."

As he gets my pants and trunks down, he grips my cock, stroking in that familiar way that I can tell my body's missed the past few days. My nerves burst with excitement, and I struggle to think straight as it courses through me. But again, there's something in Ty's expression… He looks distracted, in a way that's unsettling.

"Are you sure everything's—"

"I warned you," he says, dropping to his knees. He

pushes against my thighs, practically scooting my feet across the floor until my back's against the wall.

I can barely think straight even before he slides his tongue across my cock. "Holy fuck," I mutter.

What the hell is he doing? How did we go from jerking each other off to him already putting his tongue on my cock?

As he leans away, he grins like he's proud of himself for the effect he just had on me, the concern in his expression gone, like this has distracted him from whatever was on his mind. So I keep my question to myself, either because I selfishly want what he's doing, or because I'm happy for my dick to be the reason he's distracted. Maybe both. There will be other opportunities to ask, and now that he's had a taste of my dick, I'm curious to see what he'll do next.

He grips my cock firmly, offering another lick just under the head. Shivers rush through me, and he snickers. For a moment I wonder if he's laughing at me, like when he's pulled a prank on Alpha Theta Mu. Has this all been some epic Sigma Alpha prank? But then he runs his tongue from the head of my cock to the base of my shaft.

"Ty, fuck." I relax against the wall as he continues exploring me in slow, slick movements.

"I love how your body gets all twitchy when I do it," he says, his hot breath slamming against my wet flesh, and there's a wave of heat around the head before I feel his mouth slide around it.

This isn't happening. This can't be happening. In my wildest fantasy, this is still some messed-up prank, but now Ty's definitely taken it too far.

He pulls off my cock, leaving me wet with saliva and aching for more. "How's that?"

"You aren't seriously asking that question right now."

"Come on. I need a little validation. I like to be encouraged."

"Ty, I'm sure you're just as good with this as you are with pleasing a woman."

He winces. "I didn't want you to lie about it. I haven't had practice with this. But I guess that's what I'm doing now." He flashes a quick smile before opening his mouth and sliding back over my cock, taking me deep.

In all the times I've seen those lips, I never considered the pleasure they could give me, never could have imagined how they'd feel clamping around me, stroking back and forth.

He gradually picks up his pace, like he's taking me for a test drive. Sucking, his tongue shifting about it, it's clear he's experimenting, exploring his own capabilities. And he's reading me well too because when he pulls back to the head and sweeps his tongue around it, a moan pushes past my lips. He grips my cock, stroking as he continues working his mouth around the head.

It's no wonder the guy's so good with girls. Like that first experience, he's clearly good at picking up what feels good and when I'm most turned on. Although, with how hard I am right now, he'd have to be pretty oblivious not to catch on.

I rest my hand on his head, sliding my fingers through his smooth brown locks.

"Ty, you're so good at that," I say, offering the validation he requested, and he takes more of me into his mouth, really dedicating himself to his task. My hips jerk instinctively with his movements as he works me up, really getting me going. "Jesus Christ, if you keep it up, I'm gonna fucking shoot."

Keeping his hand on my cock, he pulls his mouth off and says, "Well, don't let me stop you." He teases the head with his tongue, driving me wild, accelerating the rush in me, this potent urgency that can only last for so long before I blow.

"Fuck, I'm so damn close," I warn so he'll be able to pull off. He jerks my cock—when the doorknob turns.

Holy shit.

Ty keeps his hand on my cock as he asks whoever's outside, "What's up?"

With his hand in place, it's like I'm suspended in this state, my body so close to the end, but also being kept from that final release. I've never felt so edged in my life, hanging in suspense for what feels like forever, until finally, a voice comes from the other side. "My bad."

Ty waits a moment, listening, making sure the guy isn't gonna keep pushing.

As soon as he's gone, Ty glances up at me. "Now where were we?"

He gives me a pump, and I don't think he realized how close I was because I shoot, my cum practically spraying across his chin and cheek as I clench my fists, enduring the powerful blast as he keeps pumping me onto his face.

"Fuck, fuck, fuck," I mutter, biting my bottom lip to keep from being too loud, until Ty's emptied the last of me. When I can think straight again, I notice the broad smile as my cum slips down his face.

"That's my dirty boy," he teases.

I roll my eyes. "I can't believe you just did that."

"I kind of can't believe it either. Or that I was so fucking good at it."

"Oh, here we go. I should have known this was coming."

"It's about to be," he says, pushing to his feet, his face still painted with my load. He unfastens his pants. "You gonna return the favor? Or am I gonna have to do this myself?"

"Suck you off?" I ask, suddenly shocked by the idea. Although, I guess that's fair.

"No, I meant just getting me off. I don't expect you

to be there yet."

Now he's triggered my competitive streak. "What is that supposed to mean?"

He sports that cocky expression I recognize from TaskFrat. "Come on. That was pretty impressive. Just give me my flowers tonight, huh? After what I did for you."

He has a point. I should simply enjoy the epic BJ and let that be that, but surely he knows I can't just let him be the victor here. Though I'm definitely not there yet, especially now that he's intimidated me with what a great job he did.

"It's okay, Lance." He pulls his cock out, wipes some of my cum from his face, and strokes it.

Holy hell.

"Just let me get off," he says, "and we'll be even."

"We'll hardly be even."

"Hard is right," he jokes. "And in that case, you owe me a BJ."

That shouldn't excite me as much as it does.

I glance down, watching as he strokes himself, and I grab his wrist. "No," I insist. "This is the least I can do."

He releases himself. "More than fine by me."

I take his cock in my grasp, noticing how hard he is from blowing me. I step closer, keeping up a good pace as he closes his eyes.

"Just like that," he whispers, so I keep my rhythm steady.

"Did you want to come on me?" I ask, hardly knowing where the idea even came from before it escaped my lips.

His eyes pop open, that grin sweeping across his face. "You want that?"

"I mean, it's only fair since I wound up coming on your face."

"Well, then I guess it'd only be fair if I came on yours too."

As I get on my knees, I continue jerking him, and there's something in his expression, like he's shocked I'm actually doing this.

I lick my lips, and his eyes are right on me as he says, "Lance, I'm about to—" His face tenses up as his eyes seal shut.

"Do it," I say, and the next second I feel a warm rush wash across my cheeks. Relief moves through me in a wave, as though all I needed to relax was for him to come on my face, and I hate myself for how I took for granted that first time when he came on me.

His body shifts and jerks about in a quick series of movements as he finishes on my face before gazing down at me, his smile revealing he's just as proud of the moment as I was when he came on me.

As the last of his cum leaves, he chuckles. "Okay, Lance, I'm sensitive now."

"Oh, sorry," I say awkwardly. It's something I should

have considered because I get the same way, but I was so into the moment, I couldn't help myself.

"It's okay," he says as I release him. He grabs my chin and runs his thumb over my cum-soaked flesh. "Fuck, that's hot."

Yes, it is.

As he pulls his thumb away, I can't help looking, seeing the way it shines in the room light. I lick my lips, thinking about that first taste I had of him. Something in me, something feral, something so lost in the pleasure of this moment, has me moving quickly, taking his thumb into my mouth.

"Oh fuck yes," he mutters as I close my eyes and enjoy the taste of him, a delicious, potent burst.

Before I know it, I'm sucking on his thumb, then offering a gentle bite at the base, running my teeth up to the end. I'm embarrassed by how hungry I was for it, what Ty must think of how I just lapped him up, but when I open my eyes to check his reaction, he says, "I had a feeling you'd want more after you had that first taste of me."

I chuckle nervously. "You weren't wrong."

"Mmmm," he says, raising his thumb to his face. He swipes it along my cum and slips it into his mouth, taking a lick. He closes his eyes, cherishing it, though I doubt he can enjoy it nearly as much as I just enjoyed his. Although, the way he lingers makes me realize there's something about this that clearly gets to both of us.

He opens his eyes again and says, "Nothing like two straight guys enjoying each other's cum." He gives his thumb another quick lick, and I burst into a laugh.

Because so much for being two straight guys.

12

Ty

Wow.

If you'd asked me a few weeks ago if I'd ever go down on a guy, let alone my frat rival, I would have laughed my ass off. But there wasn't anything funny about feeling his shaft running along the sides of my mouth, sliding up against the base of my tongue. Not sure I would have even attempted it had I not been trying to avoid talking about what Lance was catching on to.

It was a much-needed distraction, but the problem is, distractions only work for so long before reality returns. Life allows us to fly so incredibly high, but as we get too close to the sun, we inevitably come hurtling back to the earth.

After Lance and I clean up in the nearby bathroom, I collapse onto the bed, still appreciating that delicious flavor lingering on my tongue. I was out of my depth with a blowjob but took my time like I did with jerking him off that first time, trying to read his movements to determine how he would enjoy it most. Clearly, I figured it out, earning my reward.

Lance falls down beside me. "Well, fuck."

"Tell me about it. At least we know the first time wasn't a fluke."

He rolls toward me, quirking a brow. "Was there ever a question?"

"Not for me."

His gaze shifts around my face, like he's looking for something, and I fear he still might catch on to what I didn't want to talk to him about, so I turn away.

"Ty?"

"Huh, man?" I'm trying to play it cool, more than a little disappointed that I couldn't stay suspended in the bliss of what we just did.

"I know this is a lot, and I'm sorry if it's making you uncomfortable."

"What the hell are you on about?" I turn back to him, and I see the concern written all over his face.

"There's obviously something about this you don't want to talk about. And I don't know if it's trying to make sense of what you're feeling, or maybe you're worried I would tell someone, but I want you to know that I'm here to talk about any of it too. I wouldn't even tell Ash about this, and he's my best friend in the world, like ever."

His thoughtfulness, his consideration eases some of the tension balled up in my chest. Now I feel like a real asshole because I know what he's picking up on, but without a frame of reference, he's bound to think it has to do with what we shared.

"What I'm uncomfortable about doesn't have anything to do with us." I'm unable to disguise my frustration that he could even think that.

He releases an uneasy laugh. "Whew," he says in that adorable way he has. "I mean, I figured it wasn't that you didn't want to mess around because clearly you enjoyed that, but there are other aspects here, and we haven't really discussed any of them."

"The bi impulse?"

"No, the fact that you know Sigma Alpha is gonna lose the TaskFrat this year, and you're gonna be such a sore loser about it. Of course the bi impulse—and is that what we're calling it?"

I laugh. "Shut the hell up, dork. I'm definitely sorting through all that too, but about what you said—the worry that you'd tell anyone—that hasn't even crossed my mind, and I hope you know I feel the same. I won't say anything until you're ready to talk about it. You understand?"

He nods, studying my face as though trying to figure out where else my discomfort could be. How does a guy I don't even spend that much time around know me well enough to see right through me?

"It's some shit in my life," I admit. "Nothing to do with messing with you, so if you think you're getting out of that BJ you owe me, you got another thing coming."

"Sounds like that'll be another thing coming anyway," he teases, twisting his face into a goofy expression. "Well, if there is anything—and I do mean anything— you want to talk about, I'll have you know I'm a very good listener."

Since I saw that Memory pop up on my phone earlier tonight, I've felt so guarded. Clutched it tight against my chest as I've pretended to have fun throughout the night. But feeling so at ease in this bed with him, so relaxed after what we did, I find the words tensing up my throat, like they're trying to burst free, some part of me screaming for me to tell someone. No, to tell *him*.

"I have an uncle," I spit out quickly, as though if I didn't, I'd just keep this locked away in me forever.

I'm waiting for him to look shocked that I'm revealing something personal, but he simply sits there, listening, his gaze on me.

"*Had* an uncle," I clarify, nearly choking on the words. "I didn't have much of a dad. I actually have a half brother through him, who's only a year older than me. Mom only found out about her husband's other kid a few months after I was born, and you can imagine she didn't take it well, but my half brother's mom didn't seem to mind, so my dad left and started a new family. Mom got some checks, until she didn't. Sorry, it's probably weird that I was telling you about my uncle and then now I'm giving you the backstory with my dad, but it's important because Mom's brother stepped in after Dad left. He was doing well in his tech job, and she wanted to finish school so she could provide for us, so he basically helped raise me."

Lance reaches out and rests his hand on my shoulder, gripping gently, and I can see the care in his expression. It reminds me of that evening in the library when he was worried about the bruise on my arm. It's a side of Lance that assures me he's the right person to share this with.

As my gaze travels from his hand back to his face, he notices and pulls back. "Sorry, that was weird, wasn't it?"

"It was actually kind of nice," I admit, and he rests his hand back on my shoulder, giving me another burst of comfort.

There's a part of me clinging to my memories like a precious secret, fearing that if I speak about what happened, it'll somehow make it more real. Even though there's no undoing what's been done.

But the relief of sharing even what little I did is a drug, and I want more.

"It started when I was in high school. Grant would forget things, use wrong words for shit, which was strange for him. He was the smartest guy I knew. Still to this day. And he'd say the wrong person's name when he told a story. Then he would get confused by directions or when we were driving to familiar places. Sometimes we could be walking in a store, and he'd stop and look around as though he'd just woken up there. Mom pushed him to see a neurologist, and they ran some tests…FTD. Know anything about it?"

Lance shakes his head.

"Frontotemporal dementia. When people ask, I say it's similar to Alzheimer's—there are differences, for sure—but basically, it happens earlier in life than other forms of dementia. My uncle…he got it really young, and it didn't go easy on him."

I quiet. I tell myself it's to let Lance adjust to the information, but I know it's because I need a break as the memories of those early days creep back.

"Ty, I'm so sorry."

Hearing those words of comfort is like a warm cloth to my chest, easing up this ball of tension.

"Nothing you need to be sorry about. That's life, right? It's been three years since he passed. I don't turn off the notifications for photos we had on my phone. Sometimes they make me smile, like when we were hanging out at a frozen yogurt place or bowling…or trivia nights, which he killed at. But tonight, before the party, one came up, and it was from shortly before he passed. He'd had a fall, and we were at home—us and his caretaker—and he couldn't do much other than watch movies or watch us play solitaire. One day, toward the end, he said my name. Looked right at me and said it, and he hadn't in months. And he was talking to me about things that made me hope maybe something had turned. Despite knowing how it worked, this part of me wanted to believe it was gonna get better. And I took a picture." My chin quivers, my face spasming as I fight back the tears. "Because I wanted to have that moment where I felt like I saw him again. That was the last time he remembered my name."

I feel so raw, exposed, but also relieved to have gotten that out, to have said that to someone.

And yet, I hate myself for sharing it too.

And I feel like a fucking asshole. "Now I should apologize. I took what was supposed to be a fun, sexy night and fucked it up."

"You didn't fuck it up," Lance says, firming his grip on my shoulder and resting his free hand on my side. Unlike that first time, he doesn't even seem to notice himself do it, and I don't draw attention to it, since I don't want him to stop.

"That sounds like a lot," he adds. "I'm sorry you're having to deal with that."

I study his expression as he stares off, his mind clearly elsewhere. "Lance?"

As he makes eye contact, I say, "Where'd you go?"

"Sorry. Just…reminded me of something. I'm glad you felt comfortable sharing that with me. You know I'm not just good for jerking you off."

"Let's not jump to any conclusions," I tease, which makes his smile return.

And I'm proud of myself that, despite making shit so heavy, I was still able to lighten it up.

"Seriously, I appreciate your listening. You know, you can be a real sweetheart when you're not trying to stomp my ass in TaskFrat."

"Yeah, and you can be more sensitive than you let on."

"Eh, just don't tell any of the guys."

"I wouldn't," he says, like a promise.

Here I am sharing secrets with the enemy yet knowing he's far from that.

"Do they know about your uncle?" he asks, and I shake my head. "What about Ryan and Keegan?"

"They know my uncle passed, that it was hard on me, but they haven't pushed for details."

"How did it feel to share it with me?"

I consider his question before answering honestly. "Like relief."

"I'm glad." His gaze wanders. "It's like you said—life's real shit sometimes."

Again, he stares off in a way that makes me feel like I wasn't the only one holding something back. "Everything okay with you, Lance? You know, if there's something you want to share, I'd listen too."

"I…think maybe I should head out. It's getting late, and I have some homework to finish up."

A wave of disappointment pulses through me because I like just lying here, chatting with him.

"So you just came here to get me off?" I ask. "That was sweet."

I earn another smile from him.

Another win.

"I came here to get off as well, which I did. Epically, I might add."

"How else could it have been when you're fucking with Ty Lancaster?" It surprises me that, despite being terrified of sharing my secret with him, I feel better. Even more like my usual, cocky self.

Lance rolls his eyes and slides off the bed. "On that note, I'll get out of here. Give you some time to let that ego of yours deflate."

I grab my shirt, throw it back on as he heads for the door, stopping just before it.

"This was fun, Ty. I hope we do it again. And thank you, truly, for sharing that with me. It meant a lot. More than you could know."

Again, it feels like he's holding something back. Like what I shared with him might connect to something Lance has dealt with. Maybe he's lost someone close to him too?

As I study his expression, he avoids eye contact, as though afraid I'll see something I shouldn't. I consider pushing, but I would never want anyone to probe for what I just shared. It's the sort of thing that shouldn't be put out there unless you're ready.

"Thank you for listening, Lance. And like I said before, if there's anything you ever want to share with me, I hope you know I'll be here to listen too."

His gaze meets mine, and he offers a sliver of a smile, those dark eyes glistening in the room light. God, how have I never noticed how sexy he is?

"Night, Ty."

"Good night, Lance."

He heads out, leaving behind this ease within me for allowing me to share this part of myself.

And a taste I hope lingers for the rest of the night.

13

Lance

I'M IN A funk, and I know it's because of my conversation with Ty last night.

"I have an uncle… Had an uncle."

As soon as he said those words, my heart ached for him. I could tell by the way his voice cracked, how he left behind the playful Ty I'm used to seeing around campus, just how special his uncle was to him.

But now, all I can think is how shit I was at being there for Ty. I've thought of all the things I should have told him so he'd know I understand what it's like to watch someone you love fading right before your eyes.

But he knew, he must've. Not the details, of course, but the way he said it—*"Everything okay with you, Lance? If there's something you want to share, I'd listen too"*—and the way he looked at me, it was as if I were transparent and he could peer into my soul, see this part of me I'm so good at hiding from the rest of the world. I considered sharing what I went through with Kacey, but then, it felt like I'd be making his horrible tragedy all about me. And I didn't want him to feel like he had to comfort me when he was the one hurting.

The other issue was, I wasn't sure I could keep it together if I started thinking about all the fun times I shared with Kacey. Christmases and Thanksgivings. Walking around the neighborhood on Halloween with friends in our Dragon Ball Z costumes, him as Goku, me as Gohan.

I've always felt like Ty and I understood each other—our competitive streaks, the way we care about our frats and our buddies. But what we discussed last night made me feel closer to him than any of the messing around. That stuff feels special too, no doubt, but in a very different way.

Even just imagining his mouth around me, how beautiful his face looked streaked with my cum, is enough to make my cheeks hot.

But now that I know what had him in such a weird state last night, I'm wishing I could have been the one blowing him, giving him relief. Although, I know from everything we've done it wouldn't be entirely selfless of me.

As I walk around the rec center gym, picking up equipment that's migrated throughout the day, I wish it were a more hectic day so I could get my thoughts on something other than the fact that I rushed out after Ty shared something so important with me.

"Hey, sexy," I hear behind me, and turn to see Ash and Marty approaching.

I tense up.

"You headed off in a hurry this morning," Marty says.

"Yeah, we just wanted to swing by and make sure everything's all right."

I'm not surprised they noticed I was acting strange. That's one of the reasons I hurried through breakfast and left as soon as I could. And now I'm worried I'm as transparent as I was to Ty last night. That they might pick up on what's on my mind too.

"Just wanted to get to work," I lie.

"What time you get off?" Ash asks. "We were gonna grab something to eat in a bit."

"Oh, it's cool. I was gonna go straight back to the frat and finish up some homework."

"Then get ready for your beauty pageant this evening?" Marty teases.

"It's a bachelor auction, not a beauty pageant," I remind him.

Activate Kindness's auction got big a couple of years ago after Alpha Theta Mu's own Troy Locklear brought a lot of attention to the event. Now it's become an annual tradition for the frats to support the cause.

I'll be there, and so will Ty.

"Gonna get a pump in at the gym to show off the guns?" Marty asks. "Or maybe practice your speech about how to end world hunger?"

Ash and I share a laugh.

"Could you imagine if we had to listen to some Sigma Alpha ass giving a speech about the solution to climate change?" Ash jokes, and I tense up.

I normally wouldn't think twice about ragging on Sigma Alpha, but now I feel protective because of Ty.

"Sigma Alpha's not that bad." It's like I can't keep the words down, and as I say them, their expressions twist up.

"Um…" Marty says. "Ash, do you think Sigma Alpha learned how to brainwash our bros?"

"I think maybe they have. Lance, you're the one who's always ragging on Sigma Alpha. You know we don't actually hate those guys, right? It's all in good fun."

"I don't know why I said that. I'm kinda tired from being up last night."

"You left the party early," Marty notes. "Oh…wait… Oh…" His knowing look suggests he suspects something.

Did he see me head off with Ty? Did he catch something we whispered to one another when we thought no one could hear us?

"Huh? Am I missing something?" Ash asks.

My heart's racing before Marty says, "Somebody's

been hanging out with Angie an awful lot recently."

I breathe a sigh of relief as Ash prods, "Lance…"

"What? No. I mean, yes, we've hung out, but there's nothing happening between me and Angie."

Marty eyes me skeptically. "Dude, why do you have to pretend? Angie's hot, and you have fun together."

"I'm not pretending. We've only hung out once since that night she stayed at Alpha Theta Mu, and there's nothing there at all."

And if they knew whom I was really boning for, they'd really get just how not interested in Angie I am right now.

"Okay, man, I believe you," Marty says, his tone suggesting he doesn't even a little bit.

"I think Marty's projecting here," Ash chimes in.

"What? No I'm not."

Marty says that so defensively, even I don't believe him, and I use the opportunity to redirect the conversation. "You were awfully interested when she was over that first day."

Marty's shoulders square off. "Don't you have some balls to tend to? Isn't there a rule against talking to friends on the clock or something?"

"What are you gonna do?" Ash asks. "Turn him in?"

"Maybe," Marty says with a smirk.

"Okay, come on." Ash rests his hand on Marty's back. "We'll get out of your hair. Mart, you can tell me about how you're crushing on Angie over lunch."

"I'm not crushing on her!" he insists, and then we say our goodbyes and the guys leave.

I'm relieved they didn't press about my weird mood today. I love my guys, but I don't want to get into it with them. Not about this.

After my shift, I hop in my car and consider calling Mom or Dad.

I could talk to Dad and tell him about all the feelings that came up during my conversation with Ty. And we could hold space for the grief that remains from the great guy we lost. But instead, I pull up my last DMs with Ty on Insta, from last night after I got back to Alpha Theta Mu.

ME: Thank you again for sharing that. Sorry for having to head out, but hope you enjoy the rest of the party.

TY: I really appreciate your listening. And the other stuff too. ;)

Even with how heavy the night was, I smile at the thought of *other stuff* before messaging.

ME: Hey there.

I figure he might be at work, but he responds surprisingly quickly.

Ty: Hey, what's up?

I hesitate, struggling with what to tell him. *Been thinking about my dead brother all day because of our chat last night* seems like a conversation killer, so I go for the next best thing.

ME: Not much.

ME: You ready to see me earn way more money than you for charity?

TY: *You* make more than *me*? Not gonna happen.

ME: Pretty sure it will.

TY: Depends. You gonna be wearing that G-string? In which case, I'd say you're not playing fair.

I snicker. The fact that we're joking around like we normally would sets me at ease, assures me I didn't do anything to make him uneasy during our conversation.

TY: Speaking of which, not seeing any prank from Alpha Theta Mu. You guys give up?

ME: Oh, you'll be getting it.

TY: Counting on it. Looking forward to being impressed.

ME: Have I let you down before?

TY: You definitely have not.

There's a rush because I know he's talking about the stuff we've been doing.

ME: Seriously, though. Before we just go back to normal, I wanted to let you know, if you did need to talk to me again about anything...and I do mean anything, I'm open to that.

ME: And also, if you don't want to talk, I get that too.

The ellipsis appears, then disappears.

Oh, the cruel world of texting!

TY: I can think of some things I'd want to get together with you to do, but it only involves the fun stuff.

I chuckle.

ME: Could use that after the day I've had.

TY: You should swing by.

ME: Must get ready for the auction. We don't have much time.

TY: Do we need much time? ;)

I don't hesitate before replying: **Are you at Sigma Alpha now?**

I'M SURPRISED WHEN I find myself at Sigma Alpha.

But despite everything going on in my head—or maybe because of it—I want to see him again. I want to know he's truly okay after our chat.

Ty greets me at the door in a tank top and athletic shorts. His hair's a little tousled, and is it just me, or does he look even sexier than he did last night?

"Hey, man," he says. "Thank you for coming over."

"To enemy territory, you mean?" I ask, and my teasing makes him crack a smile.

He guides me up to his room and grabs me a White Claw. He sips on his own while I drink some of mine.

"I guess that was a lot for anyone to hear, and I probably shouldn't have trauma-dumped on you," he says.

"I don't think that's considered trauma-dumping. I made it clear I wanted you to share. We all go through shit, and it was a lot weighing on you. I can't imagine not having someone you can talk to about that stuff. I'm the one who should be apologizing for rushing out like that."

"You have nothing to be sorry for," Ty says. "You were great."

"I could have done better."

"I'm not really sure that's true," he insists before quieting. "Are you okay?"

There it is again. He knows something. I can see it in those bright blue eyes, set on me, like they're probing into my soul.

I start to say something, but the words catch in my throat. I remind myself this isn't just about me needing to get it off my chest. I don't want him feeling so fucking alone. Because damn, I know how alone this shit can feel.

"Last night when you asked me if I was okay," I say, "you could tell I had my own loss, couldn't you?"

He nods.

"I'm still all in my head, whether or not I should tell you, but…um…I *had* an older brother."

His expression softens.

"When I was younger. I was ten, he was twelve when he was diagnosed with cancer."

"Oh my God, Lance."

"It's okay," I say, but then stop myself. "I didn't mean that. It's not okay. It'll never be okay." I'm quiet again for a moment, struggling to find the words. "It was two years of treatments and attempts to beat it, and I really thought he was gonna make it. I think we all did, even the doctors. It was just too late, and…" My eyes water, my face twisting up, and I feel like I'm about to lose myself to emotion. "Fuck," I mutter. "And now I'm the one trauma-dumping, and I've shared all that, and I don't even know if it was a good idea."

I look to Ty, who wears a blank expression, as if it's beyond him what to do with it all.

"I'm gonna just—"

As I'm about to start for the door, get myself out of this incredibly awkward situation I created, I feel arms wrapping around me, Ty pressing his face against mine as he holds me close, like he's bracing me for the emotional fall.

It's something I didn't even realize I needed, but now I feel so at ease, this weight off me as I keep him tight against me, because I'm certain this isn't just for me, that he needs it too.

Finally, he pulls away, rubbing his hand against my arm, and his touch feels so soothing. With one arm still around me, his gaze meets mine. This isn't like last night when I feared he was looking into my eyes and seeing things he shouldn't, but like he's seeing things in me I'm allowing him to see.

"I'm sorry you had to go through all that. None of us should have to deal with this kind of pain."

Sadly, we both know that doesn't matter.

His breath slams against my face because he's so

close, and I catch my gaze drifting to his lips before licking my own. Selfishly, some part of me wants to just move forward and take a kiss.

Maybe because it felt so good to do all the other stuff we've done, hug included, I just know a kiss would feel good too—and that it would help me, not forget about Kacey, but be able to ease the searing pain in my chest.

I'm thinking this is just my own wish, but then he leans forward, his lips even closer, our gazes locking.

I'm not even sure who initiates it, but one moment we're looking at each other, and the next it's just lips before I feel my back up against the wall. It's a bit of madness as we're a frenzy of movement, excited nerves and pulsing bodies, his tongue slipping into my mouth so effortlessly, greeting mine.

And it's the distraction I need because I can barely think straight as I'm all sensation, following the inspiration of our movements as our mouths widen, as we try to get more of a taste of each other, falling into a rhythm that reminds me that there's something so naturally in sync about moving with him.

I grip the back of his head, keeping him close as his body pushes against mine, and once we've finally settled into the experience, his mouth drifts down to my chin, trailing to my neck.

I roll my head back, basking in the pleasure that pools through me as Ty shows me what he can do with that expert mouth. I find myself moaning, my breath hitching, and it seems as soon as I'm missing him against my lips, he somehow intuits this, and we're kissing again.

As he squats down, my mouth chases his before I feel his arms hook around my thighs. He pulls me right off the floor, and I hook my legs around his waist, licking at his tongue once again.

It's hard to pay much attention to anything as I'm so lost in him, but soon, I feel him pushing me against the wall, and I'm so alive, the heat in my face burning like fire as we continue licking, nibbling, sucking, escaping into the experience, letting it keep our demons at bay, at least for now.

There are a few times when I catch myself, surprised we're still making out, but then push that aside, refusing to pull out of this magical moment—when a knock at the door interrupts us.

Fuck.

But Ty doesn't stop kissing me.

"Hey, Ty," Ryan's voice comes from the other side of the door before he hammers away, shaking it.

Ty takes my bottom lip between his teeth, tugging gently before releasing it and glaring at the door. "Yeah, man?" he asks.

"We need to get ready."

"Fuck, that's right."

"Damn right! So throw some clothes on and meet me

out front in ten."

"Sounds good!"

I don't know why I'm keeping so quiet. It's not like if Ryan knew I was in here, he'd have any idea what we were up to, but I keep silent until he heads off, and Ty keeps his gaze fixed on me, both of us still quiet for a few moments before Ty says, "As good of a cause as it is, I wish I could just keep doing this."

The heat in my cheeks lingers. "Well, he did say you had ten minutes."

"You think we can find a way to make it fifteen?"

I start to laugh, but his lips clamp back down on mine, and all I know is that we must take advantage of what little time we have left.

And I fully intend to.

14

Ty

"YOU THINK WE have time to hit up Burger King?" Ryan asks as he drives us to the auction.

"Considering you barely gave me ten minutes to get ready, I think we should just get over to the convention center."

"Someone sounds pissed," Keegan adds from the back seat.

I can't disguise how annoyed I am with how quickly Ryan returned to my room. It might have been ten minutes—hell, he could have given us fifteen, and I wouldn't have known because Lance and I were so lost in each other.

Given everything else we've done together, I should have known that Lance's lips and tongue would feel as good as the rest of him, but the explosive blast took me by surprise, especially after the difficult things we'd been discussing up until that kiss.

I never could have guessed about the nightmarish loss

in his past that's been there through all our sparring and pranks, and it's amazing to think that a guy could have been through so much and still find a way to get on with his life, find moments to smile and laugh and give a damn about stuff like TaskFrat challenges, which are such bullshit next to everything we've been through. But maybe that's why we're so enthusiastic about having fun with the games…because we know how precious life is. We don't take a moment of it for granted.

"Lance has to be at the auction too," Ryan adds. "I mean, it wasn't the smartest time to plan to get together to discuss the TaskFrat Committee."

I had to make up some excuse for why he was in my room, so Ryan wouldn't know that really, I had my tongue down Lance's throat right before I opened the door.

When we arrive at the convention center, we grab our tuxes from the back and head inside. An event coordinator escorts us to a dressing room with some of the other guys—I recognize a few from school, but several aren't Peach State University guys.

Lance should be arriving too, though it's gonna take him some time since he had to hurry back to Alpha Theta Mu to grab his stuff.

I'm finishing buttoning my shirt by the time Lance heads in, acting chill, not looking my way. As he changes into his tux, I find myself watching him in my periphery so that Ryan and Keegan won't notice. Wondering if Lance is doing the same. If he's thinking about the lingering buzz from our kiss. At least, I hope he's feeling this flurry of sensation too because if not, he's missing out.

It's more than what he's stirred in my body, though. I enjoy spending time with him, talking to him. Especially now that I know we have this shared experience binding us together.

"Does this look stupid?" Ryan adjusts his bow tie in the mirror.

"I don't think it's the tie making you look stupid."

"Ouch," Ryan says. "I can tell you meant that one."

I shake my head. "Sorry, man. I'm just annoyed about being in a rush."

It's not his fault, but part of me can't help putting the blame on him for depriving me of time with Lance. And really, as much as I want to raise money for a good cause, I'd prefer to get back to that sooner rather than later.

If only we'd started this shit any other night.

Of course, life always has a way of being as inconvenient as goddamn possible.

I hate this awkwardness between Lance and me in the dressing room, both of us finishing up getting ready, not making eye contact, and I'm wondering if he also feels like if we *did* make eye contact, then suddenly Ryan will say, *Oh my God, you guys were making out in your room, weren't you?*

Just act fucking cool, I tell myself.

Somehow, we manage to keep it together before the door opens and in walk Troy Locklear and Atlas McCallister, both having graduated from Peach State last year. Atlas is the one who organizes this event, and Alpha Theta Mu alum Troy Locklear is his partner. Well, partner and stepbrother, which is like a whole deal in and of itself, but stepbrothers-turned-boyfriends is an Alpha Theta Mu thing. See Colin and Ash for more info.

"Hey, guys," Atlas says. "Just a quick heads-up about how it'll go down. Troy will introduce each of you. He's put together something with the info you filled out online. When the bidding takes place, you can flaunt it a bit. Try to keep your shirts on and keep it PG, but no harm in being playful with the audience."

"Though, if you can raise money by taking your shirt off," Troy says, "by all means."

Atlas gives his man a playful glare as the room erupts in laughter.

Lance manages to finish getting dressed as they prep us some more, and then they lead us out. As we follow them to the main stage, I wind up near Lance, not by coincidence, but because I've been inching my way closer and closer to him, even as I've tried to tell myself it'd be smart to keep my distance.

We crack at the same time, and his gaze meets mine, his lips curling into a smirk.

I hate that we have to get through this when all I want to do is attack that face again, but I take a breath, steadying myself.

"Okay, guys," Troy says as he opens a door that leads backstage, "just wait in the wings until I call you out. And once the bidding ends, you'll stay onstage with the rest of the guys until we get to the end." He turns to Atlas. "Wish me luck, A."

"As if you need any," Atlas says before Troy plants a kiss on his man. It looks like he intended it to be a peck, but Atlas hooks his arm around him, keeping him close, his tongue slipping into his mouth.

It's the sort of kiss that makes everyone quiet before Atlas pulls back and slaps Troy's ass. "Get out there and sell some beef."

Troy beams before heading out to the podium. His opening speech is dynamic, playful, his charisma on full display as he cracks a few jokes that get the audience laughing. While the bidding's taking place for the first few guys, Lance and I glance at one another again, and he winks. There's this confidence to him now, like he can read my interest so easily, unlike before when he was cautious and apprehensive.

I like this side of him.

As his gaze settles on my lips, he licks his own.

"Stop that," I say sternly, my tone taking him by surprise as his eyes widen. "I need to behave."

I'm playing with fire by talking like this so close to my Sigma Alpha buddies, but maybe that's part of the thrill.

"And next up, we have none other than the president of Sigma Alpha," Troy announces from the podium.

"Looks like you're up, Mr. Prez," Ryan says, coming up from behind me. "Get out there and make Sigma Alpha proud."

Lance rolls his eyes, simulating vomiting as I head out onto the stage.

Troy finishes his intro, and the whole thing is a bit wild—the bright lights, the sorority girls and frat guys losing it in the audience, and I can hardly think straight as numbers start getting called until I'm taken by a girl from Phi Kappa Lambda for two hundred dollars.

I join the other auctioned guys on the opposite side of the podium, watching as Keegan and then Ryan are given away next. They join me, and then a few more guys, before Troy says, "And last but certainly not least…"

Definitely not least.

"…my good friend and Alpha Theta Mu president, Lance Fehn."

He's got support from his fellow Alpha Theta Mus first, from the stage and in the audience as they lose their minds over him, but it's not their support that's grating on my nerves. I can see how some of the girls and guys are looking at him, wanting a piece of that action. Tension knots up in me at the thought of one of them winning his adorable ass.

He stands at the front of the stage, jokingly posing, but also having a bit of that bashful charm, like he's flustered by the attention. It's that charm, no doubt, that won over Alpha Theta Mu when he became president his sophomore year. There's this aura about him, and it's as though he doesn't even realize the effect he has on people.

Like he's oblivious about that sexy mug or those kissable lips.

Fuck, I can't get those lips out of my goddamn head.

"Okay," Troy says. "Let the bidding commence!"

"One hundred dollars!" I recognize Angie up front in a hoodie, waving to support her friend. I can't help feeling she's too eager, which is weird because I wasn't thinking like that at all when they were bidding on me.

Another sorority girl shouts for a hundred twenty-five.

Then one hundred fifty.

I'm annoyed by the low bids. These kids don't even know what they're missing out on.

"One sixty," comes another bid as they seem to be winding down.

One sixty? Are they fucking kidding right now? The hell?

"Two fifty!"

I look around for a sec, as though the words didn't come from my own damn mouth.

Troy glances at me. "Um…"

"What the fuck is he doing?" Keegan mutters to Ryan.

Even with the bright lights in my eyes, I see people in the audience looking around. Everyone seems confused because this is definitely a first—a bachelor onstage bidding for another bachelor.

How the hell am I gonna get out of this one?

"Dude's clearly letting that Alpha Theta Mu know who's boss," Ryan whispers to Keegan before nudging me. "Badass move, man."

Troy's looking around like he's waiting for Atlas or one of the other event organizers to come out and put a stop to this, but then just shrugs. "I guess a bid's a bid, right? So we're at two fifty for Alpha Theta Mu's president from my former frat's rival Sigma Alpha. Anyone want to save this guy from being tortured by the enemy?"

Troy's comment earns some laughs, which is a relief because hell if I knew how I was gonna explain this to the guys without straight up lying about whatever the hell is happening between Lance and me.

Of course, given our history, people would assume this is just another way of sticking it to Alpha Theta Mu.

Lance is obviously just as confused, his brows shifting as his eyes narrow.

Everything's happening so fast, I wonder if he even gets what's going on, but I'm just relieved my dumbass mouth didn't out us.

"Two sixty!" Ash calls out from the crowd as he glares at me, like he won't let his friend be owned by some Sigma Alpha bastard.

"Come on, get him," Ryan whispers to me.

Even though the first one was not on purpose, I roll with it. "Two eighty!"

Troy side-eyes me. "Um…this really isn't how…"

"Two eight-five," Lance's buddy Marty follows, then whispers something to Payton.

"Three hundred," I add, really stirring the pot on what's clearly become an Alpha Theta Mu–vs.–Sigma Alpha battle.

"Fuck," Ash mutters in the front, so I know they must be stressing about cash, but after a quick consult with his friends, he calls out, "Three fifty."

And now I'm shifting finances around in my head.

"I can spot you a hundred," Ryan says, so I call out for four.

Now things are really getting spicy. The tension is locked in, Troy not getting in the middle of it, I'm sure because despite how unconventional the bidding has become, he can't argue with the money that'll be going to the cause.

"Four fifty," Ash calls.

Fuck. I'm really cutting it close on what I can manage. I should just let it go. If I let the Alpha Theta Mus win, then I'm not out of cash, and it's not like I'm not gonna see Lance again.

As I'm working through the logic, Troy starts counting down to seal the bid when a loud, "Five hundred!" comes from the audience. My gaze shifts around before it settles on a raised hand.

One of Sigma Alpha's own: Dax.

Ryan nudges me with his elbow. "Fuck, yeah," he says. "Looks like we got that Alpha Theta Mu's ass after all."

"Right," I say, though despite my best interests, I'm tempted to outbid him. I can't, though, since that would definitely make even less sense to everyone. Hell, it barely makes sense to me.

As the Sigma Alphas start high-fiving and hugging it out in the audience, I realize I need to let this one go, even though a part of me wants to go feral and let all the guys know, especially Dax, that Lance is fucking mine.

No, not mine.

Just…fuck, he's gotten into my head with that goddamn kissing.

When the auction ends, we join our house friends on the main stage, Sigma Alphas giving Alpha Theta Mus hell, as though this was all part of some elaborate prank to pull on Lance, which normally would have amused me, but is now pissing me the fuck off.

"Guys, just act cool," I say. "This is a respectable charity."

Dax approaches me, grinning, and just like that, I'm back to being on edge. "Hey, man," he says. "Hope I was helping. Seemed like you were done bidding."

"Oh, yeah. Thanks for that," I say with clenched fists.

"No problem. I had the spare cash, and Lance is adorable as fuck, so you know…two birds, one stone. Although…I didn't know if you needed to take the date."

"No, no," I say, almost hating myself as the words come out. "It's your money. You won fair and square. And the Sigma Alphas seem content our house won his ass."

I shouldn't enjoy how good it feels to talk about owning Lance's ass, but I can't help myself.

Dax's grin expands. "In that case, I guess I can just enjoy myself."

I stifle a growl.

Rumor has it, Dax's got this keen ability to tell when guys are questioning or curious. I don't know that I believe in gaydar, but I can't help wondering if the guy has some intuition about Lance and now he's planning to make some moves, *or* if that's just my fear because Dax is apparently this amazing, epic lover who definitely understands how a man's body works and could show Lance things I couldn't. Not yet, at least.

And suddenly I find myself having particularly ragey thoughts toward one of my own Sigma Alphas.

15

Lance

WHAT WAS THAT?

The auction seemed to be going as usual, and next thing I know, I'm the one who brought in the most money of all the guys. Five hundred dollars is wild for a stupid date.

But that's not even the most confusing part.

It seemed like Ty was trying to show up Alpha Theta Mu, like this might have been a stunt, which then made me question everything else we've done. But again, if him sucking my cock was part of some epic prank, that's gotta be too far, even for a guy as competitive as Ty Lancaster.

"Sorry again, man," Ash says. "I really tried to get up there."

Everyone's disappointed they weren't able to outbid Dax.

"If we'd known beforehand," Marty says, "we could've pooled money together."

Payton adds, "This might've worked out better. We can just prank them on this so-called date."

Ah, my guys are too good to me.

"Don't worry," I say. "I didn't want you all out any savings over whatever the hell that was. And I'm the president. It's my job to take this shit in stride. I'm gonna show and be as proud as I was in my G-string and crop top, and tell them all to suck it."

The guys enjoy some laughs.

"That's the spirit," Ash says, patting my back. "Just a shame, since if you were queer, you'd definitely have a good time with Dax."

He's got this look in his eyes that, again, makes me wonder, but I don't have much time to speculate on what Ash and Colin may or may not have done with Dax before Ty's gaze catches mine from across the room. He's got his phone in his hand, and he breaks eye contact to key into it.

The buzz in my back pocket alerts me to a notification, and as the guys are chatting up friends around us, I peek at my DMs.

TY: Looks like you won after all. ;)

ME: First time I've ever seen you try to lose something.

TY: We should probably talk about that.

ME: Ya think?

TY: Can you find a way to get rid of all these frats? ;)

I stifle a laugh.

ME: I'm definitely not heading back into enemy territory after what went down. I think your boys might tie me up to a flagpole.

TY: Stop trying to turn this into something sexy.

I laugh again. Clearly, whatever went down hasn't affected what we were doing before the event.

TY: Does this mean the Alpha Theta Mus are gonna attack me if I try to come see you?

ME: Can you blame them?

TY: Nr.

I don't love being sneaky around my guys, but considering Ty and I barely know what's going on yet, that seems the safest option. Ash would understand, but I don't need all the guys in the house knowing about my sexual experimentation, and also, it's not only my call to make when Ty's involved.

Fortunately, we have the perfect opportunity.

ME: Most of the guys will be at Zeta Tau's party tonight.

TY: And you?

Eagerness wells up within me.

ME: I was considering staying in…

I watch Ty as he reads the message, and when he glances up, his mischievous smirk assures me he fully intends to pick up where we left off. He keys into his phone, and I check mine until his DM comes through.

TY: You thinking of sneaking me into Alpha Theta Mu?

TY: You fucking traitor.

We lock gazes briefly, and his wicked expression

sends a rush up my spine.

Why does the idea of sneaking around make messing with him even hotter?

All those nerves he stimulated during our kiss wait in eager anticipation for the possibility of being worked up again.

"Jesus, you're still blushing from being onstage," Ash says.

I hate how obvious I am. "Oh, really?"

My phone buzzes, and I check it.

TY: Just pissed that I have to wait until this party.

And it's on.

Ty and I continue catching up with the guys until everyone heads out. When we get back to Alpha Theta Mu, I make up a BS excuse about being tired, when really I'm wired at the thought of what Ty and I will be doing when he gets here. Two frats have stayed at the house, so I need to keep a lookout, which adds to the adrenaline coursing through me as I head through the house to meet up with Ty.

I message him when I get to the back door, opening it, poking my head out, searching around for my rival.

"Ty?" I whisper. "Ty?"

He steps around the side of the house.

Unlike me, he didn't have a chance to change out of his tux, so he's still wearing his suit pants and button-down. He looks like a secret agent as he searches around, I figure to make sure no one catches him infiltrating our house. Then he rushes to the door, hurrying inside.

"Trying to announce to the neighborhood I'm here?" he asks.

"It's just Bernie and Ted," I say as I close the door behind him. "Now come on."

I start to lead the way when he seizes my wrist. He pulls me back gently, guiding me up against the wall. It all happens so fast that soon his mouth is clamped against mine, my body coming back to life with sensation, racing back to where we left off when Ryan interrupted us before the auction. Sweeping waves of heat and eagerness move through me as he pushes up against me, wedging me between his torso and the wall.

I finally come to my senses and say between kisses, "You have…to…stop…kissing me…to get to…my room."

"Make me." He plants another kiss, and I'm not exactly fighting him off.

I cherish his lips a little longer, greedily enjoying what I've been deprived of tonight. When I manage to pry away from him, he growls, and a swirling sensation radiates in my chest. "Wow. Um…you should do that more."

He smiles. "What?"

"That growl."

"I was growling?"

Despite how turned on I am by it, I must stay focused. "We need to get up to my room."

He tenses his jaw, like he knows he'll have to restrain himself so we can get somewhere private. "Sorry," he says, "you just have no idea how long I was waiting for that tonight." He takes my hand and rubs it against that rock, making another burst of excitement pulse through me.

"Just follow me and keep quiet."

I lead him through the house, keeping a few feet ahead of him in case Ted or Bernie walk out and catch us by surprise. Once we're in my room, I lock the door behind me, and when I turn around, his lips are back against mine, his arms locking around me.

When he finally pulls back, he breathes heavily as I catch my breath.

I should just be happy we're doing this again, but a nagging thought won't let me relax and enjoy it.

"What the fuck was that shit with the bidding?"

He flinches. "I was annoyed they weren't bidding high enough."

"They were bidding as much as they did with you."

He quiets before saying, "I'm not really sure. Spoke without thinking, I guess. Maybe if you hadn't turned me on so fucking much earlier, I wouldn't have felt like I needed to get you all to myself again."

"So it wasn't like a weird Alpha Theta Mu–versus–Sigma Alpha thing?"

He chuckles. "No, that was just how I was playing it off. I figured it was better than having all the guys think I had the hots for you…for both our sakes."

Did he really spit that out without thinking? And why do I hope that's what happened?

"Smooth way out of that," I deadpan. "And now I'm going out with Dax, apparently." I chuckle awkwardly.

His nostrils flare. "You think he's hot?"

"Huh?"

He studies my expression as though trying to read whether I'm attracted to his fellow frat.

"Nothing," he says, flinching again. "It would be fine if you did think he was hot or if you wanted to enjoy the date." He tenses his jaw again.

Why is he saying it would be fine and sounding like it would not be fine at all?

"This is a weird conversation," I observe.

"Yeah, let's finish it now."

He doesn't give me a chance to respond, just takes my mouth again. He whispers between kisses, "Besides…we have better things…to do…than to talk about the auction."

His lips travel from my mouth down my throat, and I roll my head back. He kisses up along my throat, to near my ear before offering a low, rumbling growl, just the way he did downstairs. He slides his hands under my shirt, probing, exploring. My skin pricks with life before he whispers, "I think these clothes are starting to piss me the fuck off." He licks the side of my face.

There's something about the way he kisses and licks me, even that growl—it's like I've unleashed some feral beast.

As I grab my shirt and start to pull it off, Ty helps me out of it, and when I reach for my belt, he snatches it, unfastens it, and in no time, pulls open the buttons on my fly. He tugs down my boxers, exposing my hard cock before snickering, which takes me by surprise, but when I see his expression, the way he's looking at it, it definitely suggests he doesn't find anything funny about it.

"Missed this guy," he says, then wets his palm with a lick before gripping me and giving me a good, firm stroke.

"Fucking hell, Ty," I say as he slides my pants and boxers down with his other hand.

His gaze travels across my body, and he's fucking drinking me in, like there's not an inch of flesh he doesn't like. Like he's fucking obsessed with me.

"Get out of these clothes and get on your bed," he orders, his voice a lower octave than usual, which hits my ear just right.

He releases my cock, and I hurry to kick off my shoes and step out of my clothes, stripping down the rest of the way, like the part of me that just needs to get off has taken control.

As I walk to the bed, I notice Ty watching me, his gaze settling on my ass. I sit on the bed and slide back, curious what he's going to do, but he just stands in place, still staring at me.

"Are you gonna take off your clothes?" I ask, and that mischievous smirk returns.

"Not *yet*."

Between his playful tone and that determined expression, I know we're in for a fun night.

And after everything we discussed before the auction, I feel like we both deserve it.

16

Ty

FUCKING LANCE FEHN.

Lying in his bed, looking hot as sin.

There's something about him being naked when I haven't so much as taken my shirt off that excites me. He feels so vulnerable right now, like he's mine to do whatever I want to.

I approach the bed, looming over him, enjoying the uncertainty in his expression, that he doesn't know what I'll do to satisfy him first. Although, the way my mouth's watering, I already know what I want, so I lean down and hook my arms under his thighs, my face near his cock.

"You know I've been thinking about this since I last had a taste, right?"

"Yeah?" He chuckles, but I notice his dick stiffen.

"Apparently, you want me to taste it too."

"If you want it so bad, why aren't you just going for it?"

"Because I like the idea of teasing you a bit, even if it means restraining myself from everything I really want to do to you."

I offer a quick lick, then move down, starting at the base of his shaft, sliding up to the head. Just to remind him what my tongue feels like against his flesh.

"Tastes as good as I remember," I whisper. "It makes me greedy, but I don't just want to get you off tonight. I want to drive you out of your goddamn mind." Pulling my tongue back, I let him feel my breath against his flesh before offering the subtlest of licks.

He releases a deep, resonant moan that tingles in my chest.

"You keep letting me know how much you enjoy it like that," I say, "and I'm gonna have a hard time torturing you."

"Fucking hell," he says, straining.

I offer another lick, and he moans again, even louder. It still has that true ring to it, but like he isn't holding back anymore, like I lured it out of him with the promise of doing more.

Between how it hits and knowing I give him that kind of pleasure, I realize he's not the only one I'm torturing like this, so I let go. I slide the tip of his cock into my mouth, driving down to the base, enjoying that familiar sensation of it pushing up against the insides of my cheeks.

"Ty," he breathes as his fingers thread through my hair.

Never would have thought my name could sound so good, but there's something about hearing how much Lance wants this that drives me wild. Has me taking him all the way to the back of my throat. When I pull back, I work the head with my tongue, determined to impress him. His moans, the subtle movements of his body as he arches his back and thrusts into my mouth assure me it's working.

Once my mouth is satisfied, I kiss up his body, nibbling and licking, trying to taste as much of him as I can before I take his lips again, my hand gravitating to his ass.

So fucking firm.

Something animalistic rises within me, and I let that growl escape my mouth again, probably in part since he requested it earlier.

When I finally pull away from our kisses, his eyes are sealed shut. I study his face for a few moments before they flit open.

"Yeah, I think I might be figuring some things out," he says in that jokey way he has.

I laugh. "Me too."

"I notice your hand is still on my ass."

"Is that okay?"

His expression twists up. "Trust me, everything

you're doing right now is more than okay."

That makes my chest swell with pride. "Well, guess we're learning I'm just as good with guys as I am with girls."

He snorts—fucking snorts—which gets me chuckling too.

"Why's that funny?" I ask.

"It might be true, but if there's one thing that hasn't changed between you messing around with guys or girls, it's how damn full of yourself you are."

"If you got it, strut it."

"Well, don't let me stop you."

"I definitely won't," I say, kneading his ass cheek.

His gaze shifts. "Have you ever…?"

"What? Fucked a guy?"

He rolls his eyes. "No. Anal with a girl."

"Oh, yeah. One time, and it was fun."

He gulps, as though just saying I had anal before intimidates him. Although, that he even asked tells me he's considering it, and goddamn if that doesn't make my dick pulse.

Despite how turned on the thought gets me, I need to reassure him. "I hope you know I wouldn't pressure you into doing something that makes you uncomfortable."

"I'm just…I don't really know what I want right now."

"But you like this?" I grip his ass firmly.

And there's the pink in his cheeks again.

"Kinda," he says, breaking eye contact.

"Don't look away from me while I'm feeling you up." I'm just giving him hell, but his gaze meets mine again, as though he's accepted my challenge.

I stroke his warm flesh, taking my time exploring like I did when I first went for his cock. I must admit, this new, unexplored part of him has got my imagination running wild.

A part of him that would only be mine...

"So what stuff would you be interested in me doing down there?"

"I don't know that I can take a dick, but...Ash tells me about the prostate all the time, and it's not something I've ever experimented with." He seems on the verge of looking away again but stops himself.

Just like having him naked under me like this, I love him showing me this side of him. It's like now that I know his vulnerable side, all that he's been through, I don't want him holding anything back from me.

"I can try some things," I say, "see if you like it."

"But if you don't want to, then that's fine too. I don't want you to feel like you have to because I want it—"

I kiss him to shut him the hell up, and once his lips are relaxed, I pull away and say, "No. Don't do that. If you want to try something, promise you'll tell me. Maybe I won't feel comfortable, but that's what this is all about—figuring stuff out, right?"

"Okay."

"I love a one-word response from you, especially when you're agreeing with me." As he smiles, I ask, "So you want someone to explore your ass?"

His gaze wavers. "Technically…I want *you* to explore my ass."

I chuckle, but I feel a burst of eagerness sweep through me. "Well, I'm honored to do the job. And do it right."

I wait for him to roll his eyes, but his expression is serious as ever, not like he found anything funny about what I said, but like he believes me, which just means I must do everything I can not to disappoint him.

I steal another kiss, then trail some down his body until I return to his cock. I give the head a lick, making sure it's nice and firm before pulling back and lifting his legs, displaying his ass for me, that beautiful, untouched pink hole.

"I'm gonna pretend you've been saving it just for me," I whisper.

I lean down, moving close, studying that hole, familiarizing myself with it before I give it a lick, noticing the way his ass quivers, his breath hitching.

"Fuck, Ty."

That little attention getting him going encourages me to go for it, this time more confidently, swiping my tongue, then kissing like I would his mouth, slipping my tongue inside. It's enough to make me go feral, the way I did for his cock. I lock my arms around his thighs, burying myself against his flesh.

He gasps, and I feel my cock crimping in my underwear.

I press my tongue into him as much as I can manage, but it's like I'm greedy to be inside him because that isn't good enough. I pull back, wet my finger, then feel around the rim, admiring the way it twitches for me, like Lance is eagerly anticipating the pleasure I can bring him.

But there's pressure here too. I've never done this with a guy. And I refuse to be a shit experience for Lance's first time. It's the sort of thought that reminds me how far we've come from straight territory, even as I'm slipping my index finger inside him.

"That good?" I ask, assessing his expression.

"That's fine," he says in a breath.

I take my time to slide back, enjoying the way his ass grips me, studying the way his back arches, the way his mouth hangs open as he takes it.

"Another," he begs, so I slip my finger out, pushing my middle finger alongside it, gradually letting it open his ass even more. He's so damn tight, the sort of tight where I can't help but imagine how that'll feel clutching my cock.

There's a sting in my crotch.

"Fuck," I grunt, adjusting my pants with my free hand.

I push deeper, feeling around for his prostate, not really sure what it'll feel like until I reach a tender spot that makes Lance's body spasm.

"Holy fuck," he says, his eyes widening, and he looks down, clearly in shock by whatever that did to him.

I keep my finger in place, memorizing the sensation, trying to create a mental map so it'll be easy to find again.

"That's it, isn't it?" I ask, a swirl of sensation in my chest. It's the sort of feeling I usually get from winning. Adrenaline coursing through my veins.

"I think you know the answer to that."

I do, and I shouldn't be as proud as I am, but I can't help it. "This okay?" I ask, continuing to push against it.

Lance's eyes roll back, but this time, not in that way they do sometimes when he's annoyed.

As I continue playing with that spot, he relaxes against the bed, his abs shifting as he rocks his hips back and forth, like he needs more, so I push even harder, massaging.

"Jesus Christ, Ash wasn't fucking kidding," he says, and I smile at the adorable commentary.

He reaches for his cock, and I grab his hand. "Uh-uh. Let me."

Keeping my fingers on his prostate, I lean down and take his cock into my mouth, working him up from both sides.

"Ty…fuck, that feels so good. Keep doing that."

I obey, refusing to let up my work, even as my cock continues straining in my pants. I feel the moisture on the head where I know I must be leaking precum, but I can take care of myself later. Right now, Lance's satisfaction is my only concern as I work with more intensity and determination than I would in a TaskFrat challenge.

I think Lance is as hard as he can get, but his dick pulses inside my mouth, getting even firmer.

"Ty," he whispers. "You have to pull off. I'm about to—fuck…"

I grip his shaft with my free hand, continuing to stroke him as I rise off. "Just shoot in my mouth."

I don't know what's possessing me, but I'm not even thinking, just know I want to get another taste of him like I did the last time we fucked around. So I slide his cock back into my mouth, picking up my pace, really feeling that spot inside him when he starts to grunt.

"Ty, oh fuck, Ty!"

Give it to me, Lance. Give me every fucking drop.

His cock gives another pulse before there's a burst,

filling my mouth with that delicious taste. I swallow him down, continuing to work inside his ass as his body vibrates and shifts about. Fuck, I'm addicted to the way I've got him all worked up. Knowing I'm the one who did this to him.

Once I can tell I've fully drained him, I release his cock, let it fall to his abs, and lean back to get a view of him as he continues shifting about, his body jerking as he stares at me, his eyes wide like he's still in shock from how big his climax was.

"Oh, someone liked that, didn't he?"

A grin sweeps across his face as his forehead creases. "You fucking kidding me right now?"

He catches his breath, blinking a few times as though he can barely see straight after how I just blew his goddamn mind.

Then he cringes. "Ooh, it's a little sensitive," he warns, resting a hand on my bicep.

"Sorry," I say, realizing I need to take the pressure off him.

"No, it wasn't a bad feeling. Just very sensitive."

As he continues catching his breath, I slide my fingers out of him.

"Now, what are we gonna do about that?" he asks, eyeing the bulge in my pants.

I wonder if he even notices the way he licks his lips after he asks.

"You want to taste me now?"

I'm waiting for the usual, shy, uncomfortable Lance, but he doesn't pull his gaze away, just looks me directly in the eyes and says, "Yes."

It's as though he doesn't want me to doubt how much he wants this, and if there was any question about whether or not I could get harder, my cock swells even more. I hurry to undo my fly, and by the time I've tugged down my pants, Lance is on his knees, crawling toward me.

"Look who's eager for it."

"Hey, it's my turn now," he says, gripping my shaft and offering a stroke that relieves some of the tension I've worked up while I was fingering him.

He studies my cock as though there's still some debate if he's willing to take this next step, and I'm about to assure him he doesn't have to when he goes right for it, slipping the head into his mouth.

I can't stifle my moan as I roll my head back, surprised by how quickly he slips more of me into his mouth, exploring me with his tongue.

"You have no fucking idea how good that feels right now," I confess as he takes me deeper.

I rest my hand on the back of his head, massaging with my thumb as he continues working me up when he takes me to the base.

After enjoying a deeply satisfying breath, I ask, "You

trying to have fun or compete with me?”

He pulls off, glancing up long enough to say, “Maybe a bit of both,” before getting right back to it.

17

Lance

AFTER THE PLEASURE Ty showed me, the sensations that pooled through my body as he worked my prostate, I'm determined to show him a good time. Between sucking me off and sticking his fingers up my ass, I'm definitely feeling like I need to up my game.

I give him a few more pumps, noticing the way his cock throbs and stiffens when I make certain movements. I can tell why he was so damn good at blowing me. It's easier to get a sense of what works when it's in my mouth and grip. The familiar taste of his precum pushes into my mouth, setting off something in me, making me speed up.

"Seriously," Ty says. "I'm gonna come if you keep that up. Lance…Lance…"

I slide my lips off his dick, still stroking, "Give it to me."

I barely have the words out when I feel a warm rush against my lips. In a panic, I hurry back onto his cock, taking it into my mouth. A part of me feared I might have missed my opportunity, but the burst that releases onto my tongue assures me that isn't the case. My muscles relax, my mouth sliding down to the base of his cock as I swipe my tongue around to make sure I get every drop of him. It's like I've been starving and had my first meal in days—I'm blissed out, reveling in having his cock buried in my mouth, swallowing him down. There are thoughts about how I could have gone from being straight to this moment, but I'm too obsessed with Ty's cock to give any fucks.

His moans stammer, and I give his shaft another jerk. "There's no more," he says. "You fucking drained me, man."

As if I wasn't satisfied enough already, hearing that sends another wave of relief through me.

I pull off his cock, gazing up at him as he looks down at me, looking as pleased as I feel. I finally release him, and he collapses on the bed beside me, while I reposition so I'm lying alongside him.

"Whew," he says, placing his hand on his torso, just under his chest. "Thanks for that."

"Thanks for the excellent fingering."

"I was pretty good, wasn't I?"

"I'm never complimenting you again."

"I mean, you don't have to. Your body gave you away." He winks.

"Like yours did when you shot on my face before I could get you down."

"I was basically getting you back for that first time when you shot on mine."

We share a laugh, and Ty rolls toward me. "You'll have to let me know how I compare to Dax."

His jaw tenses, the playfulness in his expression gone, and part of me thinks he can't be serious, while another can tell he's as serious as ever.

"Shut up," I say.

"What? I talked to him, and the guy seems genuinely interested in you, so if you wanted him, you're already experimenting, so…"

"I don't even know Dax. Not really."

Ty's acting weird, and I don't really get why, since Dax is one of his own, and it was a fucking bachelor auction, so it's not like we're going on a real date.

"I've heard good things, though," I admit.

Ty doesn't look happy about that. "Well, maybe you should mess around with him. Might help you decide what you like and don't like…you know, since you're figuring this stuff out."

"Where the hell did that come from? We just had a good time, and now you're acting strange."

Ty shakes his head. "Sorry. Just…um…forget it. I didn't want you to think you owe me anything simply because of what we've done a few times. If you guys want to do stuff, obviously I'd be cool."

"Really? Because it sounds like you wouldn't be cool at all."

I see the muscles in his jawline shifting before he moves quickly, taking my mouth once again, his tongue expertly sliding across mine as he moves closer to me, till his body is up against mine.

"Okay, I am slightly…" He struggles with his words, which isn't like Ty at all. "I'm slightly intimidated by his experience, but I also know what I do to you."

He licks up the middle of my lips, as though trying to conjure up that feeling my body gets when he's around.

"So Ty Lancaster admits he's a little jealous?"

He growls again. "Ty Lancaster is maybe more than a little jealous, but on the other hand, it wouldn't be fair to deprive you of him showing you things."

"Dude, you're acting like we're definitely gonna hook up."

He closes his eyes and shakes his head. "Why would you put that image in my head? Whatever. It's just playing on my mind. Something about this stuff is making me not want to let anyone get their greedy hands on you—anyone else's greedy hands, at least." He grips my ass again.

As he firms his hold, a phantom sensation activates within me, reminding me of how good it felt when he was pushing up against that spot. I wonder if he's thinking the same thing I am—what would it feel like? To have his cock pushing up against it? To have him shooting while he's inside me?

Could I even get him off that way?

"What are you thinking about?" I ask him, noticing the eagerness in my chest, this hope that it's the same thing.

He gulps before pulling his gaze from my ass, finally making eye contact. "I think you might already have an idea."

"Maybe you should just say it, then," I press.

His face twists up. "How am I the one being all weird now? I think you might have rubbed off on me. But yes, I'm thinking about how it'd feel to fuck you."

Now he's swung the other way, just putting it all out there.

The back of my neck prickles with sensation.

"You don't get to encourage me to say it and then start blushing," he says.

"Shut up. I can blush whenever I want."

He smiles. "It's not something we have to jump in and do right away, but I'm curious, I guess."

"We've been very curious lately."

"There's an understatement if I ever heard one." As I laugh, he goes on, "But yeah, we don't have to rush anything. I'm enjoying this pace." He quiets, just staring into my eyes. His expression relaxes. "What we talked about before the auction… It means a lot that you shared that with me. I know you were bringing it up to help me through a tough day, and I want you to know it really helped."

It's shocking how quickly we went from having fun to him bringing up one of the biggest traumas in my life, but I understand why.

"Actually, I was surprised how good it felt to share that," I confess. "It's not something I tell a lot of people about."

And I know he can understand why.

"Well, I'm glad you shared it with me." He caresses my ass before offering a kiss.

I relax right into it. It's so easy to let go and simply enjoy moments like these with Ty. And right now, it feels like things are moving at the perfect pace.

THROUGHOUT THE NEXT week and a half, between work, school, TaskFrat, and our various other frat obligations, Ty and I manage to squeeze in time to further explore this chemistry that there's no denying exists between us. This raw desire reminds me of when I first discovered jerking off—how eager I was to get home from school and sneak away to explore this exciting new part of myself, waking to a world of pleasure.

What Ty's awakened in me adds a new rush.

I keep wondering if the novelty will wear off, but with each handjob, blowjob, touch against my prostate, and kiss, I only find myself wanting more. I'm still not ready to be fucked, but that doesn't keep me from wanting him to explore my ass with his fingers before the explosion.

And it's not just the physical stuff I enjoy either. It's our playful text exchanges, and this awareness that he understands the shit I've been through with my brother.

All these thoughts only intensify as I sit next to Ty during an emergency meeting with the Interfraternity Council, called by Zeta Tau's president after he discovered an act of vandalism against their house last night.

Six of the Peach State frat presidents sit around the conference table reserved for this meeting, Ty and I next to one another, and he scoots his chair close, glancing around before copping a feel of my leg. I don't look at him, not wanting to draw any attention to what he's doing.

The door to the conference room flies open, and Omega Psi's president, Jamie Sutton, storms in. In his usual ripped jeans and biker jacket, he looks more like the leader of a biker gang than a frat president. The perfect representative for his frat, really. He settles in a chair in the corner of the room, not at the table like everyone else. No one bothers to ask him to join the group, since you don't tell Jamie Sutton what to do.

"Last night," Zeta Tau's president, Marcus, says as the meeting begins, "we discovered the side of our house spray-painted with the words *Zeta's Glory Hole*, with arrows pointing to our back door."

It's hard not to be a bit amused by it, but Jamie is the only one who actually snickers, earning a glare from several of us.

Marcus goes on, "Now, we don't have any evidence of who was responsible, but there are rumors it was Omega Psi."

All eyes shift to Jamie, awaiting a reaction.

He glances around, taking a breath. "Okay, just to be transparent." He whips out his phone and keys into it. We're all waiting, trying to figure out what he's doing, when the door opens again, and two guys holding another by his arms come in.

The guy in the middle is just in a pair of briefs, with cartoon cocks and other graphic imagery scribbled in marker all over his body. It takes me a moment, but I recognize him from a TaskFrat challenge. He was one of the guys who cuffed Ty and me together before we got those raging boners.

"Guys," Jamie says, "meet Miles Tanner, our culprit. He confessed this morning, and we've punished him in our own Omega Psi way, as you can see. Miles, say hi."

Miles sneers, looks like he's pissed at the committee, though we haven't done anything to him…yet.

"I said, say hi, Miles," Jamie repeats.

"Hi, Miles," is all Miles gives us.

"What the hell is happening?" Ty mutters, clearly as surprised as I am by this display. Although, this wouldn't be a first for Omega Psi.

"You're just now telling us that you know who vandalized Zeta Tau?" I ask Jamie. "This could have been disclosed in an email or before the meeting."

"Whoa, you're already using words like *vandalized*. That's why I knew I should wait and do it this way."

"You thought this would set us at ease?" Ty asks.

"Eh," is all Jamie says, shrugging.

"Well, we're glad you caught him," Marcus says. "But we need to notify the authorities. We need to write up a report for the destruction of property."

"What, huh?" Jamie asks, like he's just woken up in class and been surprised with a question. "Is that really necessary? I've held a meeting, punished Miles, and we're happy to pay for the damage."

"It's important to remind everyone of the codes of conduct we all agreed upon," Marcus says, "including what falls outside the umbrella of pranks, such as destruction of property. We don't have a quote yet for the cost, but we'll have to repaint because he used permanent paint, which is specifically against the rules."

"And then we pay for the damage," Jamie says. "Problem solved, right? It was an Omega Psi guy, but Miles's action does not represent our house."

I have to speak up. "I find it convenient that every time one of your frats is involved in a situation, you say it was a one-off. Or that it doesn't reflect Omega Psi."

"It's just true," Jamie doubles down.

"The prank you pulled on Ty and me last year was not a one-off. That was done by Omega Psi on two other rival frat presidents who have since graduated. Your frat was repeatedly fined for violating our codes of conduct through several fights and pranks."

"You guys said you thought that prank with you was funny," Jamie says.

Funny, but not because we were tied up together, but because of what happened after.

Which Jamie sure as hell doesn't know.

And now, it's not just a funny memory, but a hot one.

Kind of wonder how I didn't see it that way when it was happening.

But it's beside the point.

"What if one of us had been sick?" I ask. "Or needed to go to the hospital from alcohol poisoning?"

"That didn't happen, though, did it?"

"You're missing the point," Ty says. "By creating a culture where your frats think these things are acceptable, you set the scene for something dangerous to happen."

"This is different," Jamie says. "Miles, explain what happened."

Miles continues looking around the room, as though he's in a daze from whatever weird-ass ritual took place before he arrived. "Uh…I think I was being nice to Zeta Tau calling them glory holes because I think glory holes are useful."

"What the—" Marcus starts.

"Miles," Ty says, "could you just tell us why you did that, please?"

I appreciate Ty for keeping this circus on task. At least attempting to.

"A bunch of Zeta Tau guys were bullying one of my boys at the last party, so I was just letting them know they can't get away with that."

"What do you mean by bullying?" I ask.

"Teasing him. Pushing him around. He's not as big as a lot of the guys."

A pulse of anger shoots through me. Nothing I hate more than a bunch of fucking bullies, and now Marcus is earning a few looks from us.

"I didn't know about any of this," Marcus insists.

"Okay, in that case," I say. "We'll get some names and investigate this situation further, ensuring both sides are held accountable for their actions, but, Miles, that doesn't excuse what you did. There are protocols for bullying, so next time, please consult your president, who is there to keep you all safe."

"Yeah," Jamie tells Miles. "You know you could talk to me."

"I know how to deal with assholes," Miles blurts.

It seems like he's not absorbing any of what's being said.

"I can't really do much about the fact that Omega Psi is for loners and rebels," Jamie notes.

"Thank you for coming, Miles," I say. "Can you guys head out, and we'll finish discussing this with Jamie."

The other Omega Psis escort their housemate out, and Jamie is quick to defend his frat. "So this was all just provoked by some asshats at Zeta Tau. This is what happens at frats. Can't we just call it even?"

Now he's making me feel like I'm being a Marty, but I stand my ground. "Jamie, you can't deny you have some responsibility in all this. It's our job as presidents to keep our frats safe, and Omega Psi's wild reputation and behavior have become concerning for the other frats. I think we all would like to see you encouraging your brothers to observe the rules set for all of us to abide by. Because you can pay for damages and deal with fines for this, but if your frats don't feel they can come to you when issues arise and there are more instances like this, there would be consequences. Omega Psi members can be banned from parties, events, TaskFrat challenges, and if you really overstep, we can have you disbanded as a frat altogether."

Jamie smirks. "Trying to thin out the competition?"

"Can you please be serious about this?" Marcus asks.

"I just feel like everyone is overreacting because Omega Psi has had a little fun in the past."

"You have an extracurricular fight club," Ty says.

"Who said?" Jamie inquires. "Because I think we all know rule number one of having a fight club…"

Yeah, it's a rumor, but everyone pretty much knows it's real. This is why it's hard to trust Omega Psis. They're good at keeping secrets among brothers.

"Listen," Jamie goes on, "I'm not trying to minimize what's happening here, but this campus wouldn't be as fun as it is without Omega Psi. We're freaky, yes. It's our thing. It's why people pledge Omega Psi. Let us do us, and you guys do you."

His nonchalant attitude is getting to me, so I take a breath, calming myself before trying to meet him where he's at. "Omega Psi doesn't exist in a vacuum. You are in a community, and if you want to continue existing in that community, you must follow its rules. That's all there is to it. I'm gonna motion that we penalize Omega Psi for Miles's action, if only to encourage you to reach out to your members and urge them to come to you when conflict arises. If another incident happens, we begin sanctions immediately. I motion for Zeta Tau to also be penalized, though, just a warning since this is their first infraction this year. And we should receive updates when Miles provides the names of the bullies, whom I expect Marcus to punish accordingly and ensure there are no future problems with them."

I notice Ty watching me. He looks stunned, but we move on to the vote, and my motions pass. Jamie isn't thrilled, since it'll interfere with Omega Psi's fun, but it's the right thing to do. We further agree to review all the rules with our respective frats, then call an end to the meeting.

After we finish up, Ty and I sneak off to the restroom, where Ty pulls me into a stall and shoves me against the side, his hand gravitating to my crotch.

"That was hot," he mumbles. "Watching you take charge and lay down the law for Jamie and Marcus."

"Somebody had to."

"I like when you're bossy."

He takes a kiss, and when he pulls away, I say, "Couldn't even keep your hands off me for one meeting?"

"Was pissing me off even to do that much."

He's about to move in for another kiss, when we hear the door open. He leans close, whispering, "Shh," and I feel his breath slip into my mouth.

While whoever's in here tackles the urinal, Ty unfastens my fly, slides his hand around my cock, stroking as his hot breath continues slamming against me. Once he's got me good and worked up, he pulls his hand back and takes a lick, then slips his hand under my balls, back to my ass, pushing his fingers into me.

I roll my head back against the stall, biting my lip to keep from making any noise as I hear the flush. Ty stares at me, like he's taking in every expression, as he navigates deeper into me. I know where he's going. And that's where I want him. So fucking badly.

I'm relieved the guy's finally made it to the hand dryer by the time Ty reaches that spot because I can't keep quiet anymore, and as I moan, Ty's mouth crushes down on mine, stifling the sound.

A few moments later, we hear the door swinging open again, and we're alone.

"Fuck," I say in a breath as he massages my prostate.

Ty licks my lips before pulling away. "Close call."

"Not close enough," I tease.

"Then I'd better get to work."

His mouth is on my throat in no time, licking and nibbling.

And I fucking surrender to him.

18

Ty

THE GUYS AND I are playing doubles at the indoor pickleball court of the rec center, swapping out for a person every match since there are five of us. When we finish and head to the bench for our stuff, I find myself searching around for Lance, wishing he'd swing by.

Of course, he has other things to do on the job than come see my needy ass.

I toss on my shirt. We all played shirtless, me—and I guess Dax too—out of solidarity with the guys after Ryan removed his to show off for the sorority girls on the court beside ours, and once he started the charge, no one was willing to be left behind.

Ryan takes a sip of his water before handing it to Keegan. While Ryan locks eyes with one of the girls, Keegan sips from the thermos before asking Dax, "So you got that date tonight with the prez of Alpha Theta Mu?"

I tense up.

It's not something I've been able to get my mind off since the auction two weeks ago. They both had a lot going on, which I was more than pleased about, but now that it's happening, it's all I'll be thinking of while I'm working my shift at Junkie's.

Dax shrugs. "Yeah, should be fun."

"You gonna use your magic on him?" Keegan asks.

"Magic?"

"Come on. I've heard the same things as everyone else. They say you can turn anyone."

"Turn anyone, huh? Maybe I should try *you*?" Dax teases, making Keegan laugh.

"Ooh, that a threat?"

"Do you want it to be?" Dax winks, and the guys are in hysterics.

Everyone but me, since apparently I've lost my sense of humor when it comes to Lance.

"You keep in mind that you're not gonna be an asshole to him," I blurt.

No matter how many times I ran the words through my head, it was impossible for them not to come out more than a little defensively, which earns the attention of my fratmates.

"Um…what the hell?" Ryan asks. "You have all these secret meetings with him for the TaskFrat Committee and all of a sudden you're his best friend?"

"You're my best friend," I say, sidestepping that.

Sure, Lance is my friend too, but what's happening between us is different. I guess we're friends with benefits, but it feels like more than that, especially now that I know him better than most.

"What was the point of getting the date if he can't fuck with the guy?" Keegan asks.

"Let's not assume he's not gonna fuck with the guy," Jaxon jokes, and I watch Dax's expression, waiting for him to make a dick comment—in which case I'll call the whole thing off—or give some indication of how interested he is in Lance's ass.

It's my ass.

A thought I've had a lot recently, especially as the day of their date crept up.

Just like when I initially had those weird thoughts about Lance being mine, I don't have a right to demand that, but this is all Lance's fault for being so goddamn adorable. His fault that I'm enamored with the way his eyes roll back and his mouth hangs open, that beautiful moan when I'm about to make him come yet again with my precise touch on his prostate. Having this power over his body has made me greedy for more, and it might not be my ass, but I want it to be.

Ryan nudges me. "Hey, sexy. For someone who's great at hitting on girls, you're missing the one staring you down right now. You need to get on it."

I glance over, seeing the blonde Phi Lambda clearly

giving me the eyes. She's hot. I figure she's a transfer since I don't recall seeing her last year. In the past, if this had happened, I would have been as bad as Ryan, playing the game, then making sure to swing by and chat with her before heading out, but Lance has broken me, and I don't want to be fixed.

Ryan leads the guys over to the girls, promising to get Jaxon and Keegan some time with his interest's friends, which gives me the opening I've been waiting for with Dax. "Have fun," I say through my teeth, and he eyes me uneasily.

"It doesn't sound like you want me to have fun. We cool?"

"We are, and I do want you to have fun. Just be nice to him. We were just trying to make a point at the auction, and I don't want to hear that you were a dick."

"Don't worry. I'm not planning to exact any revenge on Sigma Alpha's behalf. I actually enjoy Lance. He's a cool, funny guy."

I grit my teeth.

Now I'm wishing he'd just said he was gonna be a dick because, really, the worst thing that could happen is they hit it off and then Lance lets him hit it.

Over. My. Dead. Body.

"What are your plans?" I ask.

Dax's brows rise. "It's a surprise. I'm taking him somewhere fun."

That's what Lance told me after they made plans. What if it's a ton of fun and Dax charms the pants off him? No. Stop it!

Heat rises to my chest, where a knot has already formed, and I ball my fists to soothe my discomfort.

"You good?" Dax asks, wincing. "You look like you're about to deck me."

"Um…no. Fuck. Just thinking about how I wish I was out having fun tonight, not working." Dax is good at reading people, so I gotta bail before he catches on. Also, I'm not planning to leave the rec center without seeing Lance. "I had something I needed to bump into Lance about."

Bump into Lance about? That's not an expression.

No, but my rival scrambles my fucking brain.

"I'm gonna head out. Tell the guys for me, okay?"

I grab my backpack and sling it over my shoulder, leaving the courts, searching desperately for Lance before finding him at the front desk, where he's chatting with Ash. The knot in my chest relaxes as my cock perks up at the promise of messing around again.

What have you fucking done to me, Lance Fehn?

I approach, trying not to be so obvious that his friend will be like, *Um…you guys don't happen to be fucking around behind all the frats' backs, right? Ty, you're not like, questioning your sexuality because of how hot my buddy is, are you?*

That there was ever a question feels like a world away after all we've done the past couple of weeks.

"Hey, guys," I say, surprised at how chill I manage to sound when I'm not feeling chill at all.

Lance turns to me, his smile easing the bundle of hot tension in my chest, but also making me check to see if Ash notices because that's not how rivals are supposed to look at each other.

"There's a certain point where this becomes stalking," Ash says, though I can tell by his amused expression he's just giving me hell. Unlike some of the guys at our frats, he doesn't get too caught up in the rivalry bullshit. Of course, if he knew how obsessed I'd become with his friend, maybe he wouldn't have teased about it so casually.

"Oh, that committee thing?" Lance asks.

Good boy.

"That's good timing," Ash says. "I was gonna FaceTime with Colin, so I'll catch you at the house after your *date*." Ash sings out that last bit, and fire sears my chest, worse than whenever Alpha Theta Mu kicked our asses at the last TaskFrat.

Lance leads me back to the equipment room.

"Everything okay? What's wrong?" he asks, his voice filled with worry, and I know why. He knows me well enough to detect how on edge I am.

Fuck me for being so transparent. But fuck him for

making me this way.

"Everything's fine *now*," I assure him before I shove him back against the wall, my tongue invading his mouth, probing, exploring.

He rests one hand on my hip, the other on my cheek.

It's wild to think how awkward we were at first, and now being close to him feels like the most natural thing in the world.

"Mmmm. I like sweaty Ty Lancaster," he says into my mouth.

"You're so fucking addictive. To think we just hooked up yesterday and I'm not finished with you yet."

I'm greedy for his mouth, taking it again before pulling away.

He looks stunned by the way I went for him. "Good afternoon to you too."

I chuckle. "Good afternoon. Why didn't you come see me while I was playing with the guys?"

"We can't be too obvious, right?"

"Wish I had your self-restraint. Figured I needed to get this in before I head to work, since I'm not gonna have a chance to remind you what you'll be missing out on."

I notice the shift in his expression, and then the way his lips quirk into a smirk. "Oh, Dax...that's what this is about?"

I tense my jaw. "Don't even say his name to me until

tomorrow."

As much rage as I have around Dax taking him out tonight, another part of me likes that Lance knows he has this power over me.

"You know I'm not gonna—"

I kiss him again to stop him from finishing that sentence. When I pull away, he looks all flustered. And I must keep from kissing him so that I can make my point. "I'm not trying to stand in your way. We're exploring shit, right? And it's not like we're exclusive."

His gaze wavers. "Wait, is this your way of telling me you've been messing around with girls while we've been—"

"What? No, no, no. I haven't done anything with anyone since we started fucking around. Which is kind of amazing for me, but though we haven't even gone all the way, I'm surprised by how satisfied I am by what we have done. Well, at least until I need my Lance fix again."

Even when I took the sorority girl who won me out for dinner, it was never going to be more than that since the only one on my mind right now is Lance Fehn.

He beams, and I find my greed getting the best of me. Fuck, I'm such a selfish asshole. It's too much. It's what I've been thinking all day, especially after seeing Dax for the past hour. I don't have the self-restraint to keep it to myself.

"I do want to ask one thing before this date," I confess. "Keep in mind, if you tell me to fuck off, then that's the way it is, because I don't have any right to ask this of you."

His eyes widen, like he's starting to get concerned about what I'm about to ask, so I just spit it out so I don't leave him in suspense. "I want you to save this for me." I grip his ass.

"Huh?"

His response breaks the tension, without him even realizing it, just by him being his adorable self. Although, it also reminds me why I'm so territorial over him. Every little Lancism is perfect.

"This ass," I say, firming my hold. "I want to be in there first. So you can do whatever the hell you want with Dax, but not that."

"Ty, really, this is a bit dramatic. I'm not planning on doing anything with Dax tonight."

It shouldn't feel so good to hear him say that, nor so painful to think of him changing his mind. "I'm sure, but the guy is apparently a king in the bedroom. He's got moves."

"He's like you but with dudes?" he says, reflecting a sentiment I've brought up more than once.

"I just know I can't compete with his experience. *Yet.* But give me some more time, and I'm sure I can give him a run for his money."

"That's surprisingly humble for you."

"Just realistic. I know what I'm good at, and I know where I'm still learning, which is why I can be so confident when I am good at something."

"That's more like the Ty I'm used to." The way he grins whenever I talk like this suggests he enjoys it when I am kinda full of myself.

"Anyway," I say, "Back to what I wanted to talk to you about. We're not exclusive, so you don't owe me shit—"

"Except you want to put a reserve on my ass?"

I let out a nervous chuckle, quirking a brow. "Kinda?"

He laughs, though this time it's clear he thinks this is a joke, which just pisses me off even more.

"I'm being serious, Lance. This ass is mine. Do you understand that?"

He quiets, gulping.

"Fuck, now I've made it weird. I mean, obviously, if you don't want that, then that's another conversation, and—"

He kisses me, effectively shutting me up.

That he's even kissing me after my request assures me I haven't crossed the line.

He places his hand on mine, making me grip his ass even tighter.

"This…ass…is yours. All for my Rocky," he says

between kisses, until I've got him pressed up against the wall, grinding my crotch against him.

I'm shocked by how much his words are like a promise, offering me much-needed relief. Maybe it's wrong of me to ask so much of him, but part of me feels as though, since I was the one who stirred these feelings in him, it's my right to claim it for myself.

"Half tempted to just take what's rightfully mine," I say.

"In here?"

"No, you haven't said you're ready yet. And even if you were, I wouldn't want to fuck you in here for your first time. But don't think I'm not wishing for it."

I kiss him for a while longer, hating that I have to let him return to his friend and that I can't have this ass right here and now.

When we wrap up, he returns to Ash, and I head on to work.

Lance promising me his ass brings relief, and I know he'll be true to his word, and yet thoughts of this date night with Dax keep playing through my mind. Him putting the moves on Lance. Telling him how adorable he is. Even the thought of his hand caressing Lance's skin or him leaning in for a kiss makes me pissed. I'm a traitor to my own fratbro.

And despite managing to hold it together with Lance—barely—it's gonna be so much more difficult when I'm at work, wondering.

19

Lance

"COME ON, GIVE it to me," Dax says. He's really got me worked up. "I'll give it to you all right."

"You can do better than that."

"You're just loving this, aren't you?"

I ricochet the puck off the side of the table, and it flies into the goal.

"Dammit," he says as I throw my hands in the air.

"Hell yeah!" I shout, a swift adrenaline kick pulsing through me at my narrow 7–6 table hockey victory. I wasn't expecting this for date night, but the arcade was a welcome surprise.

"So close," Dax says.

"Yeah, you're lucky I'm having a hard time concentrating."

How can I, after that conversation with Ty?

He wants to reserve my ass. Wants it all to himself, like it's become his obsession. And his obsession is becoming my obsession.

I want to know what it'd feel like to have Ty guiding me through the experience, easing inside me, this time with his cock instead of his fingers.

I love how possessive he was of it, how he wanted to be clear it's his, though I wouldn't have done anything with Dax anyway.

"Why are you having a hard time concentrating?" Dax asks.

Fuck. Way to call me out, bro.

I can't tell him I've been thinking about Ty fucking me for most of the time we've been on our date. Or that before he came over to meet me at Alpha Theta Mu, I was checking out subreddits about anal.

"Just...stuff. What do you want to play next?" I ask, trying to get him off the scent.

"I don't know. Trying to think of things you can beat me in so that we don't wind up with another hog in the house."

I laugh. "Uh-uh. I'm never a sore loser. Besides, the hog is sooo last year. Now come on, don't go easy on me. A victory isn't a victory unless you give me your ass."

He studies me, his face twisting up as he considers his options. "Okay, then. I know what I can kick your ass at."

"Try me."

We head over to the Skee-Ball machines, competing

to see who can get the highest score. Dax is laid-back, effortlessly sinking his into the 100 corner pockets. I'm more determined throughout the game. Same end result—the score is still tight—but definitely different attitudes to get us there.

As I sink another ball into the 100 pocket, I can't help thinking about how so many of these games have something to do with getting something in a hole, which just keeps my mind going back to Ty's words…thinking about his thick dick.

I miss my pocket, and Dax wins this round.

"Dammit," I say. "You got me, frathole."

"Ooh, even when you try to sound playful, you sound annoyed as fuck when you lose. No wonder you and Ty are always at each other's throats. I'm probably betraying some kind of Sigma Alpha oath by telling you this, but Ty got so worked up last year every time Alpha Theta Mu did better at TaskFrat."

Am I a monster for how good it feels knowing how much it bothered him? Or is it exciting knowing he was thinking about me even back then?

"What about this year?" I ask. "We won the last challenge."

"He didn't seem as bothered. Maybe because it's early enough in the year, so he knows we have plenty of time to kick your asses. And as a Sigma Alpha, I must tell you, we're *definitely* gonna kick your asses. Although…I probably shouldn't say even that much now. Ty was all in my face, like I was gonna come here and haze you tonight."

"Really?"

"Oh yeah. I know we go out of our way to give you guys hell, but I think he respects you because you're a worthy adversary."

I'm not surprised to hear it, but I don't want to give away anything about my new feelings about Ty, so I just say, "Well, if you're recording to get me to say something nice about the guy, I think he's an asshole who needs to accept that Alpha Theta Mu is gonna kick your asses this year." I say all that loudly, leaning close like he's wearing a wire, and Dax chuckles.

"You guys. Have you always been this way? Like supercompetitive?"

"Pretty much," I admit. "I don't think I've mentioned this, but I had an older brother, Kacey. He passed away when I was younger. He was very competitive, couldn't really do anything without it becoming a competition."

"I'm sorry. I didn't know."

"Not the sort of thing you go around chatting about, you know?"

"I hear that. My brother is competitive too, but that had the opposite effect on me. Made me pretty chill about stuff. I enjoy friendly competition, but I'm a good sport about losing."

"I'm not like that. At all." I laugh nervously, biting my lip.

"That's sexy," he says. "When you bite your lip."

A part of me is waiting for Ty to appear out of nowhere and tackle Dax to the ground.

"That wasn't me flirting with you, man," Dax says. "Just giving you a compliment. Don't worry. I can tell you have zero interest in me."

"Huh?"

"I think you're hot as fuck, but trust me, I know when guys are into me. And the way you've been acting tonight, it's clear you just want to be friends, and I wanted to say I'm cool with that. So…who's the lucky someone?"

I eye him. "What makes you think there's a someone? You think that about everyone who's not into you?"

"Naw, you've been spacing every five seconds."

"I could be thinking about work or school. Maybe I'm working out my essay for my Tissue Mechanics class."

"So this is how you look when you think about Tissue Mechanics…" He stares off, tilting his head, a dreamy look in his eyes, giving an overdramatic performance of what I was doing.

"Okay, okay." I nudge him with my shoulder. "Enough of that. Maybe I'm caught, then. There is someone."

It feels criminal to call Ty a *someone* when he's more than that—he's Ty fucking Lancaster.

"They must be pretty special if they managed to catch your interest."

I notice Dax isn't assuming this someone is a girl, and I have a feeling he knows, but he's sensitive enough not to press. Reminds me that he's a good person to talk to, especially about some of these things running through my head, and while part of me fears he might connect that it's Ty, the reality is, it could just as easily be some guy at Alpha Theta Mu, so it's not like talking about my feelings will out his fratmate.

"Since you mentioned this person…" I say, "I have been struggling with some stuff recently. Well, *struggling* might not be the right word. I've had girlfriends, but those happened because they were usually someone I was friends with already and things developed slowly."

"You're demisexual?"

"Maybe. Seems to fit. I don't really think about it that deeply, but one-night stands aren't my thing. And I guess because my relationships always seemed to happen with girls, I assumed that meant I was straight."

"But you have reasons to doubt that now?"

I recall that moment in the equipment room, Ty's hot breath against my throat as he gripped my ass. The desire that pulsed through me. How desperately I wanted him.

"Yeah," I confess. "What was it like for you?"

"Eh, I knew early on. I was a flirt, even in middle school. Had two boyfriends at the same time."

"Holy shit. Are you serious?"

"Obviously, we like, held hands and had closed-mouth kisses, but I definitely worked out early on that I was attracted to dudes and they were attracted to me."

"Sounds nice to have gotten your head around it that early."

"We're all different, and I've been with enough guys to know that it happens in whatever way it happens. There's no right or wrong in any of it. Or really, I guess the only wrong is if you don't trust yourself and that gut impulse when you realize that maybe you don't fit into that neat little box everyone else has put you into."

It's no surprise that Dax would say some wise shit like that. "Maybe you're right."

"I am right. But it's okay if it takes you a while to sort it all out. There's no rush to any of this, and anyone who tells you otherwise is full of shit, okay?"

"Okay," I say, smiling.

"Now how about we grab something to eat? Maybe head over to Crave after and dance some?"

"I'd be down for that."

"Down for that? You're basically my hostage for tonight, and don't you forget it." He winks. "And let's invite some of the gang out and make tonight epic."

A jolt of excitement races through me.

Because I know what would really make tonight epic.

Dax stops by the restroom before we head out, and I text Ty.

ME: What are you up to after work?

I'm not expecting a reply right away, but it's like he's been waiting for a text because he responds quickly.

TY: No plans yet. Why?

ME: You should meet Dax and me at Crave. ☺

20

Ty

THERE'S SO MUCH heat in my chest, I can barely stand it.

I was so distracted throughout my shift, constantly checking my phone before Lance's text came through: **You should meet Dax and me at Crave.** ☺

As soon as my shift was over, I rushed back to the frat and changed, then got my ass over to the bar.

I shouldn't be so worked up. If Dax and Lance were vibing, surely he wouldn't have invited me. But even the thought that they're still hanging when I want Lance all to myself again has me hurrying in, nearly getting tackled by the guy checking IDs at the door. Once I get that out of the way, I go right for the dance floor. I know how Lance and Ash are at parties, and my intuition is proven right when I catch him dancing with Dax.

Lance has a smile stretched across his face, and Dax leans close and whispers something. As Lance's smile expands into a grin, my cheeks get as hot as my chest.

I want to be the reason he's smiling like that.

And there's a fear in the back of my mind—one I considered on the way over. That Lance invited me out because they clicked so much, he felt bad about what he promised me. Maybe he wanted to tell me right away that our deal about giving me his ass is off. I could see Lance wanting to tell me something like that in person.

No, it's mine. I'm the one who showed him how good he could feel. I deserve it, not Dax.

It's a selfish thought I hate myself for having.

Lance owes me jack shit.

Intellectually, I know that, but what's happening to me right now is visceral, primal. I swallow, bracing myself as I work up the courage to not act like a total creep, before approaching the guys.

Dax notices me first, and he offers that familiar smile. He's always a fun-loving guy, but I can tell he's having an even better time tonight…because of Lance? Because he knows what they might do later?

When Lance turns to me, he's still smiling, and his eyes light up in a way that's enough to make me question all my wild, intrusive thoughts.

"Hey, man, what's up?" Dax asks.

"He's mine," I blurt out. Like at the auction, the words spit right out, as though I don't have a fucking filter.

This…is all Lance's fault.

Dax's expression twists up. "What'd you say? It's hard to hear you because of the music."

I'm fucking relieved he gave me an out, so I say, "I said *hi, fine.* Sorry, I thought you said how are you…" It's the closest I can think of, but he's looking at me strangely, like he knows that doesn't fit.

"You should win some prize for making it here before the rest of the guys," Dax says.

"Yeah," Lance adds. "We got a Sigma Alpha–Alpha Theta Mu rumble going down tonight, I guess. We were gonna just do this for a while before things get going at Zeta Tau later."

"And how was the date?" I ask, searching between them for any indication that Dax has him under a sex spell.

Dax casually hooks his arm around him.

Get your greedy fucking hands off him.

I'm such an asshole. Dax is a good guy, one of my own, and it's not like he knows he's hitting on the guy I've been experimenting with. Neither is doing anything wrong, which just makes me that much more frustrated with the whole damn situation.

"We had a great time," Dax says. "Pressed him for plenty of details we can use to destroy Alpha Theta Mu."

Lance glares at him playfully. "Oh, that's what it was really about, wasn't it? Well, you did a good job getting me to let my guard down."

Dax shrugs. "Kind of my thing."

Lance laughs.

I don't make him laugh like that. Wait, yes I do.

"Come on, Ty," Dax says. "Show us what you got."

I'm usually a good dancer, but right now, I'm tense as fuck. Dax moves close to me, strutting his stuff, and it'll be less awkward to go along with him, so I do. Besides, now that it's clear they've been having a good night, I need to remind Lance I can be fun too.

I can be cool.

Which is totally not something that cool or fun people ever have to think…

Dammit.

"There you go," Dax says before getting closer to Lance, who doesn't seem fazed by the move. "Come on. You know how to work that ass."

Lance spins around and pushes back until his ass is against Dax's hips.

I've always known Dax to be a damn good dancer, and the way he's rolling his hips puts on full display the kind of rhythm I'd expect a guy like him to have. And seeing the way Lance moves that ass…

My face is on fire. I could fucking lose it and deck my Sigma Alpha bro over this stupid shit. As Lance pulls away from Dax, laughing at his move, my fists are clenched, my shoulders stiff.

"You mind if I chat with Lance for a sec?" I force out

through my teeth, summoning every ounce of strength I can muster.

"Sure, man." Dax shrugs. "Let me grab you a drink while you do that. Your usual? Tequila and soda?"

"Yeah, that works. Thanks."

He rushes off, and my nerves settle. Lance waits for me to say something, but when I just stand there, silent, he finally asks, "What did we need to talk about?"

I rest my hand on his shoulder, guiding him through the crowd to a dark spot in the corner of the dance floor, mostly to buy time to regain my senses and not say something wild or stupid, but also because I figure we need to actually hear each other.

As we settle by the wall, I turn to him. "How was the date?" I ask, unable to disguise my irritation.

"Um…fine."

"Good enough that you guys decided to hang after, apparently."

Lance's brows tug closer together. "Yeah, Dax was really cool about it all."

He is cool, something I never had an issue with until recently.

"Music's good tonight," Lance says.

"Be better if you were DJing. How else am I gonna hear the latest Tate McRae remix?"

"You pay attention to my mixes?"

"Yeah, everyone knows Alpha Theta Mu's music is

the best. And I'm not saying that just because I want to get in your ass—" I stop myself. "I really need to start filtering myself around you."

"I'm fine with you not," he says playfully.

"Speaking of your ass… I'm sorry for that shit I said earlier today. It wasn't right of me to ask that of you, and if you want—" I stop again because this is fucking killing me, but I know it's the right thing to do. And it wasn't fair to Lance. "You know you can do whatever you want with him, right?"

Lance quiets, has that deer-in-headlights look that makes it impossible to work out what's going through that pretty head of his.

"But, before you decide, know that, even though he might be more experienced, you know I know what I'm doing with girls. And I clearly know how to please you…"

"Ty—"

"Just hear me out," I say before he has a chance to go on, moving close to him, my lips just inches from his, so close that I'm tempted to take a kiss, but what I have to say is too important. "Maybe the first time with me won't be everything Dax can give you, but you're gonna feel more comfortable telling me what you need and want." I slide my hand around his hip, down to his ass, cupping his cheek. "You know we have chemistry. You know there's something here. That I'll be even more determined to impress you than anyone else."

"Ty—"

"Please, let me finish." I need to get this out, or I'm gonna stifle it, which is only making this shit worse. "No one can take care of this ass the way I will." I firm my hold on it. "I'm sure Dax would be fun, and I'm sure it'd be great, but if you tell me that whatever he does to you sparks like it sparks between us, you know I'm not gonna believe that."

I move closer to his throat, and he rolls his head back, reminding me that I still have this power over him.

That exciting rush returns. If he feels even a fraction of what I do, how could he ever deny me?

"I—" Before I have a chance to say more, Lance rests his hand against the back of my head. He guides my lips to his, and though everything we've done together has been hot as hell, in a moment, it's like an explosion, ripping right through my train of thought, and I lose myself in wet kisses and tongue. When I finally pull away, Lance looks just as shocked as I am by how intense it was, though it's definitely made me less concerned about everything that had me so worked up.

As he seems to regain his senses, he glances around, reminding me that we're still in fucking Crave.

"Sorry," he says.

"Don't you dare be sorry for that," I insist, which earns a smirk.

See, Dax, I can make him smile too.

His lips move like he's about to say something before I hear, "One tequila soda."

Dax passes me my drink, and I quickly take a sip.

I grind my teeth. The guy just bought me a drink, but now I'm annoyed with him for another reason. Because it would've been nice to know how Lance felt about everything I said. Although, given the way Lance attacked my mouth, I'd say it can't be bad.

"Did I interrupt something?" Dax asks, glancing between us, his expression confirming he knows he did, his smile suggesting he might even be proud of it.

"Let's…uh…let's dance," Lance says, still a bit out of it since that kiss.

21

Lance

Y HEAD'S STILL spinning, my cheeks warm from everything Ty said and then that kiss.

"You know there's something here. That I'll be even more determined to impress you than anyone else."

Ty's words keep playing in a loop in my head, not like a guy who was pleading for me to fuck around with him, but like a desperate man. He certainly didn't hide his jealousy of Dax when we first discussed the date, but it's clearly on another level tonight, and I notice what it does to my body, how it's got my dick a little twitchy while we're dancing. He wants my ass, and I want him to have it. I wish Dax hadn't interrupted before I could tell Ty that.

Unfortunately, our friends arrive shortly after Dax returns, so it's not like we can bail on them, but after a few songs, we manage to get some privacy again. Ty's glance toward the door is the only signal I need to know it's time to go, so we find our friends, say our goodbyes, and head out into the chilly night.

Neither of us speaks as Ty gets us an Uber, and now he's glancing at me like he's trying to work out what happens next.

"Someone's not very chatty, considering all you had to say inside," I observe, and a wry smirk tugs across his lips.

"I didn't want tonight to pass by and not have said it."

"I'm glad you did," I confess. "But there was no threat of me doing anything with Dax. We talked during dinner about the fact that I wasn't interested in him like that, but we could be friends."

"Oh…"

I laugh. "Aren't one-word responses more my thing?"

He cringes. "They really are."

"And while we were on that date, I was actually thinking about something else."

"Oh really?"

"Yeah, something I wasn't ready for before, but that I think I'm ready for tonight."

"What are you saying?"

"I guess I'm trying to work out whose place we're gonna go back to. Because you can't talk about my ass like that and not expect to follow through."

Ty's smile sends a rush through me. With all the emotions I've been through the past half hour in the club, I can only imagine what he'll do to me once we start exploring.

"Since my guys are at Crave," Ty says, "and some will have already gone to Zeta Tau, I imagine I can get you into Sigma Alpha pretty easily. And even if someone noticed, I wouldn't give a flying fuck."

"Me neither."

"My place it is," Ty says, just as our ride arrives.

It's a short trip to the Sigma Alpha house. We chat with the driver, and I try to ignore the throbbing in my crotch and the adrenaline coursing through me as I start to accept what's about to happen.

I'm gonna get fucked by Ty Lancaster, the president of our rival frat.

When we arrive, the place is pretty chill. We see a few guys around, but no one makes a big deal as Ty leads me to his room. As soon as the door's closed, his lips are on mine, and he shoves me back against the wall adjacent to the door, his hands effortlessly grasping at my body. The dam's broken, and he's finally doing all the things he clearly wanted to do to me since he arrived at Crave. That I've been wishing he would do to me.

His lips travel down to my throat, he kisses and nips, and my stomach swirls with sensation. Part of me can't believe this is really happening, that we went from getting on each other's cases, to fucking around, to me wanting him to take me completely tonight.

Ty squats, hiking my shirt up as his tongue works like wild across my abs. He licks up to my chest, pulling my shirt up and over my head, then locking it around my wrists, pushing them back against the wall, so that I'm trapped in place.

"Reminds me of a TaskFrat challenge," he teases.

"Definitely an Omega Psi thing," I joke.

"Definitely."

He plants another firm kiss on my lips, and a wave of sensation pulses through me, this potent desire activating within me.

When Ty pulls away, he grazes his lips against mine, teasing me with them. He rubs his crotch against my pelvis, so I know how hard he is.

"Feel that? That's how much I want that ass."

"You didn't leave me to speculate much at the bar. Starting to think if you overhype it, you won't be able to live up to the expectation."

He glares at me in that familiar cocky way he has. "I'm not scared your expectations will be too high. As you know, I love a challenge."

He finishes pulling my shirt off, throwing it over his shoulder before unfastening my fly. It doesn't take him long to get it loose, and then he yanks my pants down with my boxers, exposing my cock and ass. He guides me around, pushing me against the wall as his hands grip my ass cheeks.

"Fuck, there it is," he says. "Those beautiful globes, just waiting for me to slide right between them, make them all mine."

"Make them all yours." Now *I* sound like the needy one.

I hear him working his fly, and I'm waiting impatiently before I feel his girth pushing up vertically between my cheeks. For a guy who hadn't ever considered putting a dick in my ass, I'm surprised by how it feels like I need it. This is what Ty's done to me, through this spark between us and then the steady probing and experimenting.

He kisses behind my ear, growling subtly before whispering, "Stay right here. Don't move a muscle."

I follow his instruction as Ty heads over to the nightstand and retrieves a condom and lube.

Fuck, this is really happening.

He returns to me, pumps lube onto his fingers, and massages them against my hole in that masterful way he has. I can tell he's more confident than when he was first playing around back there. Now that he knows what he's doing. What gets me worked up.

He steadily pushes in, teasing at that familiar spot, and when his finger's right on it, he leans close to my ear. "There you are," he says as I roll my head back.

"Look at me, Lance. I want to see how much you enjoy it."

I obey, turning toward him. He studies my face as he continues hitting that spot, applying a subtle amount of pressure that makes me arch my back.

He hooks his free arm around me and leans in for a tongue-filled kiss.

When he pulls away, I say, "Please, Ty. I need it. Now."

He snickers. "I love that you need it."

He doesn't torture me. Pulls out steadily, then tears the condom packet open with his teeth, once again reminding me of the fuckspert he is.

I know Dax is supposed to be a great lay, but I can't imagine anyone else taking my ass other than Ty, the guy who showed me how good it could be from the start.

He readies the condom and generously pumps lube for me before lining himself up.

I shake for a moment, and Ty places his hand on my hip, rubbing gently, not rushing me. Taking his time as he rests his head against me.

"You ready to be my first bottom?"

I laugh. "You ready to be my first top?"

I glance over my shoulder, and there's this excited look in his eyes, one I recognize from when he's won a TaskFrat challenge. And I love the thought that my ass is some kind of prize to him.

He pushes in gently, nudging into me. I don't know if it's just how hot I am for him, everything he said he'd do to me, or the way he worked up my prostate already, but I push my ass back, welcoming more of him into me. Being bold with how quickly I take him. Maybe it's my competitive streak taking over.

"Fuck," Ty mutters, watching his cock push into me, and then he closes his eyes, rolling his head back. "Jesus Christ, you feel amazing, Lance."

As he pushes farther, I take him, determined to get him to that spot—"Oh," I call out, worrying for a second that I'm being too loud. Heat surges to my face as my nerves prickle in waves across my flesh.

Ty's cock continues sliding back, massaging my prostate, the movement continuing to pool sensation through me, and I notice my cock getting wet with precum.

I'm surprised he's still pushing in, until I feel his pelvis against my ass. His arms hook around me, and he kisses my neck.

"How's that feel?" he whispers.

"Fucking amazing."

"Yeah? I'm impressed with how good you are at taking me. Was thinking I was gonna have to work you up some more. How'm I doing as a top?"

I glance over my shoulder. "The worst," I tease, and he grins, clearly knowing better as he moves close.

"Then I guess I'll have to try harder." He licks up my lips before sliding out and thrusting back in subtly.

Just as I think the sensation can't get any better, he wraps his hand around my cock and strokes me as he continues thrusting. My body vibrates, feels as though Ty's bringing me to life, my nerves shouting out their excitement in a series of powerful bursts that make me lose track of anything other than this moment and what he's doing to me. He fucks and pumps at the same time, pressing my body against the wall as he kisses and nibbles at my neck, demonstrating why he was the right person to fuck me.

"So tight," he mutters before offering a quick lick. "Little virgin hole just for me."

"Only for you," I assure him as he speeds up his movements.

I call out again, but he doesn't seem to mind, speeding up, really working up into a rhythm that's got my body going wild. I'm lost in a daze, caught up in sensations I've never experienced before, lost to this delirium—when I feel his cock pull out.

"What… What are you…" I'm in a panic, my body practically losing it over the fact that he's not in me anymore.

"Relax, Lance. I just want to fuck you in my bed."

His words set me at ease, remind me that those sensations will return to me. He spins me around, kissing me and guiding me toward the bed. As the backs of my legs hit the frame, I fall back on the mattress.

Ty is on me in no time, like we're magnetized to each other, and I guess it feels like we have been for a while now.

"I want to watch your face while I fuck you." He positions my legs, opening them wide as he pulls me back toward the edge of the mattress. He slides in steadily, staring at me.

And I find myself just as lost in the sensations as before, only this time, I'm on full display, totally vulnerable beneath him as he watches all my instinctual movements, the way my mouth falls open and my face twists as his cock gives me a pleasure I've never experienced. It's so much more than what he did with his fingers against that spot. It's the pressure of him opening me up, feeling how much my ass is turning him on.

Once I've collected myself some, I open my eyes and watch his face as he fucks me. He's so damn serious, giving his everything to what he throws himself into, like he's dedicated to this so he can prove to me why he was the right guy for the job. There was never any doubt in my mind, and just when I think it can't get any better, as we make eye contact, his dick throbs in me.

"Fuck, you're even harder," I tell him.

"You think I don't notice that?" he teases, making me chuckle, though it's something I can only laugh about for a moment before I'm lost again in the intense surge of adrenaline. This angle feels even better than when he was fucking me from behind. And he's so damn hot as his forehead beads with sweat, his breath intensifying as he puts in a good workout on my ass.

For a moment I lose track of what's happening physically, consumed by the feelings he stirs within me, coming back to it as a bead of sweat drops down and lands on my lip. I lick it up, like even having Ty in my mouth like this isn't enough.

I want to experience every part of him. Taste him. Feel him.

He leans down and takes my mouth, his tongue pushing in, fucking me like his cock is my ass. I wrap my arms around him, holding him close. "Right there," I tell him because he's hitting it perfectly, the build-up moving quickly, steadily. I won't last much longer.

"You ready to come?" he asks.

"Yes," I say, and he doesn't let up his movement, taking me to the edge.

"Fuck, your ass is tightening up around my cock so much, I don't think I can… Fuck…"

His movements become more frenzied, and I hear a few quick slaps against my ass, his cock pushing deep as one thrust takes me too far and I call out, feeling the quick rush from my cock, a warm shot spreading across my abs as he continues fucking me.

Ty's arms hook under mine, keeping me close as he continues kissing me, burying himself deep within, my prostate extra sensitive to the movements as I gasp into his mouth.

His thrusts steady until coming to a halt, his body tight against mine, his torso pressed up against me, compressing the cum between us as his tongue continues toying with mine.

Finally, he takes a breath and pulls away, glancing down at me in what I can only describe as awe, and I'm sure I have a similar expression on my face.

"How was that for topping?" he asks, that cocky smile on his face, in a way that's just so Ty.

I roll my eyes. "Terrible. Tragic. You should be embarrassed, Rocky."

He laughs, a loud, uninhibited laugh. "Well, you were a perfect bottom, so good I can't even tease you about it…Stud."

I don't know why it feels so good to hear that.

He leans down and licks my cheek as though marking his territory.

Which works for me.

Because I am his territory now.

22

Ty

LANCE'S ARM AND leg are draped around me as he clings to me, his pretty head tucked against my chest. I like having him on me like this, in my bed, just listening to the sound of his breathing.

Last night was epic. Everything I could have hoped for and so much more. Being inside this tight ass that's all mine, being the one to open him up and claim it. And I'm glad Lance trusted me to be the one to do the job.

Lance finally stirs. "I guess I should go," he mutters before planting a kiss on my abdomen.

"No," I blurt out, which catches his attention, and he angles his head to look up at me. "I don't want you to go. I mean, obviously, if you need to, or if you work early or something…"

"I don't work until later in the day, but if I stay, it's not gonna be easy for me to sneak out in the morning without everyone noticing."

Despite how epic the sex was, my feelings for Lance

are beyond that. It's not just his ass I want. I enjoy spending time with him, getting to know him beyond the fun we have together.

I consider my next words carefully. "What if you didn't have to sneak out? What if we went downstairs and grabbed breakfast together?"

"Then the guys might think it weird that I was over here last night, with you."

"So what?"

He's just staring blankly at me.

"Never mind," I say. "Sorry, that's such a dick move of me. This isn't only about what I want. I want you to stay the night. I'm not ashamed of what we're doing, and I don't give a flying fuck what dumb shit comes out of Ryan's or Keegan's mouths. But you need to do what you feel comfortable with."

He's still not giving me any indication about his feelings around my invitation.

"*Why* do you want me to stay the night?" Lance finally asks.

"Stud, I thought you were a smart guy. Surely you realize I like more than just your ass. I enjoy hanging with you."

He smiles, and the tension that's built up within me dissipates.

"Is Ty Lancaster hung up on me?"

It's clear he's joking, but I can't help saying, "Yes."

I'm surprised by how serious that came out, and I can tell by his stiff expression that it takes him by surprise too.

"I like spending time with you," I confess. "And every time you're not around, I just think about getting to spend more time with you and being annoyed when you're not there, so yeah, a few more hours with you pressed up against me, offering those kisses against my abs and pecs, nestling your face against me, that would be nice."

"Even if the guys found out? All our friends?" Lance asks.

It's the practical side, which I hate that we even have to consider. "It's not a problem for me, but again, if it is for you, then fuck what I just said."

His brow twists up. "You can't say those kinds of things and then take them back. And I don't care what anyone says about what we're doing. I like the idea of you taking me downstairs tomorrow, letting all your Sigma Alpha bros know how you claimed this ass."

"And expecting many more times."

He laughs. "Well, let's hope they all live up to to-night's fuck."

"I'll make sure of it." It's my promise to him as I rest my hand against his cheek, running my thumb down his face. "I want to be inside that ass a lot more." As his cheeks light up, I say, "There's that pretty shade of pink again. Harder to get that nowadays."

"Not surprised with all the dirty things you've done to me," he says, flashing another smile.

"Stay with me tonight."

It's the last time I'll ask, and as he looks to the door, a ball of tension knots up in my chest. But then he turns back to me, and I see the playful glint in his eyes.

"It'll be weird having to explain that to Dax after we went on a date."

"Of all the guys, he'll definitely understand."

"True. But are you gonna keep the others from being mean to me at breakfast?"

"Trust me, they'll be giving me all the hell. And if Ryan says anything douchey, I'll kick his fucking ass."

"I don't doubt that. And now I'm the one getting jealous when you're threatening to do something to someone else's ass." He takes a kiss, and that easily, my uneasiness lets up. "And just to be clear," he says, "with how jealous you are about my ass, I assume, from this point on, we're not messing around with other people."

"As long as you fuck with me, that ass is mine." Again, the words come out before I can really think them through, so I quickly amend them. "And also, these lips, this dick, every part is reserved for me."

"Then that means all this"—he waves his hand over my body—"is reserved for me?"

"Yup. Totally exclusive because we wouldn't want

anyone to get hurt if I find out they're touching up on you."

He glares at me. "Yeah, I'm sure it's everyone's safety you're concerned about."

"Not *only* that." I grab his ass again, giving a subtle squeeze. "I'm just a greedy fuck when it comes to you."

"It's hot how greedy you are for me." He offers me another kiss, then pulls away and says, "Now that that's all settled, Rocky, I guess the only thing I need to be clear about is: if I find out you snore, I'm outta here."

I close my eyes and imitate a snore, which gets him laughing, but his arm and leg tighten around me, assuring me he's not going anywhere.

Granting me a moment of peace.

We cling to each other, kissing, and I feel myself drifting off in his arms.

WHEN MORNING ARRIVES, we shower, and I loan him an extra toothbrush from my last dental checkup.

He starts to put on the clothes he wore the day before.

"Uh-uh, Stud. You're not doing a walk of shame in Sigma Alpha."

"I don't think I'll fit into your pants."

"Naw. But at least you can wear one of my shirts."

I fish through my drawer, retrieving a Sigma Alpha long-sleeved henley, and he glares at me. "Has this really all been some master plan to get me looking foolish in Sigma Alpha spirit wear?"

I roll my eyes. "I thought you'd look hot in it, but fair enough."

As I continue rifling through the drawer, Lance approaches and strips off his shirt, his abs flexing, his muscles on full display. I don't know why seeing them moving around like that gets me going so much when I had all night to enjoy them, but my mouth waters.

He throws the henley on.

Is it wrong how much I love seeing my rival proudly wearing my house letters?

"Naughty." He checks himself out in the closet floor-length mirror. "Feels like I'm betraying my guys, though. They'd freak if they saw what I was doing."

He looks disappointed, but now that I've seen him in the shirt, I can't stand the thought of him being out of it. "Well, fortunately, they're not here," I say, approaching him from behind. "And I find it hot as hell."

He looks over his shoulder at me, and I take his mouth, thoroughly enjoying the naughty feeling. It might be wrong, what we're doing, but I don't give a fuck. I love him being in my Sigma Alpha shirt.

"Maybe you should bring over an Alpha Theta Mu shirt, and one night we can mess around in each other's letters."

"You dirty fuck," he says. "I might just do that."

We enjoy a few more kisses, and then we behave like good boys, finding a neutral henley for Lance that won't have him lose his status at his frat.

We're unusually quiet as we head out of my room, waiting to see whom we'll run into first and how they'll react to my sleeping with the enemy.

Keegan's door opens—of course it would be fucking Keegan—and as he steps out in only his boxers, I rest my arm across Lance's shoulders, making it clear he's my guest and that if anyone plans to say shit about him, they're not gonna have an easy morning.

"Ty, Lance…" Keegan trails off.

"Morning, Keeg," Lance says, offering a fist bump Keegan barely makes before we pass him.

I snicker. What can I say? I enjoy throwing the guys, and Lance does too.

When we get downstairs, Ryan's at the kitchen is-land, shirtless, pouring his cereal and laughing it up with Jaxon.

"Morning, guys," I announce.

Ryan's bright smile turns to me. "Morning, Ty…and Lance. Lance with Ty…Ty with Lance…"

He's having a full breakdown as he freezes there, his gaze shifting between us as he seems to be struggling to process what he's seeing. His milk overflows from his bowl, sliding across the kitchen island.

"Dude," Lance says, indicating the mess now spilling onto the front of Ryan's joggers.

"Fuckin' A," Ryan says, hurrying to grab paper towels. He packs them over his crotch.

As Jaxon helps him clean up around him, I say, "Ryan, how in the fuck did you manage to make this moment about you?"

"Couldn't let you hog all the attention, I guess." He finishes wiping himself off. "Now please tell us you found this trash snooping around because he wanted to get us back for that prank."

Even knowing Ryan's teasing, anger shoots through me. "Nah, but fuck around and find out by calling him trash one more time."

Ryan raises his hands in surrender. "Ooh, so sounds like this isn't a one-time thing. When did all this start?"

"Depends on when you want to start," Lance jokes.

"What is that supposed to mean?" Keegan asks, joining us.

"It means it's been a minute," I confess, keeping Lance close.

"Wait, but you fuck girls," Jaxon says, his brow twisted up. "Like, a lot of them."

"Well, it's pretty clear you're gonna have to add guys to the list. At least, one guy."

"You were at each other's throats at the start of the

year," Jaxon points out before blinking a few times. "That's kind of hot, actually."

"Yes, yes it is," Lance agrees.

"I guess it makes sense since you guys had to be around each other so much for all those secret TaskFrat Committee things."

Keegan and Jaxon shoot him looks.

"What?" Ryan asks. "That's—Oh, there were no secret TaskFrat Committee meetings, were there?"

"Look, it *can* learn," Keegan jokes.

"Fuck off. It just took me a minute. So you guys are what? Boyfriends?"

I feel a rush when he says *boyfriends*, like I wish that were the case, but I dismiss it. "It hasn't been *that* long. We're just having a good time. Can you all stop embarrassing me in front of the enemy?"

"Does *Alpha Theta Mu* already know?" Ryan asks, stressing Lance's frat name in a particularly condescending way—you know, the way we usually talk about it.

"You guys better stop using that tone about my house while I'm over," Lance says.

"Or what you gonna do, little man?" Ryan challenges, standing taller—not that he needs to with all that muscle packed on.

I glare at my fellow fratbro, who clearly gets the message as he gulps. "Okay, okay...we can be cool while he's over."

"Damn right you can be."

"You don't look cool. You look like you just pissed yourself," Lance tells him, indicating the milk stain, which gets Ryan roaring.

"Okay, maybe he's all right," Ryan says.

"Hey, this could work out," Jaxon adds. "Now we have an in with the Alpha Theta Mu guys. Might actually get a date over there."

"Who the fuck have you been eyeing over there?" Ryan asks. "Moaning Marty?"

The guys get laughing, but Lance says, "Hey, no one talks about my friend like that."

It doesn't surprise me that Lance managed to lead a frat his sophomore year because even my guys quiet, accepting his authority as word.

And then Dax heads in.

"Morning, guys. Hey, Lance." He offers us fist bumps, smirking in a way that suggests he had a hunch about us, at least with the way we were acting last night. "That's one of my favorite shirts of yours, Ty," he teases before heading to the fridge.

And yes, I was clearly right that he would be the least weirded out of all the guys.

"Now that we've made things as awkward as possible with your house," Lance says, "I guess I should get back to my place, start breaking the news to my guys. I'll see you later?"

I love knowing that's true, that there won't be any sneaking around anymore. Next time, he can just head on in, and we can do whatever the hell we want.

"You're damn right you'll see me later."

I proudly plant a kiss on his lips, giving zero shits about the guys seeing me, and as I pull away, I notice all the guys but Dax are a mix of surprise and amusement.

After Lance leaves, the guys are silent until Jaxon finally says, "It would be kind of funny if this was like an epic prank, though, right?"

His comment breaks the tension, the room erupting into laughter once again.

And just as I figured, the guys are cool.

Maybe a little confused, but definitely cool.

23

Lance

I'M BUZZING WITH excitement by the time I get back to Alpha Theta Mu.

Not only did I get to have an amazing time with Ty last night, but now we don't have to keep our secret anymore. I loved seeing how he didn't pull away when we were around his fellow Sigma Alphas. How he kissed me goodbye in front of them. But mostly, I love that this means we can stay over at each other's houses whenever we want without having to make excuses or keep being busy with feigned TaskFrat shit. At least, once I tell the guys about us.

Marty's in the living room, doing homework, so I grab him and we head up to find Ash because of course I can't disclose this without my best bro.

I skip some steps as I head up the stairs.

"If you don't say you won the lottery after this, I'm gonna be annoyed," Marty jokes.

Ash's door is open, so I don't think twice about

heading in, when I hear, "Fuck me, Colin. Fuck me harder."

I halt in place, but I'm too late—I already see Colin's nude back, firm ass shaking. Ash's head is rolled back as he moans.

"Holy hell!" Marty calls out, and in my periphery, I see him slip right back out the door.

"Whoa," spits out of my mouth as my mind catches up with what's happening, and Colin glances over his shoulder as Ash's gaze meets mine.

"Dude, fuck," Ash says as Colin uses himself as a shield to cover his stepbrother's body. "Did you guys need something?" Ash pokes his head around Colin.

"Um…"

"Man, don't act like this is the first time you've caught us in the act."

Fair.

"Lance, get out of there," Marty calls from the hall. "What are you *doing*?"

"You just wanna stand there?" Colin asks. "Because if you leave, I can pull out and we can actually talk about whatever you wanted to tell Ash. Or, as you know, we're happy to keep going."

I laugh nervously. "Yes, yes of course." I open my mouth to say more but realize that less is definitely more in this case, and I head out, my cheeks still hot from catching them in the act.

And maybe because it was more than a little hot.

I join Marty in the hall as he rubs his eyes.

"Oh, the images!" he calls out dramatically. "Make them go away!"

"BUT YOU DON'T even like him," Marty says.

After Ash and Colin threw on some joggers, we settled in their room, me standing, Colin and Ash sitting on the bed, Marty on the love seat, and I told them my news about Ty.

"We were never enemies," I stress.

"Yeah, that's too bad," Ash says. "Because that would have been even hotter."

"Dirty boy," Colin tells him.

"You made me dirty."

"Lies."

They're kind of self-involved in the moment, as though Marty and I have disappeared.

"Excuse me," I say. "Big news here."

"Sorry, sorry," Colin says. "It's been a while since I've seen my guy, and obviously we were—"

"We all know what you were doing," Marty interjects.

"Really? Because I thought you of all people might have forgotten what it was like."

"Shut the fuck up. I get laid."

Ash, Colin, and I glance at each other, our skepticism written all over our faces. Even Frat Cat is giving Marty a look from the end of the bed.

"Feel like I remember the last time," I say. "Last fall."

"How could you know that?" he asks.

"You were chill for a good two weeks," Ash says. "We all knew."

Marty scoffs. "I'm sorry I'm not the horny frat fuck-magnet like you guys were before you coupled off. And as I recall, Lance was just like me...or at least I thought so until he shared that he's been fucking Ty Lancaster."

"I mean, we fucked," I say, "but technically, he fucked me."

I knew how Marty meant it, but it seemed like a good opportunity to bring up this part of the experience that really intrigued me.

"Oh!" Ash says. "Lance likes to bottom?"

"I did not ask for these details," Marty insists.

"Yeah, I really *really* like it," I admit. "Like..." I raise my hands to my face and simulate an explosion radiating from my head.

"That's not where you felt it most, though," Ash teases. "Because that might be a medical issue."

I laugh. "I'm almost mad at you for not telling me how good it feels."

"I love getting fucked by my guy too," Colin says.

"But I also can tell when he just needs it."

"Maybe I should leave you all to this," Marty says.

"Chill out," Colin says. "If we want, we can talk about your relationship with your hand once we catch up with Lance about how he's just been awakened to what it feels like to get dicked down."

Marty can't fight back his laugh before he says, "You fucking bag of dicks. All of you. But sorry, I'm being an asshole right now. Lance, you did just share something really personal, so…" He rises to his feet, approaches, and rests his hand on my shoulder. "I'm here for you. It makes no difference to me, though I'm rapidly becoming the minority in our friend group."

"In the group?" Colin asks. "Try the whole frat."

"Yeah, I didn't realize when I pledged Alpha Theta Mu that it would end with me becoming a raging bottom."

"Oh, do guys who like bottoming rage all of a sudden?" I joke.

"You tell me. You gonna start raging if you don't get Ty's cock for a while?"

"Yeah, probably." I say it as a joke, but…there's some truth to it.

"Ew, gross," Marty says. "I need this visual about as much as I need Ash's sex face and Colin's jiggling ass in my head."

"You could see my sex face?" Ash asks. "Was it hot?"

"You know it's hot," Colin says. "You get plenty of feedback about that face."

"Well, I do love a compliment."

"I'm not answering that," Marty says.

"Come on," I press. "Tell Ash if his sex face is hot."

"I'm not playing this game."

"Are you insulting my man?" Colin says, pulling an overdramatically serious face and clutching his fist.

"You guys are just trying to make me keep thinking of it, and it's not gonna work." Marty covers his ears. "La, la, la, la. I can't hear you."

"Hey, why you all having a party without me?" Payton walks in, in a beanie and tracksuit jacket, and plops down in the love seat next to Marty.

"Great timing," I say. "I was just telling the guys about how I'm messing around with Ty Lancaster."

"Why wasn't I invited to the coming-out party?"

"This is not my coming-out party."

"Yeah," Ash says. "His coming-out party will be epic. What kind of best friend do you think I am?"

"So, this is like the committee meeting where we organize it? Cool."

This is one of the reasons I love my guys. As I've shared this with the gang, there's no judgment. No hate. Even Marty, who's the most high-strung of the group, is still here for me, even if he's pretending to be weirded out by the details.

"But wait, why you fucking with Ty Lancaster?" Payton asks.

"Come on," I say. "We're rivals, and we get onto each other when we can, but you know we don't actually wish harm upon anyone at Sigma Alpha."

"Speak for yourself," Payton says.

"I get that," Marty adds. "But I just don't see you and Ty together. Like at all."

"Don't be homophobic," Payton insists.

"What? That is not what I meant."

And Payton's snickering, since we all know that's not what Marty meant.

"Man, you all are the worst," Marty says. "Really, the least surprising thing in Alpha Theta Mu seems to be someone getting together with another dude. At this point, it'll be more shocking if Payton and I can graduate without getting some man-on-man action."

"You never know," I assure them, which gets Payton laughing, though it seems to make Marty think for longer than I would think he'd need to about that.

Marty shakes his head. "Well, just know, if that guy hurts you, we're gonna come down hard and destroy him and his asshole buddies."

"Us and what army?" Payton asks. "You've seen Ryan and Keegan, right?"

"We've got Colin, and we can call in Troy."

Colin and Troy, our beefy jock alums, could definitely rival Ryan and Keegan in that department.

"Those guys can easily take them on," Marty says.

"We're really talking about summoning alumni to fight our battles for us?" I joke. "But there's not any issues. Ty's cool, and we're having fun, and that's all there is to it."

"It sounds hot," Ash says.

"Yeah, I can see it," Payton adds.

"What do you mean you can see it?" Marty asks.

"Oh, come on. We've seen them all sweaty and in Speedos. I can imagine their bodies rubbing up on each other, getting all steamy…one of them teasing the hell out of the other until they blow…" Payton has this far-off look in his eyes, like he's considering my sex life way too much. As he notices us looking at him, he shrugs. "Not like I'm the only one thinking it."

"It's probably very hot," Marty concedes. "But this doesn't mean we're suddenly cool with Sigma Alphas, right?"

"Fuck no," I reply. "Rivalry continues, from the prank we're gonna pull on their asses to make up for what they did to us at the start of this semester, and then we also have to kick their asses in the TaskFrat challenges."

"That's good," Ash says, "because we still have to get them back for that prank. And actually, that was something I was gonna talk to you about."

"What? Why?"

"Last night, Colin and I were brainstorming ideas, and we got a good one, but I'm not sure we can pull it off."

Funny, because as eager as I was to share what Ty and I were up to with the guys, I'm almost as eager to even the score with my rival.

"Give it to me," I say.

"Get a lot of practice saying that last night?" Colin teases.

I'm not gonna hear the end of this.

And rightfully so.

24

Ty

"F UCK, FUCK," L ANCE says as he works his controller.

"You gotta get over here, or I'm gonna die."

We lie in his bed, naked, enjoying some *Fortnite*, which has become one of our rituals since we started staying over at each other's places. Movies, TV shows, football games, video games—the kind of stuff we can enjoy between our fuck sessions, which are everything.

"You think I'm not trying to get over there?" Lance asks.

The past few weeks with him have been incredible. We're out, giving zero shits about what we're doing. Not just having to squeeze in fun in secret, but knowing when the party's over, that ass is mine.

He's mine.

The more we fuck around, the more confident he is about bottoming, which makes me an eager top. It's not just the sex, though. I like mornings like this, when we get to play around before classes.

After I die in the game—because yeah, no way he was getting to me in time—he says, "I'm gonna have to text Taylor to see how they got past this part."

Brenner and Taylor, both Peach State alums, are his buddies he hangs with for video games occasionally. I've hung out with them a few times, and they're cool guys, and also, apparently, part of the stepbrother-partner crew in Lance's circle.

I toss my controller aside and roll on top of Lance.

"What are you doing?"

"I think someone needs a morning BJ."

One of the many perks of our zero-shits-given approach.

"Mmm. Those are my favorite," he says. "I'm surprised you have all this energy after how late we stayed up, Mr. Going-Back-for-Thirds."

"You're the one who wanted to stay up to watch that weird horror series."

One of the things I've learned about Lance since we started hanging at each other's places is that he'll get into any one- or two-season show no one's ever heard of. It's so fucking adorable, I can hardly stand it.

"Would you have rather been watching the game, bruh? Like the two straight bros that we are?"

"Sound so straight when you say *bruh*."

"Yeah, bruh? You wanna fuck me, bruh?"

"Starting to sound a little less straight."

He grabs my cock, giving it a generous stroke. "Is this straighter, bruh?"

My cock pulses in his grip. "Much straighter, Stud," I say, peeking to see his thick hard-on.

As he releases my shaft, I rub it along his thigh. "Be right back," I whisper before kissing down his body, then taking his cock into my mouth to help him rub one out before he does the same for me.

Once we've had the light snack, we eat some breakfast, then get ready and head off to class. Our little routine has quickly become the only way I'm interested in spending my mornings.

When I finish my last class for the day, I meet Ryan and Keegan for a gym session. Jaxon's tagged along too—against his will, I've learned, since Keegan is trying to whip him into shape.

"So you must really like Lance," Ryan says as he spots me on the bench press.

I'm really feeling the burn today, alive with eagerness. I finish my set and rest the bar on the rack.

"You're real perceptive these days," I tease Ryan as I sit up.

"Shut the fuck up. I know you better than anyone, even that Alpha Theta Mu you're messing with, and if you've messed around with him more than a handful of times, you've done more with him than you've ever done with any girl."

"You must not know me very well, then, because I had girlfriends in high school."

"I'm not talking about back when handholding and making out were the big intrigues."

"You think any girl who saw me only wanted to hold my hand?"

"Now I feel like you're avoiding what I'm trying to say."

"Maybe you should just say it, then."

"You're into this guy. Beyond a regular hookup."

I shrug. "Obviously."

"You guys go on dates yet?"

"What?" I ask, wincing.

"Get back to pumping. You're taking too much time between sets. Come on. We gotta get those muscles to fail."

I lie back down and get back to my presses.

But Ryan's not done prodding. "You done more than hook up with this guy? Like take him out to eat? Watch a movie?"

We definitely don't go on dates. Occasionally we watch TV when he's over, sometimes between breaks before going again, but nothing like the kind of date Ryan means.

Although, now that everyone knows about us, we *could* go on a date.

And why does that sound so nice?

I finish my set, and as I set the bar on the rack, I take a breath. "No dates. But I could see taking him out."

Ryan's face lights up, and I grind my teeth.

"Okay, okay, I do like him. I'm not hiding that, Ry."

"Just funny seeing my boy getting all wide-eyed for some Alpha Theta Mu. But if this makes you go easy on him in the TaskFrat games…"

"Whoa. That's an accusation. We did fine."

There've been two challenges since we came out to our frats, neither of which Sigma Alpha or Alpha Theta Mu won, though it has evened our overall scores, meaning we're still vying for victory.

"No one's going easy on anyone," I insist. "Neither of us would want that."

"Then we're all good. So where you think you're gonna take him? You know the fall festival is going on. That's a fun, datey thing."

"I'll think of my own dates, thank you very much."

Not a bad idea, though. When our crew's gone the past few years, we've seen Lance and his frats at the festival, and he's always having a good time.

I bet he'd like that. And I've learned I have a thing for giving Lance what he wants.

No—what he *needs*.

After Ryan and I complete our workout, we wait with Jaxon for Keegan to wrap up on the treadmill before hitting the showers. I finish first, drying off, then head to my locker. I'm in a bit of a hurry because I want to see if Lance has texted me. Maybe now would be a good time to vibe out if he'd want to go on a date with me.

"Practically skipping to your locker," I hear Ryan say behind me before I feel his towel snap me in the ass.

"Fucking prick better be careful what you start," I say, spinning around and gripping the knot in my towel.

"You think you got it, bring it."

I whip it off, giving him a slap in the side, and soon we're going at each other's asses before Jaxon slips up behind and joins me in an attack against Ryan.

"Careful!" Ryan says. "You guys are gonna bruise the meat."

"You started it." I laugh, not just because of how ridiculous and fucking cliché it is for us to be fucking around like this, but also because it's fun as hell.

"That's what you get for dragging my ass out when I could have slept in," Jaxon says.

Ryan cups either cheek as we head to the lockers. "Whatever. Still got a nice pink mark on that tail," he says, indicating my ass. "Make sure to let Lance know who did it."

I chuckle as I spin the combination lock. Removing it, I open the locker door, when I notice my duffel is gone.

"The hell?" Ryan says from his locker, echoing my thought.

"Where's my shit?" Jaxon asks.

At the bottom of my locker, there's a brown package, and as I reach inside, my mind finally catches up with what's going on.

Those little pricks.

I open the packaging of the little gift, discovering inside a piece of men's lingerie—a lacy G-string.

I can't help but laugh, and is it weird that even though Lance got me good here, I kind of hope he picked this out especially for me?

"Dude," Ryan says, and I see him assessing his own pink, lacy garment—more like trunks.

"Did they get us all?" Keegan asks.

"How did they get *me*?" Jaxon asks. "I just decided to come here last minute. Knew it was a shit idea to hit the gym today. You can see my ass in these." He peeps through the holes in the back of his lingerie, which has us all laughing.

I check inside my package, discovering our student IDs and a note, similar to the one I left for Lance when we pranked the Alpha Theta Mus, then read it aloud:

"*Ty,*

Obviously, since you guys were showering, you left your car keys and phones in your bags, which you can find back at the Sigma Alpha house. Since it's

November and we're a generous frat, we waited for a slightly warmer front, so you'll only enjoy some hard nips and small dongs.

We've left your student IDs so you can take the shuttle back in your new, sexy outfits to greet all your fellow housemates, who'll be waiting to enjoy the show, along with some very eager members of the nearest frats and sororities.

Presented to you by:

Alpha Theta Mu

PS: Didn't think we'd get you back? ;)

I'm sure they crafted the message together, but that last bit must've been from Lance.

"Clever fuck," I mutter.

"Okay, I wasn't even supposed to be here," Jaxon says. "I should be exempt."

"Uh-uh. No one's exempt."

"You think we can get someone to give us a ride?" Ryan asks.

"If we go back to the frat, everyone will be waiting for us," Jaxon observes.

He's not wrong.

"I know that guy Crews out there," Keegan says. "Bet he can get us to the mall for some shirts."

"Hey, hey," I say. "You guys are trying to avoid the spirit of the prank. Alpha Theta Mu never backed down from their challenge, and it's sixty degrees out there, so it's not like anyone's gonna get hypothermia. We're not poor sports, and we're definitely not gonna let them think they intimidated us. We're gonna strut this just like Lance and his crew strutted their adorable little G-strings and crop tops. And we're gonna look sexy as hell doing it."

Jaxon sighs. "It's days like these that I think I should have just moved into the dorms."

We all share a laugh before we start slipping into our new gear, coming to terms with just how many people will see us like this, even before we get to the humiliating moment when the frats and sororities are waiting for us to show up in these things, doing some kind of sexy fashion show for them.

But I swallow my pride.

Once we're all suited up, Ryan says, "Honestly, not too bad since we got a good pump in today."

"Everyone's gonna post this online," Jaxon says. "We're gonna be the laughingstock of Peach State. This is why I don't ever do TaskFrat shit."

"Jax, come on," I say. "You'd be lucky if anyone gave that many shits about some dumb online video. Trust me, this'll be embarrassing for a day of your life."

He takes a breath. "Fine."

Ryan checks out Jax's ass. "Plus, I think someone gave you that for a reason. I never noticed you have such a nice ass."

"Really?" Jaxon asks, checking himself out in the mirror. "Ya think?"

I assess the definition before adding, "Yeah, that's a sexy bubble butt if I ever saw one."

He bunches his face up. "Maybe those squats are doing me some favors. Wait. You guys aren't just saying this to get me to be fine with looking like this all the way back to the house, are you?"

As soon as he says that, Keegan's eyes widen. "Oh. Yeah, that's a sexy booty."

"No, we're not just saying it, Jaxon," I tell him. "Come on. Let's get through this. The sooner we get back to the house and let everyone get their laughs and videos, the sooner it'll be over."

And I must admit, I'm kind of excited about strutting in front of Lance, showing him that I don't back down from a challenge any more than he does.

We take our IDs and head to the shuttle stop, huddling close since, even though it's not freezing, it's still chilly as hell. Fortunately, it doesn't take long for the shuttle to arrive, and I recognize the driver, who's never been friendlier. We hop on the packed vehicle, standing and holding on to the rails, everyone's attention on us.

Maybe to avoid the stares, we start a game of titty twisters, having to shield our chests from each other before I manage to shut it down.

Throughout the rest of the ride, Ryan's stealing glances at Jaxon's ass, and when he sees me noticing, mouths, *"Hot ass, right?"*

"Are you checking my butt out right now?" Jaxon asks.

"Uh…no," Ryan lies.

Jaxon's skeptical expression suggests he's not convinced.

"Is it just me, or does the shuttle always take this long?" Keegan asks, and I can definitely relate because it feels like we've been on this thing for thirty minutes, though I'm sure it's more like five.

As the driver is heading down fraternity row, I see the crowd gathered outside Sigma Alpha, lining the driveway, phones out. But there's only one guy I'm looking for.

"I guess this is where you guys are headed," the driver announces, stopping the bus.

When the door chimes open, Jaxon's already preemptively tucking his head close to his chest.

"Come on, guys," I say. "Tear it up."

I go first, like a noble leader, thanking the driver before stepping off and giving my post-workout chest and abs a good flex for the phones.

It's only then that I spot Lance and his Alpha Theta Mu crew, dressed in their Greek-letter hoodies. Lance stands on the roof, raising his arms and clapping his hands, surely to demonstrate how he just owned our house.

Everyone's going wild, hamming it up to make a big spectacle of the moment our rivals got their revenge.

The crowd's so packed in the drive that it takes me a minute to get to the front porch, where I stand and announce, "Guess everyone knows where the party is today!"

The crowd cheers with excitement, and the rest of the frat is already in party mode, meaning we gotta get out the liquor we have, send some guys to grab kegs, and set up the yard and house for a full-blown party because, hell, I need it after that prank.

"Ooh, they got Jaxon's ass…literally," one of the pledges says.

"That's not what *literally* means," I hear someone nearby mutter.

I turn to see a familiar face—Miles Tanner, the guy who vandalized Zeta Tau. He's near some of the guys from Omega Psi, but keeping his distance, arms folded, glancing around like he doesn't even want to be here. For a guy who joined a frat, he doesn't really seem to dig the vibe. More of a loner, even for an Omega Psi. What's his deal?

"Hey, Rocky," I hear, pulling my attention away from Miles. Lance heads through the crowd, glancing me over in my sexy lingerie, which I haven't bothered to cover up since we started getting things together for the party. "I can tell I picked out the right piece." His hands gravitate right to my body, sliding around my waist and grabbing my ass, earning a few glances. Given our popularity, I have no doubt word's already gotten around about us, but this is probably the first time some of our peers are seeing it for themselves.

I push up close to Lance, my abs against his hoodie, the zipper cool on my flesh. "Clever little fuck," I say. "I definitely underestimated you. Is this what all this has been about? You taking my cock so that you could pull one over on me?"

"I'll have you know I didn't even have to use that to make the prank happen. It was Ash's idea, and he's smart as hell. He's been watching TikTok videos to figure out how to crack the locks. Also, in case you missed it, Crews from Omega Psi works at the gym, so it wasn't difficult to sneak in the back."

"Then I'm guessing Keegan's idea to get Crews to help us wouldn't have worked."

"Damn right. Pissed?"

"Impressed."

"Not as impressed as I am with you in these," he says, gripping my ass again.

"Oh, you thinking you want a turn back there?"

His eyes narrow. "Nah. I'm discovering I'm a greedy bottom for that dick."

"That's awfully convenient since I'm pretty sure I'm a greedy top for that ass."

"Sounds like a good fit."

We share a kiss, and I draw him closer. "I want to sneak you up to my room and get you out of these clothes," I say, "show you how proud I am of that prank. But we do have to stay at the party for a little while, right?"

"Oh, fuck yeah. I want you and your guys strutting around in these for a few hours before I let you have at this ass."

I can't help smiling, and it's not just because I want to dick down Lance. It's that fun part of him that I enjoy even more than the sexy stuff. That part that Ryan's already picked up on.

"So…" I say, "there's something I wanted to talk to you about."

"Really?"

"Yeah, I was curious if you'd want to…I don't know, head to the fall festival with me one day. I know you like that, and it doesn't have to be a big deal, but I'm enjoying what we're doing, and you're obviously enjoying it too."

He laughs.

"What?" I ask.

"You tease me about one-word responses, and here you are with verbal diarrhea. I'm pretty sure you're asking me on a date."

My cheeks flush.

"And now you're blushing."

"Well, I'm wearing these sexy lacy briefs you picked out."

He eyes me skeptically. "Pretty sure it's because you're asking me out and it's making you all feely in a way Ty Lancaster isn't used to."

I shake it off. "I do want to take you on a date, Lance Fehn."

"This isn't just because you know I'm datey as fuck, is it?"

I consider my reply. "Maybe a tad."

His smile fades.

"No," I say. "I do want to do things you like, but it's not *only* because of that."

"You don't date, though, remember?"

"Yeah, and I didn't fuck dudes either, yet here we are."

He laughs. "Here we are."

We share another kiss, and as he pulls away, he says, "Fall festival could be fun…"

25

Lance

"You've barely touched your lunch," Mom says, which must be a surprise since I usually would have devoured all my chicken teriyaki and Thai popcorn chicken by now.

"And you keep checking your phone," Dad notes in a way that's more accusatory than observational.

"You've been doing stuff like this for the past few weeks every time you've come to visit."

Ty and I agreed to have our date this afternoon, which has me excited and nervous. I figured I could swing by for lunch with Mom and Dad, but now I'm realizing I'm too distracted for them not to notice. It doesn't help that they know me better than most people.

"Okay, okay," I say. "Maybe enough of the third degree."

"This is first degree, at most," Mom insists with a loving smile.

"Well, the last text I got was from Ash. He's staying

with his boyfriend for the weekend, and he thinks Frat Cat's been acting off, so he asked me to check on him when I get back. Happy?" At least it's the truth, even if I would have rather it'd been from Ty.

"I hope everything's okay with Frat Cat," Dad says. "But you can pretend all you want. We know how you get. I'm just gonna say it. You're crushing on a girl."

I chuckle nervously. "Well…not a girl, Dad, but nice try."

I'm surprised at how effortlessly that came out…*I* came out.

Mom's jaw drops, and Dad's mouth makes an O shape.

He takes a moment before he says, "There it is, I guess."

"When were you going to tell us?" Mom asks. "No, I'm sorry, that's not what I should have said. Scratch that. We love you. We care about you. Thank you for telling us. And when *in the world* were you gonna tell us?"

"Today…?"

I certainly didn't plan it, but I didn't have any intention of lying to them when they brought it up.

"It's been a couple of months of trying to figure things out with this guy, and he's really cool. We've been hanging out, but we just decided to go on a date today, and I'm nervous."

"You always get nervous before a date," Dad says. "I remember the first girl you went out with in eighth grade. You threw up three times, then started panicking about her wanting to kiss you."

I cringe. "Can we not go down memory lane?"

"It's nice seeing you like this again," Mom says. "You always seem so happy when you're hopeful about someone, and your father and I have been hoping she was really special."

"But now we're remembering what happens when one assumes," Dad adds.

So clearly I've been very bad at hiding my feelings for Ty from them, which doesn't surprise me. If anything, they've been great at masking being aware of it.

"I mean, you couldn't have known," I say.

Dad shifts his head either way. "I think if we'd been better parents and tapped your phone, we would've."

"We could have probably taken some days off to stalk you around campus to show we cared," Mom follows.

"You guys are weird."

"Aw, come here, my big man," Dad says. He and Mom push to their feet and swarm me for hugs.

This is one of the reasons it was so easy to tell them. One of the reasons they knew I was interested in someone even before I told them. We're just close like that. And it's nice being open with them about what's going on in my life.

Although, there's a sting too. Because there's one person missing, whom I can't share this incredible news with. Who would have been just as happy for me.

"You know Kacey would have been happy for you too," Mom whispers, intuiting where my mind had gone.

"I know," I say, fighting back tears.

As they pull away and return to their seats, Dad says, "So tell us about him. We want to know everything. Talk to us until your mom gets her phone out because she's bored."

"'Scuse you," she says, shooting him a look.

I decide I might as well tell them everything. "You know that Sigma Alpha frat president I sometimes mention?"

"Ty Lancaster?" Dad asks.

"Yes…"

"A Sigma Alpha?" Dad pushes to his feet and points toward the front hall. "Get out."

He does his best to keep a stoic expression, but he finally gives, and then we're all laughing.

I tell them a PG-version of how Ty and I got together, and then we move on to more mundane topics before finishing our meal. They wish me luck on my date, and after I return to Alpha Theta Mu, I shower and get ready.

As I get dressed, I keep thinking how nice it was sharing that with my parents. But mostly, I'm thinking: *Am I really about to go on a date with Ty? The player who could have any girl he wanted? The guy I had fun giving hell to for the past few years? The guy who pranked the hell out of me at the start of the year?*

I stand before my floor-length mirror, checking my hoodie sweater and jeans to make sure they fit well, show off everything they need to so he'll struggle to keep his hands off me.

For whatever reason, I can't shake the nerves in my belly, the sort I always get before a first date.

It shouldn't matter. Ty sees me all the time. The guy was up my ass last night, and he's definitely seen me at my worst when I first wake up in the morning, so there's nothing to be nervous about. But seems like knowing him better has made me even more anxious than I was back when I was dating girls.

I check the time on my phone, and it's only five minutes until we said we'd meet at his room, so I run my fingers through my hair a couple of times, messing it in the front to give it that I-couldn't-care-less look, which is amusing considering how much I care right now. I swing by Ash's room to check on Frat Cat, who's just sleeping. He seems fine, so I text Ash to let him know before leaving for Sigma Alpha.

Once there, I head to Ty's room, approach his door,

and knock. He opens it so fast, I would've thought he was waiting for me on the other side. And as soon as I see him in his cardigan and slacks, his hair done just right, I'm taken aback, reminded why this guy could easily get the attention of any girl he wanted. And also wondering why the hell he's doing anything with me. But when his lips curl into a smirk, I suddenly forget about all that.

He steps out of his room and closes the door behind him. "You look really nice," he says.

"You've seen me in all this."

"Shut your mouth and let me compliment you on our date."

Fuck, this is so silly.

But I'm eager to share my news. "I told my Mom and Dad I'm going on a date."

"With me?"

I nod. "Yup. Dad almost kicked me out of the house for dating a rival frat."

"I'm not just *a* rival frat," he says. "I'm *the* rival frat. But it sounds like they took the whole me-dicking-you-down thing well."

"Shut the hell up. You know I didn't mention that."

He beams. "I'm glad it went well, Lance." He hooks an arm around me and tugs me close, offering a firm kiss. When he pulls back, he says, "Reminds me that I need to tell my mom about this cool guy I'm going on a date with."

"Do I know him?"

"Maybe. You familiar with Alpha Theta Mu?"

"Isn't everyone?"

"You cocky little fuck. Have me hooked on you, and now you act like you run the world."

"I mean, I do have Ty Lancaster going on a date with me, so it's earned."

He squints. "Fair."

Despite the nerves, being able to play around with him like usual emphasizes what's important—it's just Ty. I don't need to stress or worry about impressing him. Evidently, he's already into me.

While Ty and I wait for an Uber to take us to the festival, I catch him up about some of the other stuff Mom and Dad talked about—work and their social lives—and when we arrive, we grab wristbands and head in.

As we enter the festival, I notice Ty keeping some distance between us, glancing around uneasily. I must admit, it's making me insecure. "You sure about this?"

"Huh?" he says, as if pulling himself out of a daze.

"You know, it's okay not to be a date-y guy."

"Sorry, I'm overthinking it. I really don't know what to do right now. And this is not me at all."

"Let's put on the training wheels. How about we hit some rides, and you can stand closer than a foot away from me, to start."

He snickers, though I can tell by his expression he's still uncomfortable. And I'd be lying if I didn't acknowledge I'm worried that maybe he's realizing this whole dating thing isn't for him. Maybe we should have stuck to fucking around.

But then he takes my hand, playing with it, interlocking our fingers, and I see him visibly relax.

"There," he says. "Feel better already."

There go my cheeks again.

We start through the festival, and I feel a jolt of pride in being the guy he's holding hands with. As much as I enjoy our nightly fun, it's nice being out with him in daylight, knowing that everyone's seeing my hot Ty holding my hand.

"Maybe we hit the bumper cars first," he says.

"How about we do that after the jumbotron?"

"The bumper cars are right there." He indicates the line with his free hand.

"Exactly. And the jumbotron is on the other side of the festival, so unless you wanted to get rid of my hand right away, maybe just trust me on this one. I know how to date."

"Yes, sir. You know I love it when you're bossy."

I take the lead, and we enjoy some rides before he says, "You wanna go ice-skating? They already got up the indoor rink for when it transitions to the winter festival."

Tension twists up in me, but when I see how excited

Ty is, I can't say no.

It should be a fun thing, but when I get to the rink and start putting on my skates, uneasiness rises within me. I try to push it aside. I want to enjoy my day with Ty, but when I look out at the rink, I could swear I see a familiar face among the others, and I search desperately, not because I think he's really out there, but because I just want to see that face again, even if it's an illusion.

"Lance? You good?"

I notice his skates are already laced up.

"Uh…yeah. Fine."

He glares at me.

"Just had a moment."

"About Kacey?"

I'm not surprised he could tell with just a look what I was thinking about. Not when he has something similar in his past.

"Yeah," I say, and he reaches out, resting his hand on top of mine. "We took ice-skating lessons together when we were kids."

"Oh my God," he says, pulling his hand away, and starts unlacing his skates.

I take his wrist. "No, no. Please. I didn't mean to mess this up."

He turns to me, his eyes wide. "You think you're messing this up by having an emotional reaction to something that meant a lot to you and your brother?

Nothing is worth putting you through that, Lance."

"But it's not just that. Earlier when I was telling Mom and Dad about you, I was thinking how much I wish I could have told him. It would have been nice to have him there today."

As his expression turns serious, I feel like I've ruined our date, but he says, "I know the feeling. Anytime anything good happens, I pull up my uncle's number. I want to call and tell him what's going on. I want to tell him about you, just like you want to tell Kacey about me."

I rest my hand on his thigh.

"It's hard for me," he says, "because I know he'd want me to be happy, but sometimes when I'm happiest, it's harder when I remember he's not here anymore."

His words cut to my core—the words of someone who really gets what I struggle with. I take his hand and roll it on my thigh, running my thumb over his palm.

"I think one of the reasons I avoid certain things Kacey and I enjoyed together is that I feel guilty enjoying them without him. But I also know that he, more than anyone else in the world, would want me to be happy. That day when you pranked us, I was thinking of something he once told me. It's what convinced me to get out of the car in that ridiculous outfit.

"When I was in second grade, I lost some of my front teeth, and kids used to make fun of me because of it. I was so embarrassed, I didn't tell anyone, but he noticed I wasn't smiling as much. He knew something was wrong, and when I confessed, he told me he got bullied when he was my age because he had braces. I couldn't imagine anyone making fun of him, so I asked him what he did, and he said, *'Embarrassing stuff happens, and sometimes, you just gotta own it. Don't let anything keep you from being happy.'* It makes me tear up just thinking about it. "He was only in middle school, but even now, it sounds wise, profound. And I did what he said. I started smiling more, not caring if anyone saw my teeth. And I made more friends, ones who didn't mention anything about the gap. I learned he was right, and it's something I've reminded myself of anytime I get shy or insecure or worried."

Ty's quiet for a moment. "He sounds like a really great brother."

"He was," I say quietly, my voice cracking slightly.

"Grant had little bits of wisdom he passed on to me too," Ty says. "Always encouraging me whenever I was down. Always there for me. What Dad did, leaving Mom and me, was stuck in my head for a long time. I just couldn't get how he could have fathered a kid and didn't want anything to do with him. Something I thought about every Father's Day, or when I'd see other kids with their dads at school events." He's got this far-off look in his eyes, as though he's been transported into a memory, and I'm hoping I haven't brought up something horrible for him. "One day, after a soccer event, my friend was being congratulated by his dad, and Grant and Mom were doing the same for me, but it just hit me hard, and he told me, *I get why you're hurting, but don't get so hung up on the things that go wrong that you miss out on the things going right.'* Not always easy to remember, but it really reminds me to look at all the wonderful things I have in my life, even when things aren't going great."

I grip his hand tighter. "They really just wanted us to be happy. And I know they're right, and sometimes it feels like I'm betraying Kacey's memory by refusing to have any fun like this. It's just hard."

Ty moves closer, putting his arm around me, and I bury my face in his chest. I've had plenty of times where I've buried my face in a pillow, trying to stifle my scream to keep Mom or Dad from hearing my pain, but it's nice being able to hold him, someone who gets it, someone I don't fear I'll trigger by feeling this pain.

And it's easy to forget where we even are as I hold him close, taking deep breaths until I feel I can manage my emotions again.

As I pull away, he looks me in the eyes. "Do you think you're up for it? Own feeling like shit and go for it?"

I muster a smirk, appreciating how he's referencing Kacey's words of wisdom.

"Let's try." I push to my feet, collecting myself as I scan the skating rink once again for that image.

Ty and I walk up to the entrance, and I inspect the ice, taking a moment before getting on the other side and joining with the others already moving in clockwise motion around the rink. I'm a little unsteady, like I was when Kacey and I were first learning together. When I stumble, Ty grabs hold of me, keeping me on my feet.

"Whoa," I say, laughing.

"Gonna have to keep an eye on you, aren't I?"

"Maybe. It's obviously been a minute."

"You know damn well I can take it slow to begin with."

I sneak a look at him, his smirk assuring me the play on words was intentional.

We skate around the rink a few times, and I get the hang of it again. Even though memories with Kacey are coming back to me, there's something nice about being here with Ty, creating new memories.

At one point, Ty spins around and says, "Here. I wanna try to go backward." He gives it a try but doesn't really go anywhere. "What's the trick?" he asks, assessing his feet.

"They have to actually move."

"Very funny." He gives it another go, moving slowly but managing it. "Hey, come on. That's not so bad." Admittedly, it's not. And as he gets the hang of it, he stands a little taller, clearly proud of himself for his little stunt. "Fast learner, apparently."

"I could have told you that," I tease, and there's a playfulness in his expression. I'm sure he's thinking about the stuff we started messing around with a couple of months ago.

"We need to get out of everyone's way," he says, and when I make a face, he grabs my hand and guides me toward the middle of the rink, turning to me.

"If you think I'm skating backward after just remembering how to skate forward, you're out of your mind."

"Naw. It's just been too long since I kissed that sexy mouth."

"You wanna kiss me here."

"I want to kiss you everywhere." The way he says it, I can hear the desire in his tone, just how much he means it, and he moves quickly, taking my lips.

For having enjoyed our secret relationship for so long, I find that I enjoy being public like this even more.

No more need to keep our hands to ourselves.

No need for me to pretend I'm not totally into Ty.

I'm loving the way his lips and face are warming me up again. I embrace the joy I feared before we stepped out here. Don't want it to end, and he doesn't seem to either by the way he keeps nibbling at my lip before finally pulling away.

"Speaking of me not being able to keep my mouth

off you, after we catch a few more rides, whose place we wanna head back to?"

"We've gone to your place a few times, so mine?"

He winces. "Wrong answer."

"What? Why do you want to go back to your place?"

He glances around before leaning close and whispering, "Because I like fucking you in my bed."

A rush of excitement moves through me. "That's naughty, Rocky."

"Whatever. You like getting this rock there too. So you can choose the easy way or the hard way."

"What happens if I choose the hard way?"

"I haven't really thought it out, since I know you'll take the easy way."

I laugh. "Oh, so you're the bossy one today?"

"Yes, I am."

He moves close and does a little spin, making it look effortless before he grabs my hand, undermining the move when he says, "That was pretty hot, right?"

Which has me laughing.

As fun as this is, though, I'm eager to get back to his place so he can fuck me in his bed.

26

Ty

I'M GLAD LANCE opened up about Kacey. I know all too well what he was talking about, from my experience with Grant. And really, it was nice to share about these men who were so important in our lives.

Just as much, I'm proud of him for pushing through and managing to have a great time.

After skating, we enjoy a few more rides before heading back to Sigma Alpha. I'm holding his hand all the way up to my room, loving that it's not like when we did things in secret, that now I don't give a flying fuck who sees us. In fact, I want all my bros to know he's with me and that's just the way things are.

When we reach my bedroom, Lance says, "Why do I have a feeling you're gonna open the door and have some prank waiting for me?"

It's nice to see that playful, suspicious expression again, not bogged down by our heavy discussion earlier.

"A vengeance prank? Nah. You got us back fair and

square. I wouldn't do you like that. Not when there are so many other things I'd rather do to you."

I find my key card and swipe it before opening my door and leading him inside. I've barely closed the door when I shove him back against the wall and take another kiss. I unfasten his fly, opening it to loosen the waist of his jeans, sliding my hands underneath his underwear so I can grab that tight ass.

"Mmm," I say. "That's where I want to be. Claiming your ass for the thirty-second time."

"Have you been counting?"

"Hey, it's all a first for me, so it's pretty noteworthy. Why? You think that's weird?"

"Oh, it's definitely weird, but I like it."

"Of course you do. You like having this dick in your ass as much as I like having my dick there, you dirty fuck."

He doesn't deny it, just licks up my lips before pulling me closer so that my weight's against him.

We kiss and nip at each other as I lead him to the bed. We strip each other down, struggling between removing clothes and trying to keep our hands all over each other. When we wind up in bed, Lance on top of me, he reaches over, fishing through my nightstand for the lube.

I wait for him to grab a condom, but instead he says, "Um…this might be strange to bring up, but would you be interested—"

"In coming inside you?" I couldn't wait for him to finish, not when he was basically speaking my wish.

"Whoa, Rocky," he says, glancing at my cock, noticing that made me hard as stone. "We've been doing this a while, and I've been tested, obviously."

"Me too."

"If you don't want to…"

He must be able to tell the answer to that by my expression because his lips perk up.

"You know I want to fuck you raw, bro."

"Okay, *dude*."

We chuckle before he pumps some lube, massaging some across my shaft before giving his hole some. Then he lines himself up, sliding down onto my cock.

"Fuck, I love the way you make yourself comfortable in my room and on my cock," I tell him as he welcomes more of me inside him.

"I love the way it feels when you open me up like this," he confesses, taking me faster than usual, rocking up and down. He takes deep breaths, and I feel myself steadily reaching deeper and deeper.

Once he's worked into a pace, he gazes down at me with those gorgeous eyes I can never get enough of. The Alpha Theta Mu prez has become my obsession.

We get lost in our usual frenzy, swapping positions, trying out his favorites, still learning and discovering each other's bodies. While I'm giving it to him from behind, his hand on the headboard, I'm lost in the rhythm, my cock just here to serve his needs.

"How is that?" I ask, and he turns to me.

His body trembles as he replies, "That feels amazing, Ty. Just like that."

He reaches back and rests his hand on my cheek, and I move close to kiss him.

Despite our quick movements, there's something more intimate about our kiss than usual. A deep connection I feel for him in this moment. I've never felt anything like this before. It's beyond electric, an intensity I can't even describe, scary and overwhelming, yet I refuse to back down. Just kiss him more.

"You really are mine," I tell him.

"Yes, I am."

"And I'm yours."

"Yes."

"I'm greedy for you, Lance. I want to see your face and your cock when you come."

We reposition so I'm on my back, with him riding me again. I hook my arms under his legs, holding them as I drive up into him, watching his cock bob up and down, occasionally slapping me in the abs before some precum spills onto me.

"Fuck yeah," I mutter. "That's so fucking beautiful."

I stare at his cock as he leaks for me more. Then I

grip it, helping pull even more out while fucking him. His eyes roll back in that way they do when I'm jamming right up against his prostate, giving him what he needs.

"I'm just here for your pleasure, Lance. Because that's my pleasure too."

As he keeps taking me, he leans forward and rests his hand against the headboard, calling out, "Harder, Ty. Harder."

As I bend to his request, watching him writhe in pleasure becomes so overwhelming, I feel myself climbing so damn fast, maybe too fast.

"You have to slow down, or I'm not gonna last much longer," I warn him.

"Then we'll just go for round two. Don't stop. I need it."

I can't deny him. I just keep fucking away.

"Lance, I'm so close."

I feel him precome onto my belly even more. "Me too. Shoot up into me, Ty. I want all of you. Every drop."

His words pull it right from me, and as I feel my release, I call out, thrusting like I'm on a mission, loving how I'm filling Lance up.

I get another surprise as a warm rush washes over my abs.

"Fuck, that's a lot of cum," I say as Lance calls out, clearly unable to disguise his pleasure as he keeps releasing onto me in warm spurts.

I watch in awe as he finishes, a final drop marking the end.

As he catches his breath, he settles, that ass resting on my pelvis, engulfing my cock once again. His body twitches a little more, his nerves still recovering from the sensations I worked up in him.

"Jesus fucking Christ," he mutters, releasing his cock and leaning forward for another kiss.

As we continue kissing, he subtly rocks his hips. "You like that?" he whispers into my mouth. "Knowing you're shoving in me deep?"

"Yes," I confess.

"Come on. Get it up in there," he urges as he takes me to the hilt, clenching his cheeks.

Fuck, he's so greedy for me.

"Trust me, if I could get it any deeper, I would."

He smiles. "Just making sure. I like being filled up with my…"

He stops himself, his expression twisting up uncomfortably.

Even though he didn't finish his sentence, I sense I know what he was about to say, and I hate that he stopped himself.

An eagerness builds up in me again…

Feels like hope.

"Your what?" I press. "Come on. Tell me what you

were about to say."

"It's more of a conversation we should have than something I should just blurt out."

His words assure me I was right in my assumption about where this is heading. And if I'm wrong, I'll be disappointed.

No, it'll be so much worse than that.

So much so that I don't allow myself to consider it too long.

"Blurt it out anyway, and I'll let you know if I agree," I say, not breaking eye contact.

"Being filled up by my boyfriend," Lance whispers, like a part of him is worried I might laugh or tell him we're definitely not that.

I'm quiet, thinking carefully about how to respond since I don't want to fuck this up. But when I notice the flash of panic in his expression, I quickly say, "Your boyfriend, huh?" and watch his cheeks turn pink. I take his ass cheeks in either hand, giving a good squeeze. "So that means this ass would be totally mine, right?"

Lance chuckles. I can tell he's feeling vulnerable after what he just shared, but that's part of what makes it so fucking hot.

"Yeah, that means my ass would be all yours. Is that what you want?"

"Your ass?"

"To be boyfriends."

I wince. "Are you fucking kidding me right now? I took you on a date. If you think I don't want to be your boyfriend at this point, you are out of your goddamn mind."

A smile tugs at his lips, and it's too irresistible not to give him another kiss.

"Before I agree to anything, though, you might have to get me up to speed about what that involves. I haven't been in a relationship since sophomore year of high school."

His gaze narrows as he studies my face, like he's surprised this is the direction the conversation went. "Well, it definitely means more fucking."

"Ooh, I like the sound of that."

"And we'd have to go on more dates like today. You know, to get to know each other better."

"I guess I like you enough to get to know you," I tease, earning a glare. "So…movies, dinners at restaurants, clawing at each other around friends… Is that what you're hoping for?"

Please say yes.

He grins. "Pretty much."

"And then that means when we're out, I'll get to hear you say, *Oh, my boyfriend is over there. This is my hot boyfriend. This is my top boyfriend who fucks the hell out of me until I shoot all over.*"

"That's not really the kind of thing I'd have a reason to say."

"Really? You don't want to hear me say, *This is my bottom boyfriend who just needs to be stuffed with my cock and cum?*"

"Eh, talk is cheap."

"But still hot, don't lie."

He moves closer, rubs his nose against mine. "So we're doing this? Boyfriends?"

I see the eagerness in his expression, and my chest comes alive with sensation.

"I never thought I'd ever be interested in any of this," I admit. "Just never saw the point of being with one person."

"Yeah, I remember our conversation." His gaze falls, as though he's thinking this could be leading anywhere other than me being all his.

So I get to my point. "But that was before I got to know you. I used to just see sex on legs whenever someone walked by, but since messing with you, you're the only one I'm thinking about, the only one I'm interested in meeting up with. So yeah, I want to be your boyfriend, Lance. And I want you to show me all these cheesy-ass things I've been missing out on."

"It doesn't have to be cringe."

"Really? Because I don't mind being cringe with you."

I can tell he's fighting a smile.

"I want to tell my mom, but I want to do it in person, over Thanksgiving break the week after next."

"You want to tell her about me?"

"I want to call her up and shout it at the top of my lungs, but I think it'll mean more to her to see the look in my eyes when I tell her about you."

His gaze locks with mine. And I can only imagine if I look half as enamored as he looks with me right now, she'll know how happy he makes me.

"Get down here and kiss your boyfriend," I demand.

"You know you're still in me, right?" He rocks his hips again so I can feel his slick flesh sliding up and down my shaft.

"Damn right I'm still in you. And if you work me up again, we'll see if we can get you to shoot all over me like that one more time."

I pull him down, sealing our lips for another kiss—one that's more satisfying than any of the other kisses we shared today because this time, I'm not just some guy Lance is fucking.

I'm his boyfriend.

27

Lance

As I slip into the loincloth Zeta Tau sent over for tonight's TaskFrat Challenge, all I can think is how fucked up it'd be if this was another ruse. Fortunately, it's too cold to head out in just these, so I throw on my regular clothes, psyching myself up for the night, when there's a knock at my door. As soon as I open it, Ty rushes in and takes my mouth, pushing me back against my desk.

"Mmmm…you taste like mint," he says as he pulls away. "Must've gotten all brushed up because you expected to mess around a little before we leave."

"Definitely wanted to mess around, but you're not getting the main event until after."

"Want me to claim victory at the challenge before claiming that hole again?"

"So cocky. You're not claiming victory tonight, and this hole has been thoroughly claimed already."

We share another kiss before he says, "Well, now we

have your team without one of your star players, so we have the advantage."

Fall break is next week, and Ash managed to get the okay to miss classes so he and Colin could head to Maui with their family.

But the show must go on.

"Speaking of Ash being gone," I say, "how's Frat Cat doing over at Sigma Alpha?"

This past week, Frat Cat came down with something, so he needs medicine every night. Marty's already agreed to watch him while Ash is on vacation, but Ash said Frat Cat's been getting more annoyed with us making too much noise around his room, and since we're hosting the afters later, Dax agreed to watch him tonight.

"He's been loving it," Ty says. "He'll probably want to pledge Sigma Alpha next year."

"Liar. Frat Cat would never do us dirty like that."

"If I'd been smart, I would've gotten one of our pledges to knit him a little Sigma Alpha sweater."

"I wish you had. Frat Cat hates clothes. Probably would have scratched the hell out of whoever tried to force that on him."

"Well, he's very happy right now. And he's not the only Alpha Theta Mu who's happier at Sigma Alpha."

"Don't start spreading lies. You're just as happy over at Alpha Theta Mu."

"But I love dicking you down in *my* bed."

I can't lie, I love it too.

"Stop being a tool and kiss me until I can't feel my lips anymore," I insist.

"With pleasure." He leans close, and I feel his breath against my lips. He's about to attack my mouth again, when there's a knock at my door.

"The hell?" I ask.

"Is that how you greet your second favorite person in the frat?" Marty asks from the other side.

Ty grins before offering a lick up my lips and whispering, "We have unfinished business, mister." He opens the door to let Marty in.

"Nice to walk in here without seeing you two all over each other."

"Nice for whom?" I can't disguise my frustration, but the interruption is probably for the best since we don't have much time before we must get out of here. "And as far as being my second favorite in the frat, you keep me from getting dick, and you're quickly gonna fall down that scale."

For a guy who'd never had any before Ty, I'm greedy for it now. And Ty definitely doesn't mind how hungry this hole is for him.

"Besides," Payton says, coming in too, "we all know *I'm* Lance's second favorite."

"That's true."

"What?" Marty asks. "Stop being mean."

"We're already falling down the ranks here," Payton says, settling on the bed beside Marty. "First we can't compete with Ash. Then Lance starts hooking up with this guy."

Marty's jaw tenses.

"Relax," I say. "You guys are still my best buds. Nothing we do is gonna change that."

"Yeah, but you'll still always place second to a Sigma Alpha," Ty reminds them.

"Uh-uh," I protest. "You don't talk like this over here."

Ty's all smiles, raising his hands in surrender. "I can't risk being cut off, so I'll be nice."

"This is gonna be like Ash and Colin 2.0." Marty groans. "Just hearing about your sex lives all the time."

"Last I heard, you did more than hear it recently," Payton adds.

"Whoa. Lance led me into that!"

"Please, that's the most action you've had in a long time."

"I didn't say it wasn't, but I just want to be clear, when I'm with a girl, I'm gonna flaunt it around like this as much as the rest of you."

"In this house, I wouldn't assume it's gonna be a girl," Payton jokes.

"I know, right? Just waiting for my turn to tumble out of the closet. Gonna happen any day now. At this point, the idea of anyone showing me attention is better than nothing."

Payton scoots away from Marty.

"Shut the hell up!" Marty grabs one of my pillows and swats at our friend.

"Okay, okay, guys," Ty says. "We should go now. Whether you like it or not, you must let your fate play out—having your asses handed to you by Sigma Alpha, placing us in the lead for the school year."

"We would have to place third tonight for that to happen," I remind him.

"I'm counting on you being distracted by me."

We greet the other TaskFrat Alpha Theta Mus downstairs before heading over to the rec center with Ty. Since it's too cold to have the challenge outside, I lobbied for us to hold it at Peach State's basketball court.

Tonight's challenge, designed by Zeta Tau, is revealed to be a cross between strip poker and basketball, but instead of using balls, we have balloons, which is a challenge to get into the net. Eventually, all my guys are down to the loincloths, except for Payton, who still has on his shirt and athletic shorts, so we're counting on him as we help get the balloon to our goal, our teammates hollering from the sidelines.

While Ryan's chasing Payton to the net, Ryan's cloth slips down, revealing how fortunate we all already know he is, and he keeps going until the cloth slips even farther down, preventing him from moving easily, and the moment gives Payton the advantage, allowing him just enough time to sink the balloon in. The TaskFrat ref blows the whistle, signaling the end of the game and Alpha Theta Mu's victory. This puts us two points ahead of Sigma Alpha for the year, which will be a great lead to start the spring with.

I crowd around with my guys to celebrate our victory. Ryan swoops in and starts pulling down our loincloths, and Marty and Payton wind up ganging up on him and chasing him into the men's locker room while the rest of us recover. Then I catch up with Angie some before Ty finally gets away from his crew and comes over.

"Hey there," she greets Ty. "Making sure I don't try to seduce your guy?"

Even hearing her call me his guy feels incredible.

"I've done a good job marking my territory," he says, hooking his arm around me and planting a kiss on my cheek. Even though he's slightly joking, I can't help feeling there's still some part of him that feels the need to make it clear I'm his because of the time he believed I hooked up with Angie.

And I kind of love that.

She gets pulled away by one of her friends, and just as I'm about to flaunt my victory, Ty says, "Don't even—"

"What? Remind you that Alpha Theta Mu kicked your ass?"

He grinds his teeth, which sends a rush of excitement pulsing through me.

"The happier you are, Lance, the gentler I'm gonna fuck you because I know you'll hate that."

"You couldn't even if you tried," I say.

"Maybe so. We'll see."

"Hey, guys," Dax says, approaching. "I'm supposed to get back to Sigma Alpha to give Frat Cat his medicine before afters, but I've been talking to this guy, and he seems kind of curious."

"No further explanation needed," Ty says. "We can take care of Frat Cat for you. I wanted to get changed anyway before the party."

"Don't leave the loincloth behind."

"We're gonna need to put our jackets on to get home," Ty says.

"But after you have some fun, right?" Dax teases. "Get back to Frat Cat, and we'll see you at the afterparty. But don't wait for me. I plan on having a good time." He gives that signature Dax wink before slipping back into the crowd.

Ty and I say our goodbyes to the guys, then hop in the car, and I drive us back to his frat. As I pull up to fraternity row, I notice bright blue lights flashing from inside Sigma Alpha. Tension rises in me as we get closer and hear the alarm blaring inside.

"What the hell is this?" I ask.

"The fire alarm. Jaxon stayed in to study." I can hear the worry in Ty's voice. "But he's not out here."

"You think someone from one of the other frats might've pulled it?"

"Kind of a dumb prank if no one's around to suffer."

Good point.

He pulls out his phone and calls Jaxon, but it goes to voice mail. He grunts. "Fuck."

"Okay. We should grab Frat Cat and his meds and check on Jaxon." Ty nods, but I can read the concern all over his face, so I rest my hand on his thigh. "Hey, we got this. Everything will be okay."

"Yeah, you're right."

We get out of the car and jog to the house.

"Maybe we shouldn't split up," he says.

"We need to check for Jaxon, get Frat Cat, and get the fuck out of here as fast as we can."

"Just be quick, and don't be a hero," Ty says, taking a kiss before we start up the stairs.

Dax's room is one floor above Jaxon's, so I head up, noticing a funny smell—chemical almost, and maybe a bit like rubber. The hairs on the back of my neck stand on end, and when I reach the top of the stairs, I see gray smoke at the end of the hall, creeping toward Dax's room.

Holy fuck.

There's a voice in my head telling me to get the fuck out of here, followed by Ty's, *"Don't be a hero."* But I imagine Frat Cat in Dax's room, frightened as the smoke creeps around him. If we leave, the fire department won't be able to get to him in time. If there's something I can do, I need to do it.

"Ty! Ty!" I call out as I dash for the room, scanning Dax's key card. I doubt Ty heard me, though, and besides, he needs to get Jaxon the hell out of here.

As soon as I open the door, I see smoke everywhere. Must've seeped in through a vent. I fear I might already be too late as I hurry in, barely thinking straight, just in a panic, searching for our sick cat.

"Frat Cat," I call. "Come on. Uncle Lance is here."

There's not as much smoke in the room as in the hall, but it's enough to make me cough as I search around frantically, squatting down and searching under the bed before discovering him tucked in the corner. Poor guy.

"Come on. I got you, little fella." My coughing intensifies. "We gotta get out of here. I'm sorry, but I've got to do this." He doesn't budge, so I crawl under and pull him to me.

As soon as I'm out from under the bed, I notice the room's now filled with smoke, stinging my eyes. I blink, intending to open them again, but my eyes are too irritated. Fuck. This was a really shitty idea, but I can't regret coming in to save Frat Cat.

"Holy shit!" I hear Ty say in the hallway as I tuck Frat Cat under my shirt, hoping it'll provide a barrier between him and the smoke.

I hear a cough, and then Ty's, "Lance? Lance!"

"I'm here!" I call back. "I can't see."

It's not long before we're both coughing, and I push to my feet, moving toward where I think the door is, trying to keep my shirt over my nose so I won't breathe in too much of the smoke. But I can tell there's still plenty getting in.

"I've got you! I've got you, Lance. Follow my voice."

It's hard to tell where his voice is coming from, though, even as he keeps calling my name. And as the smoke gets thicker, fear grips me.

What if I led us both into danger?

What if something terrible happens?

What if I never get to tell him how amazing the past few months with him have been?

That it's all been so much more than fucking around and hanging.

It feels like a lesson I already learned with Kacey, and I should have said something sooner, told him how I really felt.

These thoughts flash by as I hear Ty beckoning me. "My voice…just follow my voice…"

I listen carefully, navigating until I hear it growing closer, and then I feel a hand, and Ty pulls me into what I assume must be the hall. Not sure, since I still can't open my eyes.

I hold his hand as he escorts me through the house, and despite being aware that there isn't as much smoke around, it's still too much. My lungs feel overwhelmed, my body trembling.

"I still can't see," I warn him.

"We're getting close to the stairs. I'm gonna pick you up. Just be ready."

I halt in place, and he practically scoops me right off the floor. I feel the jerkiness as he takes me down the stairs, still trying in vain to get the smoke to clear out of my lungs as I endure a fit that reminds me of the first time I had COVID. I can't get a breath in…starting to feel lightheaded…and then everything goes black.

28

Ty

I PACE THE ER exam room, my nerves wrecked from everything that's happened.

When I went to find Jaxon, I discovered him in his room with his earphones on, oblivious to the blaring alarm. After telling him to head out to the yard, I thought I heard Lance shouting from upstairs, so I went up, where I discovered it was all filled with smoke. When I reached Dax's room, it was so clouded, I couldn't even see Lance.

Everything else happened so fast, panic setting in as I scrambled to find my boyfriend.

I was relieved when I finally felt his hand, but he was coughing so much, and before I knew it, I was carrying him out of Sigma Alpha. After we reached safety, my relief shifted back to panic as I discovered Lance unconscious in my arms. Jaxon grabbed Frat Cat, and I called emergency services, watching as smoke billowed from the back of our house. Under normal circumstances, it would have been hard enough seeing our place being ravaged by fire, but my only concern was for my boyfriend. Making sure he was still breathing. Getting help to him as soon as possible.

The EMTs arrived on the scene before the fire trucks.

"How are you feeling?"

"Relax as much as you can. You're doing great."

The ride in the ambulance was chaotic as an EMT asked me questions while another worked with Lance, who was coming to but couldn't respond easily. "We're going to intubate you," the EMT said. "This is fairly routine for smoke inhalation injuries. Just a precautionary measure to keep your airway open." It was a struggle to watch them put that tube down his throat, but I didn't give a fuck what they had to do as long as he was okay.

When we arrived at the ER, I answered another series of questions while hospital personnel took Lance off for treatment and testing, leaving me on my own in an exam room, and so overwhelmed, I struggled to work out what to do next.

I should check in with Jaxon, who'd texted to let me know he was taking Frat Cat to the vet.

But first, I needed to call Lance's parents. An EMT had given me Lance's phone to get ahold of them, and I talked to his dad briefly to let them know what was going on. They were on the road to visit family, a few hours out already, so it would take them a while to get back here.

As I'm about to pull out my phone, I hear a familiar voice from the hall. "Which room did they say?"

The hell?

I hurry out the door, spotting Ryan and Marty heading toward me in jackets and loincloths, earning looks from the personnel and patients in the hallway. I want to call out to them, but it's a strain to get words out right now, so I flag them down, and Ryan kicks up his pace, jogging over, Marty following.

"How is he?" Marty asks, still a few yards away.

"They said everything would be fine, but I figure they tell everyone that. And he was unconscious for a minute, and they intubated him to make sure he was getting oxygen. I think he might've passed out again…or they gave him a sedative. I can't remember. Then they came and put me here. And…"

"Hey, hey, you're good." Marty steps to my side, resting his hand on my shoulder. "You don't have to explain everything at once. We're here to help and make this easier for you."

"Easier? Nothing is gonna be easier right now." I hate that I just barked out my frustration at a guy who's only trying to be helpful, especially since I wasn't expecting Marty, of all people, to be the one trying to soothe my anxiety.

"That's fine," he says. "Bad wording on my part. Let's all take some breaths together."

As he guides us back into the exam room, I mutter, "Take some breaths? That's not what I need right now. I need Lance to be okay." When the door closes behind us, I spin toward them, my gaze drifting to their loincloths. Ryan's jacket isn't even closed, and I can only imagine what the others waiting in the ER thought when they saw him in this state. "What are you two still doing in those? You look like you just got back from a Tarzan convention."

Ryan glances himself over as if unsure what I'm referring to, as Marty says, "We came right from the party. Given your text, pants weren't exactly a priority."

"How did you even get back here? Don't they have security?"

"I told them we were brothers," Ryan says. "Then this clown started rambling, trying to explain why we looked so different."

"It sounded *ridiculous*," Marty snaps, sounding more like his usual dickhead, pain-in-the-ass self.

"Ash and Colin are stepbrothers," Ryan says, "but they don't go around qualifying it. Plus, it's none of their business. They don't know us."

Marty shakes his head. "This is not important right now."

Weirdly, their spat has helped me relax—at least as much as I can under the circumstances.

"I told them we were brothers too," I admit. "Seems to work in movies. They took Lance back for tests to assess his injuries."

"And you're okay?" Ryan asks.

"Other than freaking out about him, yeah. Brianne said they might want to do some tests for me as well, but the nurse who checked me out didn't seem too concerned."

"Who the hell is Brianne?" Ryan asks.

"One of the EMTs." No idea how the hell her name suddenly came to me like that, but I'm barely thinking straight.

"Well, you still got some black and gray smudges on you."

Brianne had given me some wipes and helped me with some of it, but I've clearly missed some spots.

"Not my biggest concern," I tell Ryan. "And I need to call his parents again. I told them I would once we got situated here."

"Marty was right, though. Maybe take a few breaths first."

I'm as annoyed as when Marty suggested it. "Their son's in the hospital, and they're probably freaking out because—" I bite my tongue. I can't betray Lance's confidence and reveal what I know about his brother.

Yeah, his parents would be a mess even if Lance was their only child, but given their history with Kacey, I can only imagine how painful it must be knowing he's injured and that it'll take them a while to get to him.

"I can do it," Marty offers.

"No, it should be me," I insist. "I was there. They deserve more than a quick, panicky chat from me. Wish we'd gotten to meet under better circumstances, but here we are."

I force myself to focus, get some good breaths in, and though it's not helping much, it's better than nothing. Then Ryan and Marty leave me, saying they'll be in the waiting area.

I remind myself what Marty said, that I need to be cool when I talk to them. Not get them even more concerned than they already are. When I FaceTime them, his dad answers. They're still on the road, his mom driving. While she veers over to the side of the road, I catch them up about everything that's happened since our last conversation. I tell them the facts, but I don't mention how difficult it was seeing him pass out and then straining to talk to the EMTs, how hard he was struggling with breathing before they intubated him.

But even trying to keep my cool and get through the events that transpired after we got out of Sigma Alpha, I choke up a few times. And I see the worry written all over their faces, poking at a fear that lingers in me too.

That somehow something will happen, this will all head south fast, and Lance won't be okay.

By the time I've finished, his mom has parked, and they're both on the screen.

"We appreciate the call," she says. "We don't want to stay on much longer because we're still about three hours out, but we'll let you know when we're close."

"Okay."

"It's nice meeting you," his dad says. "Even though this isn't how we were hoping it would happen. But we're glad you were there and got him out of that house. Thank you."

"Yes, thank you," his mom adds.

"You don't owe me a thanks. I should've insisted it was a bad idea to split up, gone with him up to that room, and gotten Frat Cat out myself."

"It sounds like everything happened quickly," his mom says. "And you both did the best you could. Now we can just hope for the best. Thank you, Ty."

I tear up because there's still a part of me that's worried…that has this deep fear that something terrible is gonna happen.

I can't imagine they're free of it either.

After we say our goodbyes, I pull up another number in my phone.

Grant's.

My hand trembles.

If I ever needed him, it's now when I'm scared as fuck that the docs are gonna come in and tell me they couldn't help Lance or that he's irreparably injured with something he'll have to live with his whole life because of less than a few minutes of exposure to the smoke.

Grant would have been able to be here for me. Even when things were hard with all he was dealing with, he always had a way of making me smile.

"I wish you were here right now," I mutter.

Of course, it's not just to help me because of what's going on with Lance, but so much that we've missed out on.

Tears break free, rolling down my cheeks.

Fuckin' A.

I push through my uneasiness and call Mom, realizing just how bad it is that I've contacted so many people and she's the last on my list.

"Honey? What's that on your face? Where are you?"

I have no doubt she recognizes the inside of a hospital room. We've seen enough of them.

I hesitate before forcing out, "I'm at Peachtree Springs Medical Center. I'm fine. Mostly. I don't know. I'm not injured, but my boyfriend is."

Now's not the time to ease her into this shit. And she needs to know how important he is to me. How hard this is right now.

It's difficult to tell if Mom is more shocked by that

than she was when she first noticed my face and the hospital room, but I say, "There was a fire at Sigma Alpha tonight, and Lance, the guy you know as the prick president from Alpha Theta Mu...only he's not a prick...like, not even a little bit...and he's hurt."

I tell her what happened, from the fire up until this point, and when I finish, she says, "I'm glad you're both in the hospital right now. Hopefully they're doing what they can."

"We both know there are limits to what they can do," I snap. "What if something happens? What if he's seriously injured? What if he's not gonna be okay?"

She's quiet.

"You're not saying anything because you know there's a chance that could be true."

"As we've seen firsthand, sometimes bad things happen to really good people, Ty. And it's impossible to know what's going to happen with any of this."

Doesn't help, but she's right. I swallow the truth with an uncomfortable gulp.

"You know, I get a mammogram every year, and sometimes they find something."

"What? Why is this suddenly coming up? I don't need more things to worry about."

"It's not unusual, Ty. Sometimes they find a cyst or something they're concerned about, and I have to get more tests. During all that stuff with Grant, because of all the worry and uncertainty about him, I was paralyzed by it at times, so I wouldn't mention it to you. Because I didn't want you to be worried too."

This breaks my fucking heart. "I'm so sorry you had to go through that alone."

"I didn't bring it up to worry you about something else, but because Grant and I once had a discussion while he was sick. He said he could have just as easily been hit by a car. Or taken an unexpected fall and that be the end of it. Or had an aneurysm or heart attack or any other thing that happens to so many people every day."

"Is this supposed to cheer me up?" I ask, more than a little distressed.

"He was saying there are so many things we can't plan for that could be the end, while also reminding me that we don't go around thinking about each and every one because we'll drive ourselves out of our minds. Now, I'm obviously not saying you shouldn't worry about Lance, because you absolutely should after what happened. And yes, there is a chance that something bad might happen. But there's also a chance that he could be okay. And don't let what's happened to us make you forget that either."

My chin quivers, my eyes watering, but somehow a snicker breaks through.

"What's funny about that?" she asks.

"It does sound like something Grant would say."

She tears up too. "Yeah, I think some of my optimism comes from him."

And now I'm crying again. Fuck.

"I wish I could be half as optimistic as he had been," I say, "even when we were losing him."

"We still have Grant here with us," Mom says. "Not in the way we want, but his wisdom, his kindness, his character. We'll always have that, and don't forget it."

It's something I should remember, especially when I'm so filled with resentment and anger that he's not around anymore.

"So you care about Lance…a lot?"

A lot?

"You make it sound like a crush. It's much more than that. Lance is one of the coolest, funnest, kindest guys I've ever met. And then what he did tonight, throwing himself into danger to save Frat Cat, that's so something that dumbass would do. And I kind of fucking hate him for that, but it also makes me love—"

I stop myself.

I wasn't expecting my mind to go there.

I was already falling hard for the guy, but it's like the whirlwind we've been through tonight brought clarity, perspective.

My mind runs back through all the shit-giving and barbs we'd sling at each other. Grating on each other's nerves. That wild morning when we found ourselves bound together by Omega Psi. The TaskFrat where we realized there was more to it than we could have ever imagined. And then…everything that's happened since.

"That little prick," I say, shaking my head, smiling. I can't deny what I'm feeling. Not after what's happened.

"I love him, Mom."

"Oh, honey."

"I'm sorry I didn't tell you about him sooner. I wanted to share that over the break next week. I thought you deserved to know in person. Because I wanted you to know just how amazing this guy is."

"I'd be lying if I said I wasn't surprised, considering you've always been interested in girls. But I know that anyone who's caught your eye is incredibly lucky to have you."

"I appreciate that, Mom, but you've definitely got it the wrong way."

The door opens, and a nurse steps in.

"Mom, they're here. Lemme call you later."

We exchange I-love-yous before I get off the phone.

"Where is he?" I ask.

"Lance is fine," the nurse says. "He's been transferred to a room. We've given him some medicine to keep his airway relaxed. We don't see any obvious signs of damage to his throat, so we're hopeful everything will come back looking good. Our protocol is to keep him for a bit and observe him. The risk right now is the potential for inflammation, and we want to ensure that doesn't happen. But assuming everything's fine, he might be able to get out as soon as tomorrow."

I take a breath as the nurse leads me to the room he's in.

He's still asleep.

The nurse must see the concern in my expression because he says, "We just gave him something to relax him."

"Thank you. I should let my…brothers," I say awkwardly to keep up with our lies, "know what room we're in. They can come back here now, right?"

"Just keep it to three at a time. And if he does wake up, don't overwhelm him."

I thank him, then step beside Lance's bed and rest my hand against his chest, watching him breathe. He looks so peaceful. So vulnerable. I take his hand. "You're gonna be okay. And I'm not gonna leave your fucking side. You got that?"

As I stand there, looking at this beautiful man, I feel the depths of what I shared with Mom.

Because he's got me.

I'm so fucking in love with Lance Fehn.

29

Lance

"YOU NEED ANYTHING before we head out?" Mom asks for what must be the fifth time since I woke up maybe fifteen minutes ago.

I've been in and out all day. I had a tube down my throat for a few hours, and during that time, Ty got me a journal and a pen to communicate with him, hospital staff, Mom and Dad, and our friends. Some of the guys are still lingering in the waiting room, here for support. So on top of being tired from all that went down last night and whatever I've been pumped with while here, it's been exhausting knowing everyone's running around, worried about me.

And yet, I'm so grateful I get to see everyone again.

"I'm good," I assure them, my voice still hoarse from when the nurse took out the tube.

Ty, who's sitting beside the bed, tightens his hold on my hand, which he's been holding since before I woke up. There are some serious bags under his eyes, and he still has some soot on his face from the fire last night. I can't imagine he's gotten much sleep since we got out of Sigma Alpha. Every time I've woken up, he's been right here at my side, ready to get me anything I need.

Being in that smoke, struggling to breathe, my eyes burning, there was a moment when I thought I might never see him again. Or my parents. That I would leave them all even more grief-stricken, adding to so much existing pain. It's the sort of thought that reminds me how special they all are to me. Really reminds me of what's important in my life.

"Please don't talk too much," Dad says.

"They said I can talk a little, just need to take it easy. Now go. You said you haven't eaten since you got here."

"The guys could grab you something to eat," Ty tells them.

As helpful as he's been, I wish he hadn't offered. I love my parents, but despite how wonderful they've been and how nice it's been to see them again, it'd be even nicer to have a moment alone with him.

"No, no," Dad tells him. "Trust me, they've been helpful enough. So helpful that I think we could both use a minute to ourselves."

"I agree," Mom says, and I smile. It must've been overwhelming for my parents, though my guys would've just wanted to make sure their president's parents were comfortable. "We'll be right back, though," Mom promises, like she's feeling guilty for leaving, despite them being here most of the night and morning.

"I'm fine," I insist.

"You're right, you're right." Dad turns to Ty. "Thank you for being here."

"It's my honor, really," Ty assures them.

Mom and Dad give me some big hugs, and we exchange I-love-yous.

After they head out, Ty asks, "How you feeling?"

"I'm glad they're getting lunch. Love them, but their worrying is stressing me out."

"They're not the only ones worried about you."

I know. I've seen his concern. That's one of the reasons I wanted to be alone with him. Because while I've had so much support, he's been dealing with that on his own.

"How do *you* feel?" I press.

His gaze drifts. "It's been rough, but better now that the docs said you'll be fine."

"And I will be." I feel a tickle in my throat and cough. "Despite how I sound," I joke, which earns a smile. When I groan, he tightens his grip on my hand.

His phone buzzes, and he checks with his free hand. "It's Ash and Colin."

Last update was that the vet checked Frat Cat and he was fine. Still sick with his infection, though. There was some talk about Colin and Ash returning to be here for us, but I made sure Ty let them know they needed to go on their trip. Frat Cat and I are fine, and we'll be even better by the time they return.

"They said they almost booked a flight back but then changed their minds. Unless something happens here."

"Fair," I say as he messages them back.

"Also, there are pics on Instagram of the damage to the house." Ty shows me images of what Sigma Alpha looks like now. The fire must've progressed fast because the side with Dax's room is now an open space with charred pieces of wooden frames.

There's a sadness in Ty's eyes. It's there every time the topic of Sigma Alpha comes up.

I can't even imagine if this had happened to Alpha Theta Mu. It sucks that he has to deal with this. Still, as terrible as what happened to Sigma Alpha is, I'm just glad everyone made it out safe.

That I got to see Mom and Dad and my friends again.

That the last time I kissed Ty won't be the last.

And that he's right here next to me, where he belongs.

His gaze returns to me, and he studies my expression.

"I'm sorry," I say.

His brow creases. "Sorry?"

"Not about saving Frat Cat, obviously, but I didn't mean to put everyone through all this."

"The fire put everyone through this, not you."

He rests his phone on his thigh and cups my cheek, running his thumb over my flesh. "You didn't do anything wrong. And I don't want you thinking anything different. You were…perfect."

The way he says that, so sincerely, looking me dead in the eyes, takes me by surprise. He's been acting differently since the fire. Although, I guess it shouldn't surprise me because I'm different too.

It reminds me of those thoughts flashing through my head in the smoke. The things I wished I'd told him. How much I care for him. How strongly I feel it.

All the things I want to share with him now that we're alone, but a sound catches my attention before the door flies open and Ryan barges in, Ty practically jumping out of his seat from the shock. "Fucking hell, Ry."

His Sigma Alpha bro heads in with Marty right behind him. "Hey, buddy, how you holding up?" Ryan asks as he plops down in a chair beside Ty.

I study him for a moment. "When did you get pants?"

"I've always been wearing pants," Ryan says, glancing around as if concerned about my mental well-being. "You didn't think Marty and I would be returning to the hospital in just those loincloths from last night, did you? Dude, what are they pumping you up with?"

Marty, standing behind him, rolls his eyes.

"Did you need me to answer that still?" Ty asks.

"The guys grabbed some pants for us," Marty explains.

I open the notebook Ty gave me, pull the pen from the spiral binding, and scribble onto the page, showing the words to Ty: *Kill Ryan. Thank you.*

"What did he say?" Ryan asks.

I display the text for Ryan, and Ty shrugs. "Sorry, man. Just following orders."

Ryan slaps at his chest like he's been shot. "And by my best friend, for one of those Alpha Theta Mu assholes."

"What did you call my boyfriend?" Ty asks, but he doesn't sound like he's kidding.

"He just told you to kill me."

"It's taking you a damn long time to do it too," Marty gripes, and I can tell by his tone Ryan's gotten on his nerves since they've been here. But I also figure everyone's tired since they must've been here on and off since late last night, and it's already the afternoon.

Ty hooks his arm around Ryan's neck, pretending he's about to snap it. "Last words?"

"Can I use them to plead?" Ryan asks, which makes me laugh. "I have news."

Marty confirms this with a nod, and I jot down in the notebook: *He can live.*

"Worked this time," Ty says with a groan. "But I wouldn't push my luck if I were you. What you got? Better be good."

Ryan says, "Now, this is all unofficial…"

"He means it's rumors," Marty clarifies.

"You know what I meant. Anyway, I used to hook up with this girl over at Kappa Mu, and she was *wild*. The first time was just fun, but she wanted to pull out some toys pretty fast after, and then suddenly it's restraints and safe words. I'm down for a good time, but this was above my pay grade."

"Weird context for that expression," Marty observes.

"I thought I was a horny fuck, but this girl wouldn't let me leave her place until I was drained. Like, I didn't think it was possible to go again, and then she'd pull one more out of me."

"Uh…Ryan," Ty interjects, "you aren't here to tell us about your sexual adventures with some sorority girl, right?"

"Oh, no." He flinches, as if only now remembering his point. "She's fucking around with guys in Omega Psi, and she says one of theirs just turned himself in for starting the fire."

"Turned himself in?" Ty asks. "To the police?"

"No, to the Russian Mafia. Of course to the police. She said the Omega Psis found a way to access a master key, which gave them entry to plenty of rooms so they could pull a prank involving glitter bombs."

"We definitely need to up security," Ty says, "but looks like we'll have a while to get that sorted."

"Apparently, this guy added fireworks—some bullet cracklers—to give us a jump. Word is, the firefighters were freaking out when they did a walk-through after and the cracklers were setting off in the rooms. At first they thought there might be bombs in the frat, so they were relieved to just find themselves covered in purple and gold glitter. Probably won't be once they realize how long it takes to get that stuff out."

"I'm pretty sure they'll still be relieved to be alive," Marty says, echoing my thoughts.

Ryan ignores this. "I imagine when the guy found out how bad it went, he felt guilty. Said the glitter bombs were set up to go off with motion sensors, but one must've gone off by itself and sparked the fire."

"Do you know the name of the guy?" I ask.

"Miles Banner or something."

"Miles *Tanner*," Ty corrects.

Ty and I look at each other. Miles had also pulled that painting stunt against Zeta Tau, which he'd been reprimanded for. He seemed like a nice guy, someone who wouldn't have intended for anyone to get hurt, but the reality is, his fun prank could have had tragic consequences.

"That's probably it," Ryan says. "It's in my phone."

"Fuck," I mutter.

Ty's face flushes red. He pushes to his feet and starts for the door. "Where's the little shit at now?"

Marty jumps between him and the door, which seems like a mistake given how Ty's charging for it. I wish I had the strength to try and stop him, or even call out to him, but it's too much for me.

"He turned himself in to the police," Marty says. "He's got legal troubles and likely getting suspended, if not expelled. He's gonna pay enough for this."

"Lance could have died last night!" Ty barks, and Ryan is on his feet in no time.

"Come on, man," Ryan entreats. "Lance needs you right here."

This seems to snap Ty out of it as he turns back to me and takes a breath. "You're right."

"Miles seems like a good guy," I finally manage. "And it was brave to turn himself in, accept responsibility."

Now that Ty's thinking rather than reacting, I can tell he hears me. But I sympathize because if the situation were reversed and Ty the one in this bed, I'm not sure I'd be so understanding.

"Doesn't change that what he did was stupid and dangerous," Ty says, "which is exactly what we were talking about at the emergency meeting earlier this semester. If they think there won't be consequences for this, they've got another thing coming. It's just like we said. Their frats don't take safety into consideration, and they clearly don't do a good enough job stressing it. Fuck, I hope that guy knows Lance is hurt. I hope he knows he could have killed people last night."

"Ty, please sit down," I say.

He doesn't hesitate, like he's following a directive. I take his hand, which is cold and rigid, but as I grip, he relaxes, taking in what seems like a first decent breath.

"Sorry. I'm stressing you out," he says.

"It's fine. It's a lot."

He kisses me, rubs our cheeks together before resting his forehead against mine, like he just needs to be close to remember I'm still here. That we're safe, and that's what matters.

"So what are the Sigma Alphas doing?" I ask. "Where is everyone?"

"Here," Ryan says.

"What?"

"*Everyone's* here," Marty confirms. "All the Alpha Theta Mus and the Sigma Alphas."

"Did you guys think we were not gonna be by our presidents' sides at a time like this?" Ryan asks.

"Angie's here too," Marty adds. "I wish you could be out there to see all the guys losing their minds trying to impress her."

"I saw you chatting her up too. For like ten

minutes," Ryan observes.

"Shut up. I was trying to keep everyone else from bugging her," Marty insists, but as his friend, I can tell by the red in his cheeks that's not entirely honest. He likes her. A lot.

"I didn't want to overwhelm you with knowing they were all out there," Ty tells me.

Earlier, it probably would have been, but now it feels nice to know they came.

Doesn't surprise me, though. Despite our differences, it's clear we have frats with some amazing guys.

"And," Ty adds, "we still have to figure out where we're gonna be staying now that we don't have a house to go back to."

"Yeah," Ryan says. "The cops told us they have to finish processing the scene before we can recover our things. Also, we need to sort out the insurance."

"Let me know if you guys need help with any of the paperwork," Marty says. "Believe it or not, I'm really good at hounding insurance companies."

"No one would not believe that, Marty," Ty says. "But we appreciate it."

As much in a fog as I've been since the fire, one thing is crystal clear. "I already know where the Sigma Alphas will be staying. At Alpha Theta Mu."

Ty and Ryan both look shocked.

"There's not enough room," Ty points out.

"We could share beds until we can get air mattresses," Marty says. "Stock up on food. My guess is Ryan will need a pantry for himself."

Ryan smiles. "At least you're taking the right things into consideration."

"Are you sure?" Ty asks me.

"You think it's too early for us to move in together?" I joke, and he smiles, but then his expression turns serious.

Something's on his mind, but obviously, there's plenty to consider with all that's happened.

He bites his lip. "Yeah, I think my boyfriend might as well learn what a real cover hog I can be. It was bound to come out sooner or later."

We kiss, and Ryan says, "Okay, on that note, I'm gonna go gossip about this Miles Tanner shit with the crew while the lovebirds work out their nest situation. And now that I've been thinking about it, I might swing by Kappa Mu for a minute."

At a look from Marty, he amends, "Maybe more than a minute."

"It was the TMI part I was giving you a look for," Marty clarifies.

"TMI? That's not what I got, and not from her."

It's clear by Ryan's expression that he's joking, but Marty cringes and starts for the door. "Maybe you should room with Will…all the way on the other side of the frat."

"And here I thought we were getting along so well…"

Ty smirks. "This is gonna be interesting."

As much as I don't want to do this here, seeing him like this, and getting to be alone for what might be some time before we get back to the frat, I know what I have to tell him.

"Ty—"

"Shh. Rest your voice. Besides, I…I want to tell you something."

I quiet, wondering if there's more news that happened while I was out.

"I know we haven't been seeing each other long," he says, "but keep in mind we've known each other long before we started messing around. And I've always known you were a cool guy. Even joking around with you was fun, and…" He hesitates. "I don't expect you to feel the same."

I can tell where this is going, and I just want to assure him. "Ty—"

"No, please. Let me say this. Neither of us knows what's gonna happen next in life, and how quickly things can change, and I don't want to go another minute without saying how I feel about you. I love you, Lance. I'm in love with you."

A warm spiral swirls in my chest, soothing me. Not just from his confession, but the truth of everything he's saying.

"And I loved you before this stuff, but it took the fire to make me realize how much. And I'm sorry if this is moving too fast, but I can't pretend to feel differently. I won't. I—"

I jot down in the notebook, and he asks, "What are you doing?"

I show him the words: *I love you too, Ty.* "That's what I was trying to say," I tell him. "But you just had to win at that too, didn't you?"

He chuckles. "Guess I did win."

"Fuck you."

"I like when you say that like Darth Vader."

We share a laugh as he leans close.

"You love me?" he asks.

"Yeah. I love you."

"Funny that you said I won because it feels like you won, making me so hung up on the Alpha Theta Mu prez."

"Maybe we both won," I mutter, leaning toward him and taking a kiss.

We've kissed so many times since that first time, but this feels utterly different. There's a connection between us that's deeper than before, beyond the fun we've shared. We've been competitors and rivals all these years, but regardless of how much I've wanted to beat his ass so many times before, in this there aren't any losers. And even if there were, I wouldn't mind losing to him.

30

Ty

THE HOSPITAL RELEASES Lance a few hours later. I'm sure the staff is relieved to clear the waiting room of all the frats. Lance's parents offer for him to stay with them, but he insists he's fine and that he has to help us all navigate the new living situation at Alpha Theta Mu. They can't put up much of a fight, since the docs have cleared him, and aside from his voice still sounding scratchy, he seems to be back to his old self.

"Feels like some fucked-up karma," Ryan says from behind Lance and me as we walk up the drive of Alpha Theta Mu, both our frats following. "We have to stay with our rivals? Really?"

"You're welcome for our house saving your asses," Lance teases.

We share a look, and he's wearing a bright smile. Despite all the bullshit, things have felt lighter since I told him how I felt and I heard those magical words from him: *"I love you."*

Almost makes me feel like I don't have to track down Miles Tanner and kick his ass for what happened last night.

But only almost.

"See?" Ryan says. "Where are we even gonna talk shit about Alpha Theta Mus around here?"

"I think we just say it to their faces now," Keegan jokes as we reach the front porch.

As I turn back to the guys, Dax adds, "I'm kind of excited about the idea of staying here. Alpha Theta Mus have been good to me."

I wonder which of Lance's crew he's messed with. Not to mention, Ash and Colin are always particularly friendly with him.

"We should come up with a game to determine who'll sleep in whose room," Jaxon suggests.

"Whoever loses sleeps with Marty," Ryan teases. "And I don't just mean in his bed."

"I don't like this," Marty says.

Ryan drapes an arm over his shoulders. "I'm kidding. You know I wanna keep you all to myself."

"That's happening over my dead body," Marty says through his teeth.

"Just chill, will ya? You are so uptight. Oh wait. That's your thing, right? In that case, why don't you show us around, and maybe you can give us the breakdown of the rules so we can at least know what we're violating as we're doing it."

"That's actually not a bad idea," Lance says. "Marty, you can manage that while Ty and I…"

"Oh God, of course. I've got you, man."

Marty can act like a prick, but he's been right here for Lance and me since everything went down. I understand now why they're such good friends—Lance clearly knows a good guy when he sees one.

"You'll warm up to me," Ryan tells Marty. "I promise, I won't cuddle you too hard."

"Again, we're not rooming together," Marty insists.

Ryan simply heads into the house like he owns the place.

"Can we still get Ty to execute him?" Marty asks Lance.

"I can hear you!" Ryan calls from inside. "Going to the kitchen. I need something to eat."

"Then wait until we do a grocery run so we can stock up!" Marty calls after him.

"We should order pizza," Ryan says.

"I'm down with pizza too," Payton calls out from the crowd.

Several guys chime in, wanting pizza, which settles that.

Marty sighs, hurrying inside, and I hear him call out to Ryan, in what I'm sure is a vain attempt at controlling the uncontrollable. Something he's gonna have to get used to.

Lance is all smiles—I imagine he's happy to be back in his element, seeing everyone acting like themselves and not all worked up over him.

Although, I still feel tension twisting up in my chest. Can't go through something like we did last night without some of that lingering.

"Okay, guys," I say. "I appreciate everyone rallying around us, but Lance and I need to wash the hospital off. I'm gonna get my man to his room."

We hug it out with our guys, then go upstairs. I shower quickly and get into bed, but Lance takes some extra time before coming out in only his towel. He tosses it into the hamper by his closet, and as he approaches the bed, he notices my Sigma Alpha hoodie on the edge. The guys brought it for me to change into last night.

His lips curl into his dimples as he picks it up and throws it on, leaving the front open, as he sneaks glances toward the door, like he's waiting for the guys to rush in and catch him. "I think I deserve this after everything I've been through."

A rush of pride pulses through me, seeing my guy in our letters.

Lance retrieves an Alpha Theta Mu tank from his dresser drawer and tosses it at me. "You know what to do."

I don't hesitate. I wasn't planning on putting any

clothes back on, but this is too exciting to pass up. I toss on the shirt, and as good as it felt to see him wearing mine, I must admit I like being in his frat's letters—as if now he really has claimed me.

Lance crawls under the covers, scooting his ass back against my cock.

"What is that monstrosity?" he jokes.

I laugh. "You can't be in my hoodie like this and expect me not to be hard as hell."

"Fair," he says, tucking his ass even closer.

Fuck…

I slide my hand under the hoodie, groping at his flesh before kissing the back of his neck.

"You think Mom and Dad are gonna be okay?" he asks softly, and I know it's because of how worried they were about him.

"It definitely triggered something in all of us, but time and you being okay is all that's gonna make it better."

"I just wish I hadn't worried them."

I cling to him tighter, hoping my hold might soothe him.

"I think any worrying is outweighed by how happy they are to have you well and back in my arms."

"You're right."

He rolls toward me, rests his hand against my chest. "The whole experience made me reflect on what's important, you know?" With his free hand, he runs his thumb along my jaw. "That we have to take advantage of every moment."

"Reminds me of something I was chatting with my mom about. Something Grant had told her about how that's all we can do."

"They'd want us to be happy," he says, bringing to mind our conversation about Kacey at the skating rink. "And I'm happiest when I'm with you."

He leans close and kisses me—a gentle kiss I eagerly embrace.

As he pulls away, we gaze into each other's eyes before he says, "Okay, now just hold me close and keep appreciating your boyfriend."

"Can do," I say as he repositions with his ass tight against me. I rest my cheek against his face, kissing, then say, "The only thing you should be more concerned about is if this Sigma Alpha/Alpha Theta Mu truce is gonna work."

"Um…you mean the Alpha Theta Mu/Sigma Alpha truce? Don't forget whose house you're in."

"You said while wearing a Sigma Alpha hoodie."

"And it feels so good."

"Here I thought you were all wounded and vulnerable, and you're still the same old Lance."

"And you're the same old Ty. Unless you're gonna suddenly insist on bottoming." He glances over his shoulder, smirking.

"Not feeling any bottoming urges. But I wouldn't mind…" I caress down to those beautiful globes, copping a feel, enjoying the way my hand glides across his smooth flesh. "Mmmm," I drag out. "It'll be even nicer to get in there now that I know my man loves me."

His smile expands into a grin.

"If it makes you that happy," I tell him, "gonna be hard not to give it to you."

"It needs to be hard for you to give it to me."

I push up against his ass. "Clearly, that won't be an issue."

He reaches around, grabbing my cock and stroking.

I growl. "You're not helping any."

"How so?" He slows his pace, toying with me.

"Stop doing that. You're still recovering."

"Maybe I just need a thick dick in me to make me feel better."

"Please, you've been in the hospital all night."

"And I slept through most of it. Also, there's a reason I spent a few extra minutes in the shower."

"Fuck, now I'm really hard. I'll get the lube."

I start to roll toward the nightstand, but he keeps his grip firmly on my cock. "Or we could not."

"Oh, you don't want to do anything, then? Of course. Sorry, just my horny brain and all that teasing my cock."

He wears a mischievous expression. "That's not what I said."

"For some reason, you sound even sexier with this husky voice."

He laughs before releasing my cock and tucking his ass close so my cock runs vertically along it.

"What are we doing?"

"You can spit, can't you?"

I glare at him. "That's not something that happens in real life. That's porn shit."

"Ash says he and Colin do it all the time."

"Maybe Ash and Colin are liars. Or maybe Colin's just dicked him down enough that that hole opens right up for him."

"We could give it a try and see for ourselves. I should get what I want since I've been in the hospital."

A jolt of excitement pulses through me.

Is this some kind of sick joke?

But it sounds hot as sin, and now he's got me curious.

"Okay, we can try, but only because you're clearly wounded and horny, so you get whatever the hell you want."

He shrugs. "Truth."

"One-word Lance is back."

I wet my forefinger and middle finger before reaching down and pressing them against his tight hole.

There's no way we can do this. Maybe after I fucked him and he already had some lube in him. But knowing he wants it encourages me to give it a try.

"I guess I have kind of opened you up by dicking you down the past few months," I tease, massaging my way farther inside him.

He rolls his head back. "Fuck, that's what I need, Ty. Just get all that stress out of me." He pushes his ass back, forcing me farther in.

As I open him up, seeing how he's eased up gives me confidence that maybe I could pull this off, so with my fingers still in him, I spit in my free palm, wetting my dick a few times. I steadily pull my fingers out, switching off with the head of my dick and going slow, feeling as the head slips inside him.

He moans, but I don't go in far.

"That hurt?" I ask.

"No."

I'm cautious as I feed him some more of my cock, moving much slower than normal, waiting for any sign that he's in pain, any sound or movement, so I can pull back, until he says, "Stay right there. Don't move."

I obey, stiff like a statue to keep from doing anything that might hurt him before he says, "Okay, now...ooh," he mutters.

"Does it hurt?"

"A little."

I stop, starting to pull out steadily.

"No, it's okay." He glances over his shoulder again. "I kind of like it."

And I can read the excitement in his expression.

"You dirty fuck. I bet you do."

I lean close, taking a kiss. We linger as we continue this dance, with me easing into him as he gives me signs to proceed until my pelvis is against his ass, my cock buried in his tight hole. I love the sensation of his ass clenching around me like it's holding on for dear life.

I press my hand against his abs, keeping him close as our tongues explore each other.

"This is what I need," he whispers into my mouth.

I begin subtle movements, giving his body a chance to get used to having me inside him like this, feeling as his muscles relax, allowing me to move even more.

As skeptical as I was of the idea to begin with, this is exhilarating. It involves a greater level of care, listening to Lance's body, reading him so carefully to make sure I'm giving him what he wants.

I'm shocked as we pick up the pace to the point where I'm able to drive my cock in and out of him, him greeting each thrust with a push. I wrap my arm around his thigh and roll him on top of me, fucking from under him, his back still against my front. And as I really get going, I grab hold of his cock.

"I don't know that you've ever been this hard," I say

as I feel the precum beading out of the head.

"I need you, Ty. Come inside me."

It's more than just being in him raw, without lube. It's more than even being in each other's frat spirit wear.

I'm consumed by my desire for him.

I speed up my movements, the rush rising quickly. "Lance, I'm about to—"

"Yes," he whispers before my muscles lock up, my ass tight as I feel the release shooting right through me, coming up inside him.

Lance Fehn.

My boyfriend.

The man I've become so obsessed with.

The man I love.

But I know my work isn't done yet.

I keep drilling his ass, stroking his cock at the same time. His body shakes and trembles, and I can tell he's about to release before he moans. I glance over his shoulder, watching as he shoots across his abs, some settling by the hoodie zipper that's draped across his torso.

I kiss the side of his face, feeling his hole tighten up, so I still inside him, breathing in sync with him.

As he comes down, he laughs before saying, "Impossible, huh?"

"Guess you proved me wrong," I say, reveling in knowing he's stuffed with me. "I should grab us a towel."

He reaches back. "No. Stay like this. Just roll me over and cuddle me again."

I follow his instruction, keeping deep in him as he relaxes against me.

"It's always good," I note.

"I think we need to do more of that."

"I agree. Unless of course you want me to bottom for you, but I'm sure you wouldn't want that because then I'd have to be a better bottom than you, and I wouldn't want to make you feel embarrassed about being the second best top and bottom in the relationship."

He twists his head back for another kiss, and as our lips part, I whisper, "This whole staying-with-you-guys thing is a really bad idea."

"Huh?"

"I actually have to study and attend classes, but if I'm staying with you, I have no reason to do anything other than fuck the hell out of you every day and night."

He smiles like he knows how right I am...that I won't be able to keep my hands off my guy for long.

I kiss him again, relaxing until it feels like our usual kisses. The sort that make me feel safe and like all is right in the world. I take his hand, running my finger along the inside of his palm.

It's been a wild journey to get to this point, where Lance Fehn went from being my seemingly straight frat nemesis to us sharing a bed and him being filled with me. We've both been through a lot of shit, and I know there will be more, especially as we navigate this shared-premises situation for our frats.

"Grant and Kacey were right," I say. "Grant saying we can't spend our lives worrying about whatever might happen, and Kacey saying we can't let anything keep us from being happy. We have to cherish moments like these, that I'm lucky enough to lie in this bed with an amazing guy, knowing there's nowhere in the goddamn world I'd rather be right now."

Lance is quiet before adding, "I hate that we lost them. But it's nice that we have our memories…and the things they shared with us. That we learned how important it is to grab hold of love when we find it."

It's true. As hellish as the experience was for both of us, at least I know I don't take having Lance in my arms for granted. And I never will.

"I love you, Stud," I whisper against his ear.

"I love you, Rocky."

He turns back to me once again, and we share another kiss.

I surrender to this moment, lose myself entirely to the bliss of being here with him, knowing he's mine and I'm his.

Nothing else matters.

EPILOGUE

Lance

"**I**'M SO ON edge," Ty says, arms wrapped around me as we lie in my bed.

It's not the first time Ty's said this today, since we called an emergency meeting for both frats.

After the fire, the guys stuck around at Alpha Theta Mu through finals. It took about a week before they could recover their belongings. Then Ty went to North Carolina to visit his mom, and I stayed with my parents for the holiday. After Christmas, I flew out to stay with him at his mom's place for a bit, since FaceTime and calls weren't enough and I was missing my man. Plus, I was excited to meet his mom.

Throughout finals and the break, Ty's been navigating insurance and consulting with Sigma Alpha's attorney, working through the details of the complex situation and the whole insurance runaround more than a few times.

Now we're back at Alpha Theta Mu, and today he

finally got some answers, even if they weren't the ones we were hoping for.

We share a kiss, one of the many we've shared since that very first kiss.

But it's much different since the first time.

Really, since we exchanged I-love-yous.

It means so much more than those passionate, tongue-filled kisses that set my flesh on fire. It's not just the heat anymore; it's something deeper that reaches into my soul. Knowing Ty sees more of me than most, just like I see more of him.

As I pull away, I admire the Alpha Theta Mu tee he's wearing, short because I cut it into a crop top for TaskFrat. Since we first began exploring this naughty pleasure, we've had maybe a little too much fun wearing each other's frat spirit wear.

"I don't want to do it." Ty groans. "Why don't you run the meeting today?"

"We're both running it, and you know you wouldn't want me delivering the news."

"The guys aren't gonna be happy. Maybe if I fuck you one more time, that'll make it easier." He practically attacks me, his mouth on mine, his greedy hands all over my body, sending that familiar rush through me. Soon, his face is buried against my neck as he licks and nibbles.

"This is something that should be a reward *after* the meeting," I tell him.

"I don't think you really want that." He seizes my hard cock, stroking.

As a surge of excitement pulses through me, I grit my teeth. "Seriously, though. You said you had five minutes like ten minutes ago."

"It hasn't been that long."

"It really has."

He grunts, prying away from me before checking his phone on the nightstand. "Oh, fucking hell."

He hops up and starts for the door.

"Ty—"

He spins around, and I grab at my own top, his Sigma Alpha hoodie.

"Oh…" he says, flustered. "Guess they don't need to know about this…just yet."

"Naughty Rocky," I tease.

We grab fresh shirts, wearing the ones for our appropriate houses—though that's not nearly as fun—before heading downstairs to join our Greek brothers for a combined meeting between Sigma Alpha and Alpha Theta Mu.

With chairs set up around the living area, the room's basically divided into two halves, Alpha Theta Mus on one side, Sigma Alphas on the other, but the guys are cutting it up with each side, no one seeming to give much thought to the fact that we're rival houses.

Frat Cat sits in Ash's lap as Ash makes a claw with his

hand, giving Frat Cat something to slap at. Fortunately, he didn't have any issues from the smoke, and he recovered from his infection fairly quickly. It's nice seeing him back to his usual self.

Colin sits at Ash's side, arm draped around his boyfriend. He's still got another week before he has to be back at law school, and he's taking advantage of every moment.

Ty approaches the podium we set up earlier in the day so he could talk to the guys. I stand right behind him, feeling the tension practically radiating off him, which has me on edge too.

"Okay, okay, everyone." Marty pushes to his feet from the chair beside Ash. "The meeting is in session. That means even you, Sigma Asshats, must pipe down."

This earns some rebellious noise, but everyone quiets soon enough, allowing Ty to begin. "Thank you, Marty, for the unsolicited help. Um...I know everyone wants an update on the state of Sigma Alpha, and we've been coordinating with the insurance company to find a solution to housing while they work on repairs. That said, the solution we came up with isn't ideal, but it's all they could offer us. There are three places we can relocate to so that everyone has a place to stay. Insurance will cover the expense, fortunately. But—"

"Three locations?" Dax asks. "As in, they're gonna separate us?"

This is the bad news.

Ty tenses his jaw, and I step closer, resting my hand on his back. He takes a breath before continuing. "I did everything I could, and the insurance did their best to accommodate, but there's just not enough room for twenty guys in any one location. They can get a temporary lease at Wilfred Complex, and the Highland in town is offering up space, and—"

"Those aren't even near each other," Keegan points out.

"Yeah," Ty agrees, "and the other hotel is Wayford Hall."

"How are we gonna have parties?" another Sigma Alpha asks.

I can see that my fellow Alpha Theta Mus are uncomfortable, but I'm hoping they'll realize why we called them here too, and that they'll sympathize with our rival frat.

"It's not ideal," Ty says. "And the problem is the damage is extensive enough that we're looking at having to deal with this through a good chunk of the semester, if not through the spring."

"This is my senior year," Ryan says, obviously rattled by the news, and surely speaking for more than just himself. "These are my guys."

"Lance and I have discussed a possible alternative, but it would involve both Sigma Alpha and Alpha Theta

Mu agreeing to it. Lance will take it from here."

He gives me space at the podium, and I step up for my part.

I always get a little nervous when I have to get up in front of everyone like this, especially when it's not just my own house, but I remember the day I pledged to be president of the frat—it's not a responsibility I've ever taken lightly, so I power through. "It's been tough with everyone on top of each other like this. It'll be messy if we do it through the semester, but to keep Sigma Alpha together, I've offered to take a vote with Alpha Theta Mu to see if we're willing to share our space." I can read the apprehension on some of the guys' expressions. "It's not what any of you signed up for. And that's why Ty and I agreed we won't do this unless we have a unanimous vote and everyone's happy with this. But before we take a vote, I want everyone to keep in mind how we would feel if ours was the house that burned down, and we were the ones who were gonna be separated, especially for the seniors."

"It doesn't have to be all bad either," Ty chimes in. "Could mean bigger and better parties. More hands to tend to responsibilities around the house."

"I think we can go ahead and take a vote," Ash says.

"Yeah," Marty agrees. "Alpha Theta Mus who want to help Sigma Alpha out, show of hands?"

I notice my crew—Ash's, Marty's, and Payton's

hands—pop up, followed shortly by the rest of the house. A lump forms in my throat. I'm choked up seeing what a cool crew we have here at our house, the sort of thing that makes me proud to be Alpha Theta Mu.

Ty sidles up beside me, and I see the admiration in his expression. "Regardless of what Sigma Alpha decides, thank you for that. We've always been rival houses, and we still want to kick your asses, but it means a lot that you would invite us into your space. Now let's find out if my Sigma Alphas are cool with this solution."

"Oh, we're cool," Ryan says.

"What are you, the spokesperson for the frat?" Jaxon asks.

"You not cool?"

"I'm fine with it, but we need to take a vote."

"Come on," Ryan says to the guys, pushing to his feet. "Show of hands? Who's in? Let's see those palms high."

All their hands pop up in an instant, and Ty and I sneak a look at each other.

"Is that all we needed to talk about?" Ash asks.

"Well, yeah," Ty says, our guys having showed us that all our stress had been for nothing.

"Then I think there's one thing left to do," Colin adds. "You obviously must have a huge-ass party to celebrate Sigma Alpha staying here."

"First party of the season!" Ryan hollers, and it's on.

The guys aren't in the living area long. They're off

getting things ready to bring it, sending out group texts to get the neighboring frats and sororities over here. By the time we're finished setting up, I'm at a DJ table in the living area, playing my mix, chatting up Ash and Colin.

"This'll be interesting," Ash says.

"Yeah," Colin follows. "In all my time at Peach State, this was the last thing I ever expected would happen between Alpha Theta Mu and Sigma Alpha."

"Tell me about it," I say, reflecting on my own personal rivalry with their president.

Marty approaches with some drinks for us, handing them out.

"You see Ty around?" I ask as I take mine, and he smiles; he knows how hung up I am on my man.

"Can't even be away from the guy for a whole hour," Marty observes.

"It's taken us longer than that to set this up," I insist.

"Barely."

"It's cute," Ash says. "Trust me, I don't like being away from this guy for too long. I miss my Colin when he's gone." He's already got his arm around Colin, and tugs him closer.

"And I miss my Ash Ketchum," Colin says before they share a kiss.

Marty makes like he's about to throw up. "I hope you guys don't become this bad."

"No promises," I say.

Marty cringes, and Ash and Colin are so involved in each other, I doubt they even heard him.

"Glad we got that sorted out," Marty adds. "But I'm not thrilled that little asshole is still going to school with us."

Marty's not the only one who has ill feelings toward Miles Tanner since the incident, and I get it. It's been a huge catastrophe caused by his recklessness. But I have to stand up for him. "It was an accident. And he turned himself in, fully cooperated with the police, and will be doing community service with this on his record. Does he really need to also get expelled?"

"We both know," Marty says, "it's likely because his daddy had the cash and Peach State didn't want to lose his generous donations. Anyone else would've been kicked to the curb. At least Omega Psi expelled him."

Not that they had any say in it. The IFC voted, so he was out regardless, unless Omega Psi wanted to face even more sanctions than they already were because of the incident.

"Hey, guys," Angie says, approaching the booth.

"Oh, hey, Angie." Marty's frustration with Miles Tanner vanishes, a grin flashing across his face, his eyes lighting up. He's been getting this way more around Angie recently, and I know my friend well enough to know he's got a bit of a crush on her. It's adorable, but Angie seems totally oblivious to it.

As they chat, I notice Ty and Ryan on their way

over. Ty comes right around the table, wrapping his arms around me from behind and nibbling at my neck. "That worked out well, didn't it?"

"Very," I say. "Now we just have to make sure the guys don't kill each other."

"Yeah, Mart," Ryan says. "You hear that? You're gonna have to make sure not to kill me."

Marty shifts his attention from Angie, with a very different look than the one he gave her. "Maybe if you bothered to pick up around your side of the room," Marty says pointedly. "Or put on some earphones…or wore some goddamn underwear."

"Oh, come on." Ryan nudges him with his shoulder. "You gave me all that hell about not wanting to room with me, but now we're roomies."

"Because I fear for any of my friends having to be the ones to suffer with you."

"I haven't been that bad."

"*Yet.*"

"The rulebreaker and the obsessive rule follower," Ty whispers in my ear. "What could possibly go wrong?"

I spin around to him. "Guess they'll have to work that out, since I'm gonna be too busy having my way with my man to deal with their bullshit." I take his hand, sliding it onto my ass. "You know that's where your hand belongs," I remind him, and he beams with pride.

I push up close, feeling him getting hard for me already.

"Stud, we need to enjoy the party."

"I have a playlist set up. And we can make a quick trip to the bedroom."

"If I get you in your bedroom, we might not make it back."

"That better be a promise," I say, and he takes my mouth.

When he pulls away, he assures me, "It definitely is."

He's eyeing me, sporting that cocky smile.

The one that used to grate on my nerves.

The one that now gets me hard as hell.

It's the smile I've become so familiar with, since he wears it every day, as if the thing that makes him cockiest is that he bagged me.

I cherish that smile now the way I cherish every moment with him. As we've both learned the hard way, there's no telling what could happen tomorrow. All we can do is enjoy every moment we can with each other. Never take any of it for granted.

And that's exactly what I intend to do, with my guy, Ty Lancaster.

THE END

Order Marty and Ryan's story today!

mybook.to/TheFrathole

Follow Devon on Social Media:

linktr.ee/devonmccormack

BONUS CHAPTER

The following scene takes place before Chapter 1 of *Frat Around and Find Out*, during spring semester.

It's probably exactly what you think it is.

Enjoy! ;)

xoxo Devon

Lance

THE PRESSURE IN my head reminds me of the time Ash accidentally bumped my head with a baseball bat during a TaskFrat game. Considering how it's throbbing, I figure it's gonna be a hell of a hangover, which serves me right for agreeing to play another round of beer pong at Omega Psi's party last night.

Although, this doesn't explain this other pressure against my body. It's like someone's lying on top of me, and after forcing my eyes open, I realize...oh, that's because there's a guy lying on top of me—I assume another frat from the party.

The morning light stings my eyes.

Fuckin' hell.

How did I wind up here?

And who the fuck is on top of me?

It must be a little after dawn, and judging by my surroundings, my new friend and I are behind the shed at Sigma Alpha.

The frat's face is practically buried against my neck, brown hairs pricking at my cheek.

"Dude," I mutter, struggling to move, without success either way I try. "What the—?"

I wiggle some more, discovering what looks like plastic stretch wrap, the kind I've used to pack up things when moving in and out of the frat. It loops around his nude back, binding us together…

Oh fuck. We're not wearing any clothes. Of course we're not.

"Hey, wake up, man," I say, wiggling some more to get his attention.

The guy stirs, groaning like I just kicked him out of a deep sleep.

My senses continue awakening, and I notice how intense his body heat is against me, that he's even sweating a little.

And there's something pressed against my hip. It's uncomfortable as fuck.

I start to detect a familiar scent, recognizing it even before he turns to me and says, "Lance?"

There's that face.

"Ty fucking Lancaster?"

"Fuck…" He winces, his eyes clearly struggling the way mine were when I first woke. He smirks. "Omega Psi must've had a fun time getting this together. Fuck, is that tape?"

"No, it's not quite that fucked up. Just stretch wrap."

Assessing our predicament through his slitted gaze, he struggles with me.

That thing against my side is really putting a lot of pressure on me, and I grit my teeth. "Will you stop moving? There's something against my hip. It's like they put a rock between us."

He tilts his head. "Dude, you must know that's not a rock."

I'm barely thinking straight, let alone making sense of what he's saying, but as I focus on his look and the sensation—too much give for it to be a rock—it dawns on me what he's getting at.

"Wait, what? Why are you doing that?"

"Doing that? It's the morning—"

"I know what it is, but usually I don't have someone else's on me. Fuck, Ty. Just stop."

"You know that's not how it works. I think the better question is, why aren't *you* hard?"

"My dick's jammed up against you. I don't think I could get hard if I wanted to."

"Well, maybe you should be relieved because this isn't exactly comfortable for me either."

I struggle to get his cock off me.

"Okay, when you move like that, it's not helping."

"I'm not gonna lie here with your dick on me like…"

His eyes bulge, panic in his expression. "Really, Lance, you have to stop."

"Just move it a little." I feel a sensation on my side. It's warm, and more than slightly alarming.

"Stop, please!" he insists.

I freeze in place beneath him, my cheeks hot because this is an embarrassing-as-fuck situation.

"Did I just make you…"

"It's only precum. Trust me, you'd know if it was more than that. Now will you listen to me and not move?"

Knowing what happened when I didn't listen the first time keeps me in place, and he leans back, chuckling as he gazes down at me.

"What?" I ask.

His expression stretches into a grin. "I kind of like it when you follow my orders. Bet your guys would love to see you having to do what Sigma Alpha's prez says."

"Just get it off—"

"I don't think you want that."

"I was gonna say *me*—get it off me."

"You didn't say it fast enough, and besides, if we

can't make jokes, what else are we gonna do?" He searches around, blinking a few times. "Yeah, I'll have to figure out how to get out of this. They wrapped us together pretty tight."

"I'm assuming we can't just call your fratbros to come get us."

"That's clearly what Omega Psi wants us to do so that everyone can know what they did to us. I say we don't give them the satisfaction."

"We're on the same page there. Although, gotta hand it to them. This was clever."

"It was, wasn't it? Not gonna keep us from sanctioning their asses, though, right?"

"Nope." I sigh. "So now the question is, how are we getting out of this?"

Ty tenses his jaw. "Yeah…that's a good question…"

Ty

LAST THING I remember was chatting up a hot girl at the party last night. When I woke up, I was hoping the person I was face-planted into was her, but of course, I can't be that lucky. Instead, clearly, the wildest frat thought it'd be hilarious to tie me up to my rival.

And they would really be getting a kick out of me having a raging boner against him…

I don't know that I've ever woken up this hard before, but with my cock wedged between us, pressed against his smooth flesh…well…it's definitely not helping anything. At least he's not moving anymore, so maybe we can find a way to get out of this before I blow my load all over him.

Lance is dead quiet beneath me while I work my arms, trying to get some wiggle room so I can free an arm.

"What are you doing?" Lance asks.

"If I can reposition, I can make enough space to pull apart, and maybe then one of us can crawl out."

"Just make it quick."

I stop, glaring at him. "You think I'm not trying?"

Careful as I'm being, I can't avoid subtle movements against Lance's body, and the pressure inches me closer to what I know will be the end if I don't pace this out, but as I take a break, I can tell Lance is getting annoyed.

"Why can't you move faster?" he asks.

"I think I made that pretty clear."

He grunts. "We might as well call your guys out here if it's gonna take you this long."

I really don't want them to see me with this hard-on, though, and Lance must understand because he says, "I'll wait."

I take deep breaths, feeling that pressure subsiding, bringing me some relief before I start shifting about again.

"Do you need any help?" he asks.

"Yeah, give it a try."

"You'll tell me if something's happening down there, right?"

"Just. Help."

We work together. Feels like something we might do in a TaskFrat challenge, minus the being fully erect against him.

As I feel the wrap give, I say, "I'm gonna try to crawl up you. Stay still while I do that."

Because of our efforts, I can actually lift my pelvis up some, so it's just the head touching him, but it means I have some space, so I start to crawl forward.

I don't know what it is about this position, or the way my cock is gliding across his flesh, but that was definitely the wrong move because a surge of excitement rushes through me. I freeze in place. "Oh fuck."

"What? Why are you making that face?"

I take deep breaths, trying to will my dick down, but for some reason, feels like that only makes it harder.

"I'm, like, right on the edge," I warn.

He's frozen once again, giving me a moment to re-cover.

When that excitement relaxes, he must see the relief in my expression because he says, "Maybe think of something gross or weird."

"Like?"

"Think about having sex with your grandma."

"Ew."

"Or me. I don't know how that isn't enough to make this go away."

"With how much I drank last night, I'm as shocked as you are. Now just push out at the sides some more. We loosened it some already, and if we can do it a little more, maybe I can get off the head."

"The head?"

"Of my dick," I explain.

"This is so fucked up," he mumbles, but follows my instruction. We work together for a bit, but then he starts wiggling again. "I think a part must be loose over here because I really feel it. I just need to…"

"Um…Lance…" There's that surge again, moving even faster than last time.

"Just let me do this real quick, Ty, and we'll be out of here."

"You have to stop."

"I'm barely moving," he says, refusing to heed my warning.

And I know it's too late as adrenaline shoots up my spine, every nerve in my body electrified. "Stop, stop, stop," I plead as his movement seems just the thing my body needed to betray me. My muscles lock up as I jerk about in a series of movements, feeling the warmth wedging between us as I grunt through my teeth.

"Oh no," Lance says, surely feeling what's happening.

With my eyes shut as I recover from the explosive release, I gasp before opening my eyes and seeing him frozen, mouth agape.

"Did you just…"

"I told you to stop moving," I snap, even as I'm still emptying onto him.

He cringes. "Dude, gross. That's nasty. It's like sliding around now. Fuck."

I'm panting, my body still working through this.

"I can't believe you just did that."

"Would you feel less weird about it if I gave you a little kiss?" I say in as sarcastic a tone as I can muster, and the look he shoots me makes it clear he doesn't appreciate it.

But just as quickly, he cracks a smile.

"The hell?" I ask, still catching my breath.

"This is so fucking ridiculous." He can barely get the words out before he's laughing. His eyes light up as he rolls his head back, and now he's got me laughing too. "Seriously, Ty. I can't *believe* you just did that," he reiterates.

"You made me do that."

"I am never letting you live this down, by the way."

"I think that's more than fair."

Now we're in stitches, he's covered in my cum, and

neither of us can get it together enough to get the hell out of here.

"I'm going to fucking destroy Omega Psi when we get out of this," I say, feeling more clearheaded now that that load got out of my system.

"I think you at least have to take me on a date first," he teases. "And here I thought you didn't like me."

Fucking Lance Fehn.

I'm never gonna hear the end of this.

ABOUT THE AUTHOR

Devon McCormack

Devon McCormack grew up in the Georgia suburbs with his two younger brothers and an older sister. At a very young age, he spun tales the old-fashioned way, lying to anyone and everyone he encountered. He claimed he was an orphan. He claimed to be a king from another planet. He claimed to have supernatural powers. He has since harnessed this penchant for tall tales by crafting worlds and characters that allow him to live out whatever fantasy he chooses. Devon is an out and proud queer man living in Atlanta, Georgia.

Find Devon:

www.devonmccormack.com